About the Author

Haley Klinge wrote her first novel when she was ten years old. It was trash and riddled with plot holes, but she never stopped loving to write. Unfortunately, she felt that her dream of being an author was too far-fetched and didn't get the guts to actually start writing until she turned thirty. Now she can't stop. She currently lives in Indianapolis with her husband and two children, aspiring to continue to write smut novels for as long as her fingers can type.

A Highly Improbable Meet Cute

Haley Klinge

A Highly Improbable Meet Cute

Olympia Publishers
London

www.olympiapublishers.com
OLYMPIA PAPERBACK EDITION

Copyright © Haley Klinge 2024

The right of Haley Klinge to be identified as author of
this work has been asserted in accordance with sections 77 and 78 of
the Copyright, Designs and Patents Act 1988.

All Rights Reserved

No reproduction, copy or transmission of this publication
may be made without written permission.
No paragraph of this publication may be reproduced,
copied or transmitted save with the written permission of the publisher,
or in accordance with the provisions
of the Copyright Act 1956 (as amended).

Any person who commits any unauthorized act in relation to
this publication may be liable to criminal
prosecution and civil claims for damage.

A CIP catalogue record for this title is
available from the British Library.

ISBN: 978-1-80439-907-1

This is a work of fiction.
Names, characters, places and incidents originate from the writer's
imagination. Any resemblance to actual persons, living or dead, is
purely coincidental.

First Published in 2024

Olympia Publishers
Tallis House
2 Tallis Street
London
EC4Y 0AB

Printed in Great Britain

Dedication

This book is for my husband, Zach, the king of dicking me down. I love you more than you'll ever know.
(If you're related to me and still choose to keep reading, please refrain from ever looking me in the eye again. Just kidding, but seriously, read at your own risk).

Acknowledgments

There are so many people to thank I wouldn't even know where to begin, but here I go. To my husband first and foremost, for never doubting for a second that I'd actually be able to publish my book. To Christian and Lana, for beta-reading my book and telling me I don't know how to make a pie or stop saying the word lust. To my mom, who taught me to love reading, especially romance. To the friends that are more like my family and supported me every step of the way: Rudi, Hannah, Megan, Sarabeth, Nicole, Christian, Lana, and April. Your encouraging words and optimism kept me going when my imposter syndrome was getting the best of me. To the family members that supported me any time I said this was too good to be true. To the people who helped me crowd-fund enough money for this to even happen, thank you so much for helping me achieve my dream: Hannah, Lauren, Mandee, Maddy, Josh, Kaia, Zach and Sarabeth, Effie, Mandy, Tina, Sadie, Eliza, and Katie. And lastly, to the team at Olympia. Thank you for taking a chance on a nobody author with a penchant for swear words. This is a dream come true.

Trigger Warning:

This book contains:
A single parent home, anxiety, sex, and panic attacks.
If any of these are a trigger for you, please do not read.

Always put yourself first, and know you are loved.

Highly Improbable

Vinyl Edition

Side A:
1. Hot Mess By: Cobra Starship
2. Trip By: Ella Mai
3. Oh My God By: Adele
4. See You Again (feat. Kali Uchis) By: Tyler The Creator
5. Crazy Train By: Ozzy Osbourne
6. Killing Me Slowly By: Bad Wolves
7. Electric Touch (feat. Fall Out Boy) By: Taylor Swift (Taylor's Version)
8. Leather and Lace By: Stevie Nicks, Don Henley
9. Honey, Honey By: ABBA
10. Don't You (Forget About Me) By: Simple Minds
11. Golden Hour By: Kacey Musgraves

Chapter One
Ella

Here's the fucking tea... I shouldn't even be here right now, but due to some unforeseen circumstances, and a general lack of a happily ever after, here I am.

My God, a friend should never revel in her best-friend's unhappiness, but if a (mostly) free trip to Jamaica is thrown into the mix one might be inclined to reevaluate such things. Internally, obviously.

Jamaica in July is exactly how it sounds. Walking along the concrete path, I can feel the heat radiating through my five-year-old plastic white Old Navy flipflops, to the point where there may or may not be a slight chance that the scuffed bottoms are melting as we speak. The grit of the sand slides underneath them while the sun burns against my flesh. A small relief of a breeze rolls in that glides against my pale skin, a balm to help soothe the general lack of protective clothing a bikini top and coochie clincher shorts can offer.

As I suck in an uneasy breath, the humidity palpable and all encompassing, I consider, how Josie and I found ourselves on an engagement moon together. If you're wondering what the fuck an engagement moon is, join the club, before this I didn't know either.

Apparently, it's when rich people celebrate their engagement by going on vacation. What was supposed to be the launching off point of a beautiful future together ended up being more of a Challenger situation and not even making it into the atmosphere.

Namely, Trevor, the bane of my fucking existence and heart breaker of my best friend, cheated on Josie a month into their engagement.

The insane part? He's a lawyer at his parent's firm and cheated on her with his receptionist. The biggest cliché in the book. You've seen this Lifetime movie character before I can assure you.

He's exactly what you would picture a lawyer named Trevor looking like: gelled back hair, smarmy face, and looks like what would happen if every man in the Republican party fused together like a transformer into one super douche. Needless to say, I didn't like him before, but I truly hate him now.

His family gave them this trip as an engagement present, and Josie told Trevor to fuck off and that the least he could do was give her this trip. To my complete and utter shock, he didn't argue, and his dumbass is stuck in Indianapolis while we get drunk on the beach. Well, that was my plan anyway, except Josie won't come out of our room.

Which brings us to now, me walking back to our room, salty air licking my skin, with a blueberry scone (her favorite) and mimosa in hand to coax her out. When I tap the key card onto the reader, I brace myself, and get my no-nonsense face on.

As I walk into the room, a burst of cool air hits my face, and a small sigh of relief escapes my throat before I muster the courage to pry this woman out of the dark hovel she's created for herself. "All right, Jos, enough is enough, no more wallowing!"

I fling open the heavy white curtains dramatically like they do in the movies and hear what sounds like a hiss come out from underneath the covers. "Seriously, Jos, we've been here for three days, and you've barely come out of this damn room! For Christ's sake, you just hissed at me like a damn vampire!"

When I jump onto the bed next to her, I peel back the covers to reveal a very grumpy Josie glaring back at me with dark brown eyes. Her purple silk bonnet is slightly askew, and a dark springy curl falls out of it. This is not the Josie I know and love, and once again I'm cursing fucking Trevor and all his stuck-up ancestors before him for making my best friend hurt so much.

"Oh, I'm sorry! Are you the one that is supposed to be on vacation with the love of your life, but instead you're with your pain in the ass friend, Ella, who won't let you wallow in peace?" Josie says, not even pretending to mask her irritation.

"First of all, I'm the love of your life, so jot that down, and secondly, no, but this pain in the ass friend is trying to get you outside in some fresh air! Look, I brought you a blueberry scone and a mimosa!" I know I'm placating, but desperate times and all that. I shake the bag with the food in it at her, as if that would make it more enticing.

"Why does this feel like the equivalent of you dangling a carrot in front of a rabbit? Are you just going to shake them around in front of me and keep moving until I somehow end up out of this hotel room?" At this point, the edges of her glaring are starting to soften into more of a smirk, but progress is progress.

I smile teasingly and toss my humidity induced frizz ball of blonde hair over my shoulder, "The thought may have crossed my mind…"

Josie sits up in the bed, again progress, and takes the scone from my hand. Gingerly picking it apart and delicately popping a piece into her mouth. She sighs once the first bite hits her tongue. I knew bribing her with food and alcohol would smooth her over.

As I scooch in next to her, I hand her the mimosa and hope that the bubbles and orange juice relax her even further. "We really need to get you out of this room, not only because at this current time you're borderline agoraphobic, but also because this entire room looks like a Hallmark Valentine's Day movie threw up all over it."

It's true, and when we first got here and walked into the room it was much, much worse. Red rose petals in the shape of a heart on the bed, champagne chilling in an ice bucket with two glasses, a jetted tub with, you guessed it, more red rose petals laying on a bubbly layer of lavender scented bubble bath. Not to mention the hanging door knob sign that flips to 'Honeymoon in Progress' along with a sweet note from the hotel staff congratulating Josie and Trevor on their 'Happily Ever After.' When she read it, Josie promptly burst into tears.

In a frenzy I started draining the bath and scooping up as many rose petals as I could into the toilet to flush them. Looking back on it, that was a completely idiotic idea, considering rose petals will go ahead and clog the toilet so bad that it backs up and overflows onto the fancy bathroom tile, thus forcing you to call housekeeping to shut it off within the first twenty minutes of your stay.

If you're wondering if housekeeping looked at me like I was a few beers short of a six pack, yes, yes, they did.

"Is it just me, or do you want me to get out of this room?" She says sarcastically as she takes the last bite of her scone and washes it down with a sip of mimosa.

I snort, and steal Josie's mimosa out of her hand to take a sip, "Yes, smart ass, I do. Everyone knows the best way to get over a break-up is to get back out there! Find a hot guy you'll never see again and get some vitamin-D."

Josie reaches up and stretches out her long arms, exposing some of the deeply tanned skin on her belly. Josie is all curves, long limbs, tan skin, and springy curls. Even in her misery, she is undeniably beautiful.

She narrows her eyes at me, "Ugh, I wouldn't even know what to do with another man's penis. The only one I've ever touched is Trev's."

I glare back at her, refusing to let her make yet another excuse why she can't leave this room. I'm not going to pretend I understand what she's going through. I've never been in a relationship before because I prefer my dicks with an expiration date, let alone know what it's like to be with the same person since college, but something has to give. She can't stay like this forever.

My stare earns me a massive Josie Jones eye roll, "Jesus fine okay I'll leave this damn room if you stop talking about it and never refer to a penis as vitamin-D again." She drags her hands down her face, "Ugh, I don't get why we can't just do M^3? I'd rather do that than be around other human beings."

I hop out of the bed and very dramatically roll my eyes, "Jos, you know you can't invoke Millennial Movie Marathon without the proper tools in place. We don't have Netflix or peanut butter M&M's so you're just going to have to get the fuck over it and put on the bikini that let's your ass cheeks hang out so they can tan properly."

The promise of tan lines seems to be enough to propel her out of bed and into the closet to grab the aforementioned bikini.

While Josie changes, I grab my SPF 70 and begin to lather it generously on my already red tinged skin. Looking in the mirror, I try to make sure I don't miss a spot, and I can feel my critical eye start to sharpen on myself.

My hips are wide set and coated in fleshy skin with lightly colored stretch marks on either side. The marks are accompanied by what Josie calls 'an ass that won't quit without a two weeks' notice' whatever the hell that means, and my large breasts sag slightly. If it wasn't for the tie holding my pink floral bikini top up, they would sag even more.

After I finish coating myself in enough SPF that every one of my pores is drowning in submission, I French braid my red blonde hair back away from my face in hopes of taming my frizz.

When my gray eyes begin to fall appraisingly in the mirror, I smile at myself reassuringly, and say the same thing that I do whenever the critical eye comes out. This *body may not be perfect, but it's beautiful and it's mine.*

Josie rounds the corner toward the mirror in the makeshift mudroom of our hotel suite, her neon green bikini making her impossible to miss, and gives me a sideways glare, "You're afraid of someone judging you, aren't you?"

I return her glare back at her through the mirror as she places her reflective aviator sunglasses on her head to hold back her curls, "No! I'm just trying to work through my shit and say my affirmations. I'm in Jamaica with my best-friend, and I'll never see any of these people again. Why would I be afraid of someone judging me?" I say way too quickly and with a slightly higher pitch than normal.

Logically yes, I know these things, and on vacation I want to be the confident woman that can strut around in a bikini and is unapologetically herself, but if you can't make it, fake it.

With narrowed eyes Josie grabs her tie dye beach bag full of essentials and hauls it over her shoulder, "Okay. Good, because you're fine as hell. I have the required smut reading materials, towels, and sunscreen. Anything else?"

I grab my oversized sunglasses and place them on my head, "Nope, just alcohol but we can get that from the bar on the beach. Is it just me or is this giving Maple Grove Neighborhood Pool Vibes?"

Josie giggles and opens the door to exit the hotel room, "Yes very much so. All that's missing is a Seagram's Jamaican Me Happy to really seal the deal."

Summers in high school with Josie were a lot like this. We would pack a beach bag during the day while my mom and stepdad were at work and sneak some of my mom's Seagram's, along with one of her many smut books featuring a bare-chested pirate/highlander/CEO or any other number of your classic leading male characters in those type of books on the cover.

We would lay out by the pool and read passages out loud to each other laughing hysterically while taking a sip of Seagram's and convincing ourselves we were tipsy.

When we got too hot, we'd jump in the pool and cool off, just to repeat the same process all over again. Being that most of the residents in Maple grove were elderly, Josie and I had the pool to ourselves about ninety percent of the time.

The other ten percent of the time we would join in on the water aerobics class they would have sporadically throughout the season, kicking and pushing the water while listening to the seniors gossip about their families.

Those summers together were some of my favorite memories, so I try not to get too sentimental and mushy at the nostalgia of it all as I close the door behind me and follow Josie down the sand dusted pathway leading onto the beach.

*

"His quivering member was ripe with passion, strong enough to break my will in half." Josie reads sensually before snorting loud enough that the very tan and leathery woman on the blanket in front of us turns around and glares at us. She clearly takes her sunbathing very seriously. I dubbed her the sun goddess because I noticed since the first day we were here that she's always the first person on the beach, and the last to leave. When I told Josie this, she decided to call her beef jerky Barbie, and unfortunately for her, the nickname stuck. Not like I'd ever mention that obviously.

Beef Jerky Barbie's ire just makes me giggle even more as I watch her turn back around, "If a man's dick was 'quivering' near me I feel like I would be inclined to smack it away."

As I say this Josie is taking a big gulp of her margarita and laughs so hard that she fights unsuccessfully to keep all the liquid in her mouth. Watching her laugh this hard I can't help but smirk. Yesterday I didn't even think I would be able to get her out of our room, so the fact that she's not only outside on the beach, but also laughing gives me hope that she'll be getting over the flaming bag of dicks formerly known as Trevor sooner rather than later.

As I revel in the current bliss that is being on the beach with a smiling and tipsy Josie, I polish off the remaining lime margarita in my hand to the dregs. It's so fucking hot. Like if I were wearing foundation it would melt off my face hot, and this is how I justify that I just sucked down my second margarita in the span of an hour to myself.

Josie and I are laying on our crisp white towels side by side facing out toward the ocean, and I can feel the warm sand underneath heating my body from head to toe. Between the burning sand beneath me, and the sun beating down above me, I feel like a baked potato in a bikini, and this beach is my oven.

As I look out at the green and blue of the crashing waves, I once again have a fourth wall breaking moment that equates to me not believing that I'm here. Jamaica is just so unbelievably beautiful that it doesn't even seem like a place that could be real, like Oz or Narnia.

I'm used to flat as hell Indiana where the local treasure is corn, soybeans, and winter snowstorms so frigid you can feel the cold sinking its teeth into your bones. Truly this whole endeavor feels like an out of body experience. It may be an oven here, but it's a beautiful one.

I hear a slurping sound come from the towel next to me, and peer over to see that like me, Josie also just polished off her second marg. "Looks like there's a third round in our future, Jos." I say while already standing up and getting ready to trek down to the bar to get us another.

"Wow, if I would've known that getting cheated on by my fiancé meant being catered to like this, I would've set him and his receptionist up sooner," Josie deadpans as she settles back onto the blanket and opens her book back to the page that she left off.

"Ha fucking ha. Don't get used to it, once your heart is properly put back together it's back to regularly scheduled programming. Don't try and milk it either, I'll know!" at that I put on my cheap ass flip flops and turn toward the bar.

I hear Josie yell behind me to not get murdered and what looks like a singular middle finger in the air. Typical.

As I walk toward the bar, I see two guys, two very hot guys, and try to subtly look at them through the side of my sunglasses without them seeing. Both of them have dark hair that seems to absorb the sunlight and exposed chests that glisten with a slight coating of sweat. One is tall with a lighter complexion, muscular broad shoulders, and curls that are currently falling into his right eye. The other guy has olive skin and arms covered in tattoos, but both are extremely attractive.

They seem to be getting closer, the taller and less tan one with curly dark hair turns his back toward me while the other poses to throw a neon orange frisbee. I find myself watching the one facing away from me in particular, not failing to notice how his back and shoulder muscles flex as he anticipates the throw.

Quickly, I avert my eyes, realizing that I have been staring for longer than what is considered socially acceptable, and keep walking. Looking straight ahead, the bar is the last thing I see before a shirtless man runs directly into me so hard that I get knocked down to the ground, feeling the burn and grit of the sand on my ass as I look up. Only then do I realize the man I'm prepping to tell off is the exact hot frisbee man I was just ogling.

Chapter Two
Liam

Shit. Double shit. I just ran into someone. Mortified, I am literally mortified. I immediately look down to see a woman, albeit a very attractive woman, with her ass in the sand and her oversized sunglasses falling off her face revealing sharp gray eyes.

"I can't believe I did that, holy shit I am so sorry!" I go to try and help her up, but she promptly swats my hand away and stands up, dusting herself off.

"I have sand in my ass crack!" She yells, so loud in fact that the people at the bar peer over to see what exactly is going on. Her voice is high pitched, but not grating, like even when she's cussing and angry, a stranger literally just ran into her, she sounds amused. Like there's a joke that I missed.

"I know, I know, I'm so sorry." I look over and see my friend Max, who at this exact moment couldn't get his eyes any wider if he pried them open with his fingers. He seems to be suffering from sympathetic embarrassment on my behalf, how generous.

I currently feel my face burning, and not from the sun, but from sheer humiliation. As I turn to look back at her I'm met with those eyes, gray like steel, that look as if they're enjoying watching me squirm. My God, if I hadn't made an idiot of myself just now, I'd ask if I could buy her a drink.

"Oh, don't worry about it, if I had a dollar for every time a hot guy knocked me on my ass so he could catch a frisbee, well I'd have a whole dollar." She smirks, clearly enjoying herself. I, however, am much more focused on the fact that she just openly told me I was hot. *I can't remember the last time someone called me that... Oh, wait yeah, I can, it was Blair, back when we were actually happy together.*

Well, no need to dwell on that now Liam, Jesus. I shrug and wave the neon orange disc in front of me, "If it makes you feel any better, I caught the frisbee."

She smiles wide, like she's been waiting for me to make a joke back at her from the moment she peered up at me from the sand. That smile, holy shit, makes me grin like a fucking idiot. She's one of those people that when they smile, it would be impossible to not reciprocate. "Well yeah then I mean it was totally worth it. I guess this is just our fun little meet cute." *Huh?*

"I have no idea what that means," I look at her, confused as ever, but she just shrugs and tosses her bright blonde hair over her shoulder. She turns to leave and waves goodbye, effectively ending the conversation. It happens so quickly in fact, that if Max didn't just see that entire interaction unfold, I would question whether it really even happened at all.

*

After spending the remaining sunlight of the day at the beach we head back to the room to get changed and ready to go to one of the nightclubs at our hotel. The air conditioning is running full blast in hopes of combating the blazing heat we were in all day, and when I walk into our room I instantly relax.

Once I've kicked off the excess sand from my feet by the door, I decide to shower, and for the first few minutes I just stand there and let the water run down my body. I can feel it washing away the sand and salt from the beach, and I close my eyes, enjoying the peace.

My peace, however, is quickly interrupted by my brain that immediately thinks of a pair of steel gray eyes looking up at me with an amused expression. What the fuck, why am I thinking about a woman I had a two-minute interaction with, in the shower? *Because she was fucking beautiful,* I hear the little voice in my head reply, *should've asked to buy her a drink dummy.*

As if he and the voice in my head are in cahoots, I hear Max tap his razor against the sink. "You should've asked the sandy ass crack girl to meet you tonight."

I groan in irritation, because, of course, he won't let this go even if I ask him to. He's been insistent on finding me someone to hook up with ever since Blair and I broke up, which I'm embarrassed to admit was months ago. I'd like to think it didn't rattle me, but it obviously did. It wasn't a shock really, but getting dumped by someone you thought you would marry really knocks your confidence down a notch. Me pre-Blair wouldn't have hesitated to buy her a drink.

Even though Max's longest relationship he's ever had was with his hand he still manages to give me advice on how to get over a breakup, which is namely to fuck someone new and get over it. However, I guess, I can't confirm or deny if that would actually work because I haven't been with anyone since Blair.

"Oh, and what exactly would've been my opening line? 'Hey sorry I knocked you on your ass, but if you're interested, I'd love another opportunity to sweep you off of your feet." I rinse my hair and turn off the faucet, grabbing my towel off the rack on the side of the shower and tying it around my waist.

He taps his razor on the sink again and brings it back to his face to remove the last remnants of shaving cream while looking at me through the mirror, "Actually yeah, you should've... That was smooth as fuck."

"Of course, you think that. What does it matter anyway, I wouldn't see her after today. We fly back home tomorrow." I head to the closet and grab one of my many short-sleeved button up shirts with a weird print on it. I decide to go with my navy one with tiny flamingos on it. I love these shirts mostly because my students have come to know me for them, and now it's like my thing.

"Liam, that's the point you dumb ass, you don't hook up with someone on vacation because you plan on marrying them. You're supposed to have fun, it's literally the reason I brought you on this trip in the first place." He wipes off his face on the towel next to him while I glare at him and grab my cologne to spray my shirt.

"You literally told me to come with you on your nonsense business trip, which by the way I'm still not entirely convinced you don't smuggle drugs back and forth from all these places, to help me get my mind off Blaire. Getting my mind off my ex doesn't mean I just fuck anyone I run into on the beach."

This is not the first time I've even tried to wrap my head around what the hell my best friend does for a living. He's explained to me countless times that he's not doing anything illegal, and that he reviews hotels as a legitimate business, but I'm not convinced. If I didn't love science and teaching so much, I would say I picked the wrong career path.

"Fine. Be boring if you want, but don't wait up for me. Just because one of us plans on being celibate for the remainder of our lives doesn't mean the other one can't have fun. Now let's go." With that we walk out the door and down the outdoor hallway, the humidity instantly surrounding me and causing me to tug on my shirt.

*

As we enter the club, my senses are immediately overcome by the multitude of overwhelming sensations that are all happening at once.

It's open air, meaning that instead of walls it's open on all but one side, letting the light breeze trail in from the ocean. The music is all encompassing and the vibration from the synthesized pop can be felt through the tile on the floor. It's dark outside, but you wouldn't be able to tell in here because between the strobe lights and color alternating ones it looks like daylight.

If it's noticeable that this isn't my element directly on my face, Max seems not to notice, and I follow him to the center of the floor. The air is thick, like how it could only be in a place this humid with what seems to be a hundred people gyrating and breathing in the same space. No wonder they don't have walls, we would all suffocate.

Max is in his element, and he absolutely lives for this shit. He loves to dance and have fun, which suits his personality because he's the most social person I've ever met. He can travel to all these places and meet new people every time without it even seeming difficult.

He says it's because he was an Army brat and had to learn to adapt to new environments every few years, but I still think he would be this way regardless. Needless to say, Maximiliano Rossi and I are about as opposite as could be, and if it wasn't for us being roommates in college we probably would've never met.

Even now he's already found a woman to dance with and will soon enough be whispering the one sentence he knows in Italian against her ear, a sign that his master plan is already in motion. If I'm even going to be able to pretend to keep up, I need a drink.

I make my way toward the bar and order a rum and coke. While I wait for the overwhelmed bartender to make the drink, I rest my elbow on the sticky counter.

I look out toward the crowd of people, and that's when I see her, the woman from the beach. There's that smile from earlier, the one that made me grin like an idiot, and I can already feel the upward tug of my lips involuntarily.

Maybe this is proof that Max was right, and that I should've offered to buy her a drink. As soon as the bartender hands me my rum and coke, I'm going to force myself to go talk to her. I turn quickly back to the bar to see that he's putting the stirrer in my drink, so I hand him the cash including the tip, with a little extra because the poor guy is clearly overwhelmed, and quickly walk away to see if I can find her.

However, once I turn around, she's gone, and again I'm wondering if I really actually saw her at all.

*

Knowing there's no way I'm staying here alone; I decide to leave probably an hour after what may or may not have been the beach woman sighting. Max meets someone and naturally, he leaves with her, and I'm left to my own devices.

I end up sitting in a chair on the back patio of our room and smoke a cigar to help clear my mind. I light the cigar and inhale, relaxing a little. I'm not a smoker, but on occasion I do appreciate a good cigar, and my last night on vacation with the vast darkness of the ocean and sky intermingling with one another as my view seems as good a time as any.

I close my eyes, trying not to think of Blair, but am shocked when the image of a pair of glinting steel gray eyes breaks through. *You know, a totally normal reaction to have toward someone you had a two-minute interaction with, pathetic,* I scold myself once more.

I open my eyes in time to see a woman walk in front of me, but not just any woman, the one from the beach. *Is she a witch? Am I going fucking crazy, and this is a mirage? Maybe this is the equivalent of being stranded in the desert and seeing a river. I haven't been with a woman in so long that I'm literally hallucinating.* That must be it, I'm losing it.

Just then she spots me, "Hey you're the hot guy that got sand in my ass crack," she says already smiling. *Damn it don't grin like an idiot.*

I'm grinning like an idiot, "Hey! You're sand crack." *What the fuck Liam*, I yell to myself as I feel the heat of embarrassment creep up my neck.

To my complete and utter shock, she giggles, "Mind if I take a pull?" She motions toward my cigar.

"Go for it," I say, handing her the cigar with one hand and standing to pull out a chair for her with the other, the grate of the steal pulling against the concrete.

"Oh my, what a gentleman," she says with a trace of a southern accent that wasn't there before, alluding to the fact that she's playing a southern bell.

With her sitting next to me this close, I can see her in even more detail. With her reddish blonde hair braided back away from her face I can see the dusting of freckles across her nose and cheeks. Her fair skin looks soft enough to touch, and as she takes a pull from the cigar, I see her chest slightly expand, pushing her breasts upward. I notice then that she's wearing the weirdest necklace I've ever seen. Except it's not a necklace, but more of a neon shot glass on a chain.

"What does your shot glass say?" I ask as she passes me back the cigar, her fingers lightly brushing mine as she does. *So, fucking soft.*

She chuckles, "It says 'Swallow like a lady,' my best friend bet me that I wouldn't wear it all night, and at this stage I would do just about anything to cheer her up, so I did it."

As she says this, I'm inhaling a puff of cigar, and I laugh so abruptly that I cough erratically while I exhale the smoke. "Good to know," I say while coughing.

She smirks, her eyes smoldering and turning into liquid steel, "What? That I swallow?"

I blanch, "Oh, god no!" I'm backpedaling as quickly as I can, "I just meant that you're a good friend. It's good to know."

Her eyes crinkle at the edges, clearly enjoying teasing me, "Yeah well joke's on her, I'm one shot drunker and now I have a new necklace." That makes me laugh, she's funny and beautiful. Why did I have to meet her while in another country? If we were back home, I would immediately ask her out.

"What brings you guys to Jamaica?" I ask as I pass her back the cigar. She takes it from me, gingerly.

"Why? Planning on murdering me and seeing how easy it would be to get away with it? I've got to tell you my friend thinks I'm on my way back to our room, and if I'm not back soon she'll come looking for me." She wraps her pouty pink lips around the cigar again, the image stirring something in me that makes me need to adjust in my seat.

"If I recall, you walked up to me, and asked me for my cigar. How do I know you're not a serial killer or some sort of siren luring me to my doom?" Around the cigar, I watch her lips turn up, smiling around it. The image of my dick in her mouth as she smiles flashes behind my eyes. *Jesus Christ brain calm the fuck down.*

"If I'm the siren and you're the sailor in this scenario, I think the inevitable shipwreck would be worth the ride." As she says this I wonder if she's the type of person who is comfortable saying this to me because I'm a stranger she'll never see again, or if she's normally this confident. I wish I could find out.

"But, to answer your question I'm here as sort of a fill in. My best friend got engaged and this trip was supposed to be for her and her fiancé. His parents bought it for them as an engagement present to celebrate. Except right before we left, she found out that he was cheating on her with his receptionist, and demanded she get the trip and bring me instead."

"That is absolutely fucked. With his receptionist? That's not even creative," I retort while pushing back the dark curls that keep falling in my face from the wind.

"My sentiments exactly. A total dick Trevor move. I barely found him acceptable before, but now I want to put his number on every loan website I can find so his phone just rings and rings until he descends into madness." As she says this, I watch the breeze blow back her blonde braid, exposing her neck and the silken skin there.

"His name is Trevor? Yikes, that's not a good sign. I've yet to meet a Trevor that wasn't an asshole. I'm sure that's the least of what he deserves."

That makes her grin maniacally, "That's exactly what I always say. I've never met a Trevor and was like, 'He seems to be a standup guy that doesn't wear boat shoes or is patiently waiting for Vineyard Vines to be a publicly traded company."

She tilts the cigar toward me, using the gesture to ask if I want more. I shake my head no and she promptly stamps out the end on the edge of the metal table.

"I wanted to be excited to go on this trip with her, but seeing her so miserable, it was hard to enjoy it knowing she was hurting so bad. The whole atmosphere is so romantic and beautiful, and the room we're staying in is literally the honeymoon suite. When we walked in it looked like a red rose petal factory had exploded and they hadn't cleaned it up yet. When she saw it, she immediately burst into tears."

I grimace at that, "That sounds miserable. What did you do?"

Her eyes sparkle as she chuckles, "Well I went into panic mode. I wasn't thinking clearly. My best friend was crying, and I just wanted to get rid of it all as soon as possible, so I started grabbing all the rose petals and flushing them down the toilet..."

"Oh my God, that's a terrible idea," I say while shaking my head.

"Yes. Yes, it was. The toilet started to back up and overflow all the rose petals all over the bathroom. We called housekeeping and they rightfully gave me the death glare while they cleaned up a shit ton of rose petals and water that were all over the bathroom. I made some enemies that day."

She looks down at her flipflops, clearly thinking about something, and I wish I could read her mind. "What about you?" she questions, "What brought you here?"

I decide to omit the heartbroken portion of the decision to come here and instead say, "My best friend reviews hotels for a travel site. He decided to let me come along while he 'works' aka getting drunk and playing frisbee on the beach during the day and dancing at the club at night."

"That's a job? Jesus I'm jealous! I picked the wrong career path apparently. Are you sure he's not in the mob?" she chuckles, the sound is infectious.

I laugh at the knowledge that I'm not alone in questioning the legitimacy of Max's job, "Believe me I've asked him many times and he swears that he is in fact working for an actual business. He's just a lucky bastard, or so he says anyway."

We're silent for a beat, and I look up to see her eyes peering directly at me. She doesn't look embarrassed for being caught staring, but more like she's trying to read my thoughts. I watch her bite her pouty pink bottom lip and desperately wish I was the one biting it instead.

Chapter Three
Ella

He catches me staring, but I lean into it, continuing to hold his gaze. I feel hot all over, not only because the humidity of the night wraps around me like a warm blanket, but because of the magnetism I feel toward him.

With his amber eyes on me, I feel confident. I say what I feel and don't hold back, which is absolutely insane because I don't know this man, and after today I won't ever see him again. I decide then that this newfound confidence may be fleeting, but I'll enjoy it while I can.

I break the tension filled silence, "What's on your mind slick?" *Slick? Am I a private investigator from the 1930s? Lord Jesus help me.*

If he finds my words bizarre, he doesn't say anything, and I smooth out my blue floral body-con dress under his gaze as his amber eyes meet mine once more. He's looking at me like I'm a puzzle he hasn't put together yet. "I'm just trying to remember if I've ever talked to a stranger like this before. I don't think I have."

I watch that strong jaw clench for a fleeting moment. My gaze dips down to his mouth, his lips quirking up, acknowledging that he knows I'm appraising him. How could I not? My God this man is gorgeous.

His inky black hair is slightly longer on top than it is on the sides and a head full of perfectly messy curls. His amber eyes make me want to melt under their gaze while his strong sharp jaw peppered with stubble makes me want to lick along the edges of it.

For not the first time today I imagine those massive broad shoulders between my thighs and my pussy clenches at the thought. *Am I a feral fucking animal? Come on Ella, get your shit together.*

The sad truth is yes, I am feral for this man I just met, and I may never see him again, but I'm going to revel in that amber gaze for what little time I have it.

I muster up the confidence that has been building since I met him, and aided by Jose Cuervo, to walk over to his chair. His eyes dart to mine, like he's trying to figure out what my plan is. Joke's on him, I have no plan. I'm operating on feral woman energy alone.

I gingerly straddle his lap, not quite sitting yet, and hear a sharp intake of breath come from his throat. "We aren't strangers remember? We had a whole romcom collision earlier that will make sure I chafe for weeks to come."

His breath is more gravely now, deeper and hungrier while he chuckles, "Oh right. How could I forget? I'll be sure to tell our grandchildren someday."

A laugh escapes me, he's teasing obviously. We both know that whatever this is will only last one singular moment in our timelines. We're ships just passing through that happen to be stopping at the same port before we move on toward our final destination.

The air between us is getting thinner by the second, the tension feeling like a rubber band being pulled as far as it can go before it snaps. His eyes are burning now, looking at me like he wants to devour me whole, and at this point I want him so badly that if he did, I'd let it happen with a smile on my face.

I can't take it anymore; I need his lips on mine. I plunge my mouth toward his, and audibly groan at how good he tastes, like rum and smoke and slightly sweet. His tongue sweeps against my lips, trying to gain entrance into my mouth. I let him in willingly and run my tongue against his in return.

It feels like our lips are warring with one another in rapid movements, and his mouth is soft and strong. He sucks my lip between his teeth and gently nibbles on it. The small prick of pain makes me shiver.

"You like that pretty girl?" He whispers against my mouth, "Because I've been thinking about those lips on mine all day long."

My legs go wobbly with his breathy words and standing on them is taking away the energy that should otherwise be diverted toward that fucking mouth of his.

I sink down onto his lap and feel sheer euphoria when I do. He's hard, so beautifully bulging against my pussy that I'm thankful I decided to wear a dress tonight, if only because that means one less scrap of clothing between us.

"That for me?" I whisper against the place where his jaw and throat meet, the light stubble scraping against the skin of my lips. I can smell him now and it's suffocatingly intoxicating. A mixture of musk and salt from the air. I wonder if he tastes as good as he smells there, so I kiss up his throat and lick along his jaw. *Fuck, yes, he really does,* I think before my lips return to his.

"Goddamn," he moans against my mouth, "Of course, it is. Look how beautiful you are." His strong hand grips my chin, forcing me to look into a molten gaze that could set me on fire. "Now be a good girl and take off that necklace. It's cumbersome and I want it out of the way so I can I have those perfect tits in my mouth."

His words make me spiral into a corkscrew of need. For someone who seemed unsure of himself at first, he definitely isn't when someone is writhing on top of him. His commanding tone is a drug and I want more, so I listen and set the necklace by my phone on the table next to us.

"So good pretty girl, now ride the ridge of my cock until I tell you to stop," he commands as his lips go to my throat and kiss all the way down to the top of my breast. I stuck in a sharp breath in anticipation as his finger plays with the fabric at the top of my dress.

He's teasing me while all I can do is grind my hips against his erection and try to get more friction to my clit, and because my body has not a scrap of self-control while I'm on top of this man I wrap my arms around his shoulders and lift my breast closer to him, prodding him to take me into his mouth.

He chuckles huskily and pulls down my dress and bra over my left breast, exposing it to the warm air. My traitorous nipple is already pebbled with want, and he can't control the grunt that comes from his mouth as he sucks my nipple past his teeth. I smile, knowing I undo him just as much as he does me, and decide to torture him more.

I grind my pussy down harder on his bulge, feeling the grating of his zipper against my flimsy panties, which at this point are so soaked with my need for him I know I'll leave a wet spot behind...

As if he can read my thoughts, he lets my breast fall from his mouth and smiles up at me, "I can feel how wet you are beautiful, and I bet if I stick my fingers under your dress, you'll soak me."

I writhe on him more, trying to get enough pressure to my clit to relieve even just a little of the ache between my legs.

"Yes," I whine.

His hand palms the breast still in my dress as his mouth grabs another hungry kiss from my lips. "Good," he smirks, lord this man's cockiness with how he affects me should be unnerving, but instead it just turns me on more.

His hand slowly, painfully slowly, grazes down my torso, my hips. He plays with the hem on the bottom of my dress. I think his hand is going to go upward, when suddenly my phone vibrates on the table next to me.

"Don't answer it," he whispers against my neck. I look over to see that Josie is facetiming me. *Shit.*

"Fuck. I have to go. My friend probably thinks I've been murdered. I texted her like an hour ago that I was on my way back to the room. She's got to be freaking out." I look into his disappointed gaze, looking pained with need, and I know mine must look equally so, but Josie will always come before potential one-night stands that I'll never see again.

"I get it," he says while giving me a half-smile. Quickly I put my boob back in my dress and straighten my skirt out since it had basically run all the way up to the bottom of my ass.

I bend down and look in his eyes, trying to memorize them even though there's no reason to. "I had fun," I whisper, hoping he knows I genuinely mean that, and give him a kiss on the cheek.

As I turn to walk away, I hear him call after me, "Wait! I don't even know your name!"

I shout back grinning as I do, "Does it matter? It's not like we'll ever seen each other again, this isn't an actual romcom."

He shouts back, "What about your necklace? How else will everyone you meet know that you swallow like a lady?"

I look back at him then and stop, "Keep it," I yell back. "And if you really want to find me again you can put it on every fair maiden you see until you find your way back to me, like Cinderella."

I keep walking, laughing at my own dumb joke. Clearly it was wasted on him that I made a Cinderella joke, because my name is Ella and he doesn't even know my name, but I entertained myself none the less.

On my way home I feel cold for the first time since I've been here, the bubble of desire now popped, and my body lacking the extra heat that his gave me. I think about how exactly I'm going to explain to Josie that the reason I've been M.I.A. for the last hour was because I was so engulfed in a man that I was basically humping him with my titty out for all the world to see.

*

The next morning, our alarm blares into my consciousness, and it feels like my brain has been rattled inside of my skull. Josie pops up like a meerkat, like she was already awake and waiting for the alarm to go off.

A trait about her that I truly hate? She's a morning person. It makes me want to vomit. Actually, I think that might be the tequila shots from last night.

"Wakey wakey sleepy head!" Her chipper voice echoes around my ear canal like someone just put on a Korn album at full blast.

She's already wetting her toothbrush when I crack my eyes open to glare at her. This is the happiest I've seen her in weeks, and all I can think about is what body part I would need to sell, and to who, in order for me to get just five more minutes of sleep.

"This is an inhuman hour, you monster." I grumble and wipe my eyes with the heel of my hand.

My head feels like a concrete block that's being actively drilled into, and I have the acrid taste of last night's cigar and tequila laden heavy in my mouth.

The cigar... and I'm remembering him. His hands on my breasts, his lips on my collarbone, his tongue in my mouth. The way he smelled like musk from his cologne and salt from the ocean air; *the fucking smell of him, the taste of him, the way his voice commanded me.* It permeated every cell of my body in the best way possible.

The sheer thought replaying in my mind makes the spot between my legs liquid. *Jesus Ella you cannot be this unhinged about a man you'll never see again.*

Maybe I just need to get him out of my system. We did get very abruptly interrupted and didn't get to finish what we started. *When I get home, I'll bust out Ol' Reliable and go to town. Maybe after an orgasm or three I'll be able to stop thinking about him,* I think to myself before shoving the comforter over my head.

"Ma'am you knew we had a flight this morning. That's what you get for swallowing like a lady so many times last night," she says as she squirts cinnamon flavored toothpaste on her brush. Just add the fact that she has to be the only human on Earth who uses that stuff to her long list of serial killer traits.

"An act you incited by betting me in the first place!" I protest and throw the cover off my head.

"Speaking of which, El you never actually told me what happened last night." she said slightly muffled by the toothbrush in her mouth.

I get up to wash my face and brush my teeth alongside her, thinking about how exactly I'm going to explain this. It's not that I think she's going to judge me, far from it, she's my best friend and has been for over a decade now, but more than that I'm not even sure how to explain to myself what happened last night.

I sigh as I scrub my face, washing the remnants of last night's mascara I was too lazy to take off. *I look like a racoon that got drunk in a dumpster*, I think to myself. "So, um, you know the guy that ran into me at the beach?"

Her eyes meet mine in the mirror while she runs product through her curls, "The sandman? Yes, I remember."

"Oh cool, didn't realize you gave him a name. Um, yes, Sandman. Well, I was walking back to the room and there he was, on the porch, smoking a cigar. So, I thought hey I'm going to go up to him and say something, and I did, and then one thing led to another, and I ended up on his lap with my tit out grinding on his dick with our clothes on like I was in fucking high school." Saying this out loud just makes me realize just how completely unhinged I had become. I tamp down the urge to feel embarrassed. It's not like I'll ever see this man again anyway.

Her eyes widen in response before she smirks at me and chuckles, "No you didn't."

"Oh, but I did."

"That doesn't sound like something you'd do. You'd care far too much what people would think if they caught you topless and dry humping a man in public where anyone could see."

"Yes, while I agree that sounds more like me, apparently with the right amount of motivation I can become someone who doesn't care about social norms or public indecency." I finish moisturizing and begin packing up all my toiletries, feeling my cheeks heat at reliving the memory.

"We love to see it. You could afford to not care so much about what people think sometimes. Social norms and public indecency be damned!" She stops zipping up her suitcase to ball her fist into the air and shake it for dramatic effect.

"Yeah well, sorry in advance, but in my panic to get back to the room I left the shot glass necklace on the table. He tried giving it back, but I told him to keep it, like it was Cinderella's glass slipper or something." As I say this, I do a final sweep of the bathroom, shut off the light, and put all of my toiletries in my suitcase.

I hear her snort loudly, "I get it. Because Ella."

I smirk because I knew she'd get my reference, "Yeah well, the joke was lost on him because he didn't even know my name, and now he never will." I zip up my suitcase before continuing. "In hindsight I am sad that I left that necklace there though because I planned on leaving that in my will to my grandchildren someday."

"A potential treasured family heirloom to be sure, but I guess now we'll never know." Her eyes crinkle around the edges as she says it, barely containing her mirth. "Now hurry up and finish packing. We can't miss our flight. We have a big week ahead of us, especially you, considering this is your first-year teaching at Valley."

My nausea returns, twisting my stomach into an anxious knot, and this time it's not the aftermath of the tequila but the anxiety of starting at a new school.

It feels like starting all over again, and if I think about what happened at my last job it will send me into a shame spiral, making the anxious knot worse. Valley Creek Middle School should be a fresh start for me. At least that's what I'm hoping for.

After last year's debacle at my old school, I couldn't go back. Thankfully the school Josie is a counselor at had an opening for an 8th grade Social Studies teacher. A silver lining in the shit storm that was last school year is that now Josie and I get to be at the same school together, a dream we've had since we were teenagers.

"Thank you so much, Jos, I don't know what I would've done if you hadn't gotten me this job." A brief flash of a thought smacks me in the face, me having to move in with my mom and stepdad, comes to forefront of my mind, and I shudder.

I love my mom, and after everything he's done for my mom and I, I love my stepdad too. He helped raise me through the last of my formative high school years when he didn't have to, and I'm grateful for everything he's done for me. However, going back to Maple Grove and having to explain to all of my mother's tantric yoga friends why I'm living with them again would be a painful torture I never want to experience.

Yes, my mother does tantric yoga, and yes, it has scarred me on numerous occasions. If the next question is does she have a crystal shelf, the answer is also yes.

"El, what that place did to you was fucked up, and it's their loss. Valley is lucky to have you." She says this with such a matter-of-fact tone that it's almost enough to convince me.

As we pack up the last of our remaining things from the room, I pull up the bar on my suitcase and wheel it out the door. I'm sad to say goodbye right after I was finally able to get Josie to start enjoying herself, but she's right. We have a huge week ahead of us.

Before I turn to walk down the corridor, I look back at Josie. "Speaking of fucked up things that are their own loss, has the disappointing pocket rocket with a low-grade buzz, formerly known as Trevor, tried texting you this morning?"

A big smile takes over her entire face, "No... well he could have, but I wouldn't know. I blocked his number this morning when I woke up. He called me for the seven hundredth time, and I just couldn't take it anymore."

I squeal and fling my suitcase to the side to pull Josie in for a giant hug, squeezing her mercilessly. "I'm so damn proud of you, Jos!"

She returns the hug and lays her head against mine, "Yeah well, the time for self-pity is over. I told myself I needed to get my shit together by the time this trip was over." She shuffles her neon green duffle bag onto her shoulder, crushing her curls.

"I had my allotted time to grieve, and damn it I'm a strong, independent woman. I'm tired of wasting tears and dehydrating myself over that dumb idiot. Now let's get to the airport." And with that we exit the corridor and we're met with chilly morning air.

A swell of pride rushes through me. Sometimes I wish I was like Josie, confident and put together enough to be able to cut off any guilt or shame I feel because I know, in the end, it's what's best for me. I've never been like that, able to see the end result and know I did the right thing. Instead, I'm constantly plagued by all the different ways I've messed everything up, and eventually I get so triggered by it that I lock it away in a box in my mind and never visit or acknowledge it again, like the super healthy person that I am.

Chapter Four
Ella

Before I know it, it's Monday, the first teacher workday before school starts back from summer break. My first official day as the 8th grade Social Studies teacher for Valley Creek Middle School. Even though I won't meet my students for another couple days, I'm an anxious wreck.

As I stand in front of the full-length mirror in my bedroom, I can feel that critical eye start to come out once more. My brain won't shut up for longer than five seconds and therefore I've changed my outfit for what is now the fourth time. I have no doubt it's going to find yet another problem with this outfit too. Various band tees, jeans, and tank tops have all been thrown into the no pile. *Too tight, too lose, too casual, not casual enough, a Marilyn Manson shirt is probably not considered appropriate in the Middle School setting...* My head is a mess.

I look onto my bed, or what can now be more accurately described as my closet graveyard, and sigh. *Just shut the fuck up for five seconds brain so I can move on already.* The way things are currently going my brain's going to exhaust itself thinking of every possible scenario before I even leave the house.

I want to make a good first impression, but I don't want to overdo it either. Considering I'm going to be setting up my classroom a majority of the day I just give up and decide what I'm wearing is good enough, a yellow sundress with white flowers and lacy white Toms.

I check my makeup and run a brush through my tangled blonde hair before heading out the door toward my car. Most people think that when I wear a dress, it's because I'm trying to be fancy, but honestly if I can avoid wearing pants at any given time, I'm going to do it. Especially, when it's fucking August in Indiana, and the air is so thick with humidity that my skin becomes sticky with sweat the second I leave my house.

Yes, a sundress was the way to go, I think to myself as I open the door to my Prius and get immediately blasted in the face by the heat trapped inside. *Shit, my concealer is probably melting down my face already.*

I instantly turn my air conditioning on full blast and pray that I make it to the school before I sweat so much that I look like a drowned rat pulled from White River.

Fleetwood Mac's *Rhiannon* comes on through my speakers and Stevie's voice transports me to a place where I can't see literal heat waves coming off the concrete. I'm momentarily soothed enough to start driving and decide to leave before the anxious knot gets the best of me and I make a run for it.

*

I park the Prius in front of the side entrance where my classroom is so I can unload my boxes easier. I pop the trunk and take a good look at the building before taking a deep breath. It's obvious that this school has been well taken care of, and its massive red brick walls look new even though I know they're not. This school has been around for decades.

That's good, I can tell everyone really cares about this place. Coming from teaching at a charter school I'm not fully sure what to expect the differences will be transitioning to a public school, but I know from what Josie has told me it sounds a hell of a lot less toxic than the last place I was at.

After lugging in my last box and re-parking my car I give myself a second behind my new desk. I breathe in the familiar scent of school and enjoy my classroom before I finish setting it up.

It may be nerdy, but I fucking love the way that school smells like floor polish, books, and a little like chlorine. Growing up, before my mom met Hank, my stepdad, we moved around a lot. Anytime my mom would meet a new guy she would think was the one, we would move in with them.

Inevitably, it wouldn't work out. They would get in an argument or something that my mom didn't have the patience to work through, and we'd pick up and leave again. Even though every school was different, it really wasn't. The smell of a new school was one of the few familiar constants from my childhood, and even now it comforts me when my gut instinct is to panic.

I would throw myself into my schoolwork because it was easier than constantly meeting new people. I developed my love of history then. I think it was because my present and future always seemed unknown and constantly changing, but history wasn't something you could change. What's already happened in the past, can't be undone, but it can be learned from.

It was yet another constant in a world where I had none. Eventually, I gave up trying to make friends at all because I was tired of having to say goodbye. It just hurt too much. We would always promise to text or call each other only for it to never happen.

They would get busy with their friends that were still there and their activities and lives and would eventually stop reaching out. I couldn't blame them after all, it wasn't like I ever stayed long enough to make an actual long-distance friendship worth hanging onto. They were usually surface level friendships at best, at least until I met Josie.

When my mom met Hank, I figured it was going to be the same as any other guy my mom dated. Eventually I thought shit would hit the fan and we would pick up and leave Indianapolis to move on to the next place, but to my complete shock, we stayed.

It wasn't for lack of trying on my mom's part, but Hank fell in love with her, and when they got in an argument and my mom tried to do what she always did, run, he found us and convinced us to come home. After that, it seemed like my mom figured out how to stay put, with Hank's help, of course, and they got married.

Despite the fact that I was a stubborn and surly fourteen-year-old, I started to open up to Hank. In some ways, I feel like he sees me as the daughter he never had, considering I never knew my biological father and he doesn't have any kids of his own. According to mom, she hooked up with my bio dad at a Grateful Dead concert after he offered her his blunt and two months later, she found out she was pregnant with me. Hank is the closest I'd ever get to having a dad anyway.

Once I realized that we were actually going to stay this time, I started to open up more. I entered a program at school that was supposed to help you decide if you wanted to become a teacher that also provided college prep, which is where I met Josie. After I met her, there wasn't a doubt in my mind that Indianapolis was my home.

After I've finished putting the final touches on my classroom, it's time for me to head to the theater room where our first administrative meeting is being held. I look at the walls a final time to make sure it looks as inviting and comfortable as possible before grabbing the school map off my desk and walking out the door.

As I listen to my shoes squeak against the polished floor, I realize that I didn't even need a map at all because the theater is directly down the hall from me in the center of the building. I push open the wide oak door to find theater seating that leads down to a small stage where I see Josie sitting near the front, her wild curls tied up in a knot on her head with a scrunchy.

Immediately I rush toward her, just in time for her to turn around and see me. We both squeal and give each other a giant hug. "I can't believe you're here El! I'm so excited."

I sit down in the open seat that she saved for me and wrap my arm around hers, "I know, I am too! This is going to be so much fun. If only little El and Jos could see us now!" With a giggle we settle in as Principal Bledsoe walks up the wood-splintered steps onto the stage.

As Bledsoe walks across the stage, it is very clear that he commands authority as well as the room. He's tall and broad shouldered with deep set eyes and skin with perfectly coiffed waves in his hair. I suspect that this man has not once had an embarrassing moment or bad hair day in his life.

His deep timbre echoes through the theater as he begins his speech, "Welcome everyone to what I'm sure will be yet another successful school year here at Valley Creek Middle School--"

"And my last!" An elderly woman in the front row interrupts as she raises a maroon-painted fingernail defiantly into the air.

Bledsoe chuckles, a deep rumble that reverberates off the walls and revealing a small gap between his two front teeth. *Oh, good, he has a sense of humor.* "Yes Stella, as I'm sure you will remind us constantly over the upcoming year, you're retiring."

Bledsoe starts launching into expectations for the upcoming school year, and I try to listen, I really do, but my eyes start to glaze over and succumb to a daydream. A daydream of amber eyes and the taste of a smoke and rum flavored tongue against mine…

"And yes, though some of you may be retiring or moving onto different paths in your teaching career; the cycle of education continues with new educators. Educators who are ready to help inspire the students at Valley Creek Middle School. Helping prepare the next generation for what comes next. With that in mind, please help me welcome our new 8th grade social studies teacher, Ms. Ella Jacobs." *Shit did he just say my name?*

"Come on up Ella, and introduce yourself to everyone," Bledsoe's voice echoes as he waves me up onto the stage. *Oh, okay, I guess I'm standing in front of a giant group of people today…*

A polite clap comes from the crowd as a deep flush crawls up my chest and leaks into my cheeks. My skin feels hot and itchy under everyone's gaze as I walk up the steps.

I lightly clear my throat and in the cheeriest voice I can muster I begin to speak, "Hi everyone! I'm Ella Jacobs, and as Principal Bledsoe said, I'm the newest addition to the 8th grade Social Studies department. I graduated from Indiana University, go Hoosiers!"

I hear a few excited yells from my peers out in the seats and could only be from what I would assume are fellow I.U. grads, "I majored in education with a focus in history, and up until-" I stop mid-sentence because when I look into the middle of the crowd of teachers and staff, I see him. The man I haven't been able to stop thinking about for the last few days, the man that Josie so delicately refers to as Sandman. The man that's forced me to test out the battery life of Ol' Reliable over the last couple days.

I try to speak, but the words are caught in my throat, and my eyes must be the widest they've ever been, a look I can see he's currently matching. He clearly remembers who I am because those amber eyes I was just daydreaming about only minutes before look like they're going to pop out of his head if they got any bigger. His mouth is open in complete shock. *I've got to be hallucinating...*

"Ms. Jacobs?" I hear Bledsoe's voice, but I feel like I just ate a popsicle with my front teeth and now my entire body has brain-freeze. I literally cannot do anything but stand there gawking, unable to speak or move until what clearly is a hallucination is over. *Did my mom give me ayahuasca tea again...?*

"Ms. Jacobs? Are you ok?" His deep voice is growing more and more urgent until I'm finally rendered mobile again.

My words come out jumbled and fall out of my mouth all at once, "Sorry yep, um, can't wait to get to know everyone!" I panic and awkwardly leave the stage in what could be considered a half walk half jog that I don't think any human being has ever done, and probably could never recreate again. I quickly sink down into my seat and cover my face.

"Did you just have a stroke? Do you smell burnt toast? That's a sign you know." Josie whispers in a I'm-whispering-but-I've-never-actually-whispered-in-my-goddamn-life way. Honestly, I want to say I didn't, but with who I just saw, a stroke seems like the most logical explanation. With how stale this auditorium smells I kind of wish I could smell burnt toast.

What a great way to introduce yourself Ella, I'm sure every person in here right now is thinking about how totally normal and not spastic you are. I sink down farther into my seat and try to listen to the rest of the diatribe Bledsoe spouts off, but the thought of focusing is completely overshadowed by the fact that I saw the man whose mouth had my nipple in it mere days ago while simultaneously embarrassing the shit out of myself in the span of thirty seconds.

Chapter Five
Liam

What. The. Actual. Fuck. This can't possibly be real. As I watch Ella, which is apparently her name and not beach siren like I've previously been calling her, walk up to the stage my pulse quickens instantly.

I feel like every cartoon character whose eyes bulge out of their sockets and turn into pounding hearts. I know I was joking before, but I think there's a very strong possibility that she is in fact a witch. It's the only explanation.

Not just because this entire scenario is extremely unlikely, but that I've thought of little else since I was with her the other night. My thoughts have been plagued by her every moment since then.

Every daydream I have is of her grinding on my dick outside of my pants. Her skintight dress riding up to cup her ass, the smell of her skin, like lemon and fresh air, that resides at the crook of her neck. I can still hear her panting in my ear. The moan I pulled from her when I took her perfect pink nipple into my mouth. The way her tongue was so greedy against mine, like no matter how many times she tasted me, it would never be enough, matching me stroke for stroke. I've fisted my cock to the thought more times than is probably normal for an interaction that didn't even lead farther than our clothes being removed.

In Jamaica I just kept wishing that I could see her again, and maybe, this is it, my chance. Call it fate, God, luck or whatever, but I'm not going to waste this, even though every logical thought in my brain is telling me that this is just a glitch in the matrix.

A small part of me wonders if she even remembers me, but then I see it, or rather she sees me and immediately stops mid-sentence, looking directly into my eyes. *Oh, fuck, yes, she recognizes me all right.*

I watch Bledsoe prompt her multiple times before she realizes she's supposed to respond and then runs off the stage. *Holy shit, she really is as beautiful as I remember.* Her long strawberry blonde waves cascade down her back, and the sundress she's wearing hugging her along the curves that I ran my hands down only days before. From a distance I can't see them, but I know they're there, those piercing gray eyes that could burn a hold right through me.

She's perfect, and the thought of needing to taste her again overwhelms my brain, and it takes all of my effort to focus enough to at least pretend I'm paying attention.

*

Whatever Bledsoe talked about for the rest of the meeting I couldn't say, my brain had short-circuited. *Ella. Ella. Ella.* Playing over and over again in my head, like a record that had been scratched, and it was the only word I could hear through the static. *I have to talk to her.*

When the meeting is over, I see her rush out of her seat and head back down the hallway. *My hallway? Does she know where my classroom is?* No, she doesn't, but instead runs into the classroom across from mine. And then I remember, she's replacing the 8th grade Social Studies teacher, the one who taught across the hall from me. *Her classroom is across from mine.*

As I walk toward the doorway she rushed into, I see the name Ms. Jacobs on the door. My thoughts are confirmed, she is most definitely in the classroom across the hall. *This should be interesting...*

I enter through the doorway, and I immediately notice how much effort she's put into making her students feel comfortable. The desks are arranged in three pods with the names of the different branches of government: legislative, judicial, and executive, hanging on signs above them. Along the top of the wall by the white board is a picture of every U.S. President and their name in order of term, and the room smells lightly like apples coming from the candle warmer in the corner. Her desk is decorated with pictures of friends and family, and a framed picture of former Supreme Court Justice Ruth Bader Ginsberg. Just seeing how much effort she put into her classroom makes me smile.

When I look over in the corner where her bookshelf is at, I see her pacing back and forth with one of her hands balled up into the other, wringing them together. She looks deep in thought, and I stand there watching her for a minute, worried that if I say something I'll scare her out of her trance.

I'm just close enough to see where the top of her dress hugs her chest before meeting the curve of her waist and flaring out. *I remember that curve, and I'm itching to touch it again.*

Finally, I decide to break the trance by lightly clearing my throat, "*Umm...* hi?" I say in the most even tone I can muster, which is not at all, and my voice comes out uneven and gravely.

Her blonde hair whips over her shoulder while her head jerks to the side to see who was speaking. Once she registers that it's me standing in her doorway, I see her eyes go wide like an owl. "Oh, um, hello."

I'm close enough now that I can see the freckles dusting over her nose and cheeks, her sharp gray eyes looking as if they could peer directly into my soul.

"So not sure if you remember me..." I trail off as I say this, I realize I'm giving her an out; a way to pretend that we've never met. I see the way she's looking at me, and I know if she spins it that way, she'd be lying to the both of us, but I can't imagine what this must feel like from her perspective. I want her to at least have the option to have a fresh start.

"I don't really have a habit of making out with a ton of different men in various tropical locations, so yes I remember." I watch her gray eyes crinkle at the edges, her pink lips tugging slightly upwards like she's suppressing a smile. *She's at least acknowledging that we've met, so I guess that's a good thing.*

I'm trying to be casual, I really am, but my body is a fucking traitor. I feel my heart rate accelerate, my skin prickling with the memory of the way she felt against me. "Oh, cool, yeah, I guess if I would've known you'd be here I could've brought your shot glass with me..."

She's actually smiling now, a chuckle escaping from her, and I can't help but grin back at her. "Are you saying you kept it...?

I watch her tuck a strawberry blonde lock of hair behind her ear, exposing more of her neck and collarbone. *I kissed that exact place on her collarbone, nibbled on that spot on her neck.* I internally groan at the memory of it.

"Well, if I recall you told me to and I quote 'Keep it and try it on every fair maiden like Cinderella,' and because I don't make a habit of making out with a ton of different women in various tropical places, as you say, I kept it." I know I'm smiling like a smug idiot, but I honestly don't think I have control over what my body does when it's around her. Everything just has a mind of its own.

"Ha. Cute. Very cute." She says as she wrings her hands in front of her.

A realization dawns on me, "Wait. Was the Cinderella joke because your name is Ella?"

A cackle rips from her throat, immediately making me laugh in response, "Yeah I thought I was pretty clever with that one."

There's a moment of dead air, where neither of us are talking, and it seems like we're both barely even breathing. "So, listen, I wanted to come talk to you. Since I'm right across the hall…"

She holds her hand up interrupting what was the beginning of a ramble, "Wait. Your room is across the hall from mine?"

"Yes…" I trail off.

Her eyes narrow in response, "So let me try and comprehend what's happening, in case this is real and not actually a fever dream resulting from one of my mother's questionable teas, like I think it is. You and I met in a completely different country and made out. We potentially would've taken it even further than that, but we were interrupted. It was pretty great…"

I smile, glad that I'm not the only one who enjoyed myself. "Agreed. Though I'd argue it was more than pretty great if I say so myself."

Her hand wringing has picked up momentum now, shaking her hands out every few seconds as a result. "But we figured we would never see each other again. I didn't even bother asking your name because of that. Yet, here I am, my first day teaching at a new school, and you, hot guy that got sand up my ass, not only teach here, but do so across the hall from me?"

I feel a blush crawl up my neck because she called me hot so blatantly and my body can't hear one compliment before getting embarrassed. God Blair really did a number on me. "I think that the fact that I teach across the hall is less shocking than the fact that I teach in the same school and live in the same city, but overall, yeah that's a great summary of events."

She stops fidgeting with her hands, and I watch her place them on her perfect, wide, hips before I continue. "However, since we're in a professional setting, being colleagues and all, I feel like Mr. Hot Guy that got sand up my ass would be more appropriate. However, I understand that might be too long winded, so you can call me by my government name which is Liam, or Mr. Scott."

She snorts, "Well Mr. Scott, if you came here to tell me that we should just remain colleagues, then have no fear. I have no interest in dating someone I work with. The waters at my last school got muddied and I never want to experience that again."

Well, this isn't going how I want it to at all. *What does she mean the waters got muddied at her last school?* I'm not in the business of making a woman uncomfortable when she has no interest in me. I can take a hint. If she doesn't want to be with me, then at least I'll have closure, and I'll be able to get over this insane infatuation I have with her. *It's probably just because we met on vacation, in the real world this wouldn't work.* Not to mention how embarrassing it is that I clearly am way more into her than she is me. Story of my life. Having a professional relationship won't be hard, it was just a one-time thing.

"Well obviously, I can respect that. I just wanted to clear the air. Your professionalism has been noted, Ms. Jacobs." On the outside, I'm trying to seem confident and unaffected, but on the inside, I feel like there's a rock of disappointment sitting on my chest. A fact that is truly insane if only for the fact that I don't know this woman really at all.

I give her a slight wave and turn around to go to my classroom across the hall. I'm almost out of the doorway when I hear her say, "Wait, Li—I mean Mr. Scott, I meant to ask you what class do you teach?"

I feel a cocky grin she can't see spreading across my face. Thinking of the best way to deliver my exiting line, I turn to her and simply say "Chemistry," and wink at her before I close the door behind me. *Flirting is not the way to start a professional relationship between colleagues Liam,* I scold myself, and walk into my classroom.

Chapter Six
Ella

Holy shit. Fuck. Double fuck. If there's a cussword in the English language, it's running through my mind right now. The moment I heard his voice, my body responded, anxiety and desire dumping into my bloodstream and mixing together into a cocktail that surely would be lethal.

Anxiety because this is exactly what I don't need. I need a fresh start, a new beginning at a new school where I can teach what I love in peace. Desire because, well that man is so fucking hot that if I touched him and he burned me, I'd say thank you and then lean in for more.

Telling Liam that we just needed to be coworkers felt wrong, like drinking black coffee when you want a macchiato, but it had to be done. Do I ache between my legs just thinking about finishing what we started? Yes, but a good job needs to preside over good dick. Checks before sex and all that...

If I would've been able to see three moves ahead at my last job, then maybe, I could've prevented what happened. Inky curls, strong arms, and broad shoulders be damned, I couldn't get distracted. *And if I bust out Ol' Reliable tonight and think of him while using it, then well a win is a win.*

Oh lord I need to tell Josie this right fucking now. I quickly shut off the lights in my classroom and lock the door so I can run down to her office. As I walk down the hallway, listening to my Toms squeak against the freshly polished floor, I try to quiet my brain that's working a mile a minute.

I've heard of people that can quiet their brain and sometimes think nothing at all, but mine is the opposite, I can't stop thinking. My mind is the equivalent of a security guard in front of thirty different monitors, switching screens back and forth and sometimes watching two at once. I'm a medicated Queen, so now it's like fifteen monitors, but I don't think I'll ever be able to fully quiet my brain no matter how hard I try and calm it.

I do a rapid-fire shave and a haircut knock before opening the door to Josie's office and bursting through the door. I didn't realize how quickly I was walking, or how out of shape I am, until I stop in front of her desk and start breathing erratically.

She looks up at me and immediate concern crosses her face, "El? What the hell are you ok?" She rounds her desk and wraps me in a hug of soft skin and coconut smell.

Through rapid breaths I manage to get out, "Jos, oh my God." I rest my arms on my knees because that's what people do in movies to help them breathe deeper. It did nothing for me, but then again, those people probably can remember the last time they ran. Which I can't.

Her dark brown eyes bore into me as she pulls herself slightly away from me and shakes my shoulders. "Is someone trying to murder you?" Her first response in any situation. She watches a truly disturbing amount of true crime and it's done her exactly zero favors.

I chuckle a little at that, "No, but the most insane thing has just happened."

I look at the desk in her office as I wait for my breathing to quiet down. She has pictures all over, of us on the beach in Jamaica, dressed up for Halloween our sophomore year of college as Salt n Peppa, and Mr. and Mrs. Jones standing on either side of their daughter with an I.U. diploma and a giant smile on her face. My heart warms at the sight and now I'm finally breathing at a normal pace and can speak. "I think the most unlikely coincidence in the entire world has just happened. You remember sandman, from our trip?"

Her brown eyes go wide, and I think she would look less skeptical if I told her, I won the Nobel Peace Prize by playing 'Can't Buy Me Love' on the harmonica. "Yes... why?"

"Well, I think I got sucked into a wormhole that sent me into another universe."

She rolls her eyes at that, "Your penchant for dramatics is as strong as ever."

My eyes narrow back at her, "Your snark has been noted and filed away for a later date, but how well do you know Mr. Scott?

I seem to have sufficiently confused her because her head has cocked to the side questioningly, "Liam? We've worked together since I started here. We're on the activities committee together... why?"

"Well, I wanted to tell you how I know him," I pause slightly for dramatic effect, "Because I know him from sticking my tongue down his throat while we were in Jamaica. He's the sandman."

Her mouth gapes and every part of her body language is reading shock, I truly think, I would've had better luck of convincing her of the harmonica thing. "You're telling me that Liam Scott, 8th grade Chemistry teacher, is the sandman? You're full of shit."

I chuckle, "Believe me you don't have to explain to me how unhinged all of this is, but my God even in fluorescent lighting that man is so hot."

Josie rubs her neck with black painted nails, "Yeah

definitely. If he wasn't only thirty, I would think the song '*Hot for Teacher*' was written about him. All of the students love him."

"I'm not shocked by that at all," I muse.

She smirks at me then, "No one's really gone for him recently because he was dating Blair up until a few months ago..."

"Wait, as in Blair the school nurse?" I vaguely remember seeing her at the meeting. I obviously looked at the staff directory before I started here, and I remember that even before I saw her in person, I registered how pretty she was.

She has long chestnut hair that flows down to her mid back and is beautiful, undeniably so. I remember thinking that she looks like the woman Ursula from 'The Little Mermaid' turned into so she could marry Prince Eric. Me, well, I give off more of a Flounder vibe.

"One in the same." Still smirking and giving a playful wink, "But she broke up with him a couple months ago so if you're interested in an Act II, he's single and ready to mingle. That is if you're interested in 'mingling' with him anyway."

I audibly groan, "I would love nothing more than to climb that man like a rock wall, but I can't risk going through what I went through last year."

Visions of everyone's eyes boring into me, like I brought leprosy to the school or something, whispering behind hands, and ignoring my general existence flood my brain. "I've sworn off 'mingling' with coworkers."

Her deep brown eyes soften at that, her hands clasping mine, "El you don't know that it would--"

I interrupt her, "It's not about whether or not I know it will be the same. No matter how devastating his eyes are or how his forearms look with the sleeves of his button-up rolled to his elbows, I must resist. It's not worth the risk."

She gives me a slightly appraising look, "If you say so, but I've seen this plot in enough romantic comedies to know that the inability to be together just makes it hotter."

I roll my eyes at that. "I'm not an animal. I can control myself," I say more confidently than I feel.

Dying for a subject change I ask, "Want to go get coffee from the lounge?" She nods before we walk out of her office and head down the hallway.

Chapter Seven
Liam

It's my free period, and I have approximately seventy-five scientific method worksheets to grade and a back-to-school night presentation for the student's parents to finish. I haven't started any of it.

Why? Well, because my door is open and so is Ella's, *sorry, Ms. Jacobs's*, and I can't stop listening to her voice. Even though I can't see her, I hear her, and believe me my brain loves to fill in the gaps. The animated tone she has in her voice when she talks to her students is what I imagine sunshine would sound like if it talked. She's currently talking about the Boston Tea Party, and just said the phrase, 'And that's the tea.' I can't help but laugh, she's so great with these kids.

I'm not really a history buff by any means, but I could listen to her talk all day long, although, that might have more to do with my infatuation with her and less with the actual history, but still. I could close my door to avoid distraction but keeping it open leaves the opportunity for her to come by my room and talk to me. Clearly, I'm a martyr, and our frequent talks about music and the insanity of our students between passing periods have become the part of my day I look forward to the most.

It's been two weeks since Ella told me that she wanted to keep things professional, and though I thought that would be easy enough, it's clear my brain disagrees. I'm addicted to her, and not even just in the physical sense, although, that too, but I also seem to find any excuse I can to talk to her.

Half the time I don't even realize I'm doing it, it's like I think about her smile or making her laugh and the impulse propels me forward, only to come to when I reach her doorway or I'm across from her in the hallway.

Any time I think I've got her out of my system, I smell lemon and think of that spot on her neck or see the color of gray steel and think of her eyes. It should be noted that trying to go an entire day without smelling lemon or seeing the color gray is virtually impossible, so it can be imagined how successful I've been.

Hell, just thinking of that smell has my skin buzzing. Without my students here during my free period to keep me focused on the lesson my brain might as well be a puddle of smut soup.

I think of sitting on that chair on the porch, Ella straddling me, and the warm Jamaican air smelling of salt and ocean cocooned around us. How soft and warm she was beneath my touch. How her skin tasted as I licked and nibbled up her neck.

I have truly lost all sense of rational thought, which is really unlike me. I dated a woman for a year, and I don't think she had this kind of effect on me, but then again maybe, that was the problem.

Blair was a nice enough person, and I thought that at one point we would get married, but in the end, we just didn't see our lives going in the same direction. She wanted a fancy Carmel wife life, the richest suburb in the city.

Unfortunately, that's just not something that can be provided on a middle school chemistry teacher's pay. We had gotten into a couple arguments about how I had a degree in chemistry, and she felt like I was wasting it as a teacher, but I love my students. Even though science is my passion, I was never meant to be in a lab all day. My calling is to inspire young people who also love science, or to teach those who don't love it that it can actually be fun.

I may not be the next George Washington Carver or Marie Curie, but I'd love to think I could be teaching them. No matter how much I tried to explain that she just didn't understand.

I wanted to make the relationship work, but eventually she dumped me and told me that she knew what kind of life she wanted to lead and that it didn't coincide with mine. I felt heartbroken, but I respected her honesty, and now that I think back on it, I wonder if I ever actually even loved her or just the idea of having a forever with someone. I think we both stayed together so long because we thought we could change the other's mind.

My dads have that relationship that's so idyllic that I just wanted to have it too. A best friend I could spend my life and grow old with. I feel like deep down I knew that Blair wouldn't be that person for me, but that didn't mean getting dumped by her hurt any less.

I roll my shirt sleeves up to my elbows so I can buckle down and focus, but when I pull out my red pen to start grading, I think of perfect pouty lips opening around a cigar and sucking. *Oh, great, I lasted all of one minute without thinking about her.*

I need a voice of reason, so I pull my phone out of my pocket and text the only other person that knows about Ella and me, Max.

Me: Talk me off the ledge.

Maximiliano the douche: ooh what ledge? Are we finally going cliff diving?

Me: No dumb ass I'm talking about a metaphorical ledge.

Maximiliano the douche: well, that's what you get when you try and use nuance with me. What metaphorical ledge are you on?

Maximiliano the douche: ooh wait, let me guess, still hot for teacher?

Me: You've got to stop making that joke. It's losing its luster. I'm pretty sure Eddie Van Halen said the phrase less.

Maximiliano the douche: can't stop won't stop. Just ask her out.

Me: She already said it wasn't happening.

Me: She has a no dating colleague's rule.

Maximiliano the douche: That's a dumb rule. Maybe you should just try and woo her. *Waggles eyebrows suggestively*

Me: I'm not going to be that guy that thinks he knows what a woman wants more than she does. She said she doesn't want to date, so I'm respecting that.

Maximiliano the douche: A gentleman as always good sir.

Me: I guess she said something happened at her old school.

Maximiliano the douche: Shit. What?

Me: Idk, didn't ask.

Maximiliano the douche: Wow talk about a cliff hanger. How are you going to set up for a big reveal and know nothing?

Maximiliano the douche: But if you aren't going to ask her out…

Me: Shut the fuck up.

Me: Why did I text you? You're absolutely no help.

Maximiliano the douche: Just saying it's a missed opportunity to not finish what you guys started, and if you aren't going to then…

Me: I know you're joking, but I also think, I could shove the Bunsen burner next to me down your throat and feel no remorse.

Maximiliano the douche: ooh kinky.

I set my phone down and roll my eyes. I should've known better than to think Max would ever be a voice of reason. I love him, he's like a brother to me, but really, he is the last person I should ask for relationship advice. Considering my actual brother and I don't see each other very often because he lives in Tennessee, and is equally terrible at advice, I don't have a lot of options.

Respecting Ella's desire for discretion really doesn't allow for anyone else to know or talk to about the situation, and since everyone else I hang out with works at Valley with me, Max is pretty much my only option. I guess this is just going to have to be a learn as you go situation, which means I need to get over this very irritating crush I have on Ella and try to be friends with her, because it looks like friends is all we'll ever be.

Chapter Eight
Ella

Well… that went fine, I guess…

I try not to be overly critical of myself and how my presentation to the parents went. It's not like this is my first back to school night by any means, but it's my first one at Valley, and I wanted to make a good first impression. I know the parents trusting me with something as important as their child's education is a big deal, and I don't take that lightly.

I move to the back of the room where I set up a refreshment table for the parents and start to clean up. I scrape the crumbs from the leftover cookies to the side of the table and into my cupped hand to dump them into the trashcan.

My worry was only amplified by the fact that I could hear all of the parents laughing across the hall in Liam's room. I feel like at one point during my presentation I looked to the back row of parents to see Ava's father physically straining to keep his eyes open.

I'll try not to take that one personally… As I'm clearing the rest of the cups from around the punch bowl, I hear a light tap come from my door.

I turn to see Liam, in all his rolled-up shirt-sleeve glory, standing in my doorway. The longer top part of his dark curly hair is slightly falling into his eyes and the sight of that makes my stomach feel like it's competing for Olympic gold in gymnastics. *He's really trying to torture me, isn't he? This definitely feels like some sort of sadistic torture.*

"Ms. Jacobs?" *Shit, I think he realized I was looking a little too closely at him.* There's a cocky smile starting to play toward the edge of his lips. *Yep... he saw.*

"Mr. Scott," I reply in the most professional tone that I'm currently capable of after just moments ago staring at his arms. *Ugh, I wish I could feel those arms wrapped around my body again... no. Bad Ella! Colleagues don't think about other colleagues' arms being wrapped around them.* Lord what I wouldn't give right now to have one of those fancy brains that can shut off occasionally right now.

"So how did your first Valley back-to-school night go?" he asks while leaning against the doorway. As I watch the movement, I try not to think about how his broad shoulders take up an absurd amount of space and how good he looks while doing it.

I roll my eyes dramatically, "Not nearly as entertaining as yours apparently. At one point I looked back to see Ava's dad physically prying open his eyes, so he didn't fall asleep."

He chuckles, that cocky smile still lingering on his lips, "Don't take it personally, he works third shift, so he barely sleeps. I do have a penchant for showmanship when it comes to science, but I think that has more to do with the fact that a couple years ago I learned that if the parents like you, they don't cuss you out."

His grin is full of mirth "Well, they cuss you out less anyway when their perfect little angel gets an F because I caught them cheating on their Chemistry test and 'they would never do that,' he says while making air quotes with his fingers."

The idea of this makes me laugh, "Wow you should teach a master class. I'll have to remember that next year."

He shuffles his feet a little bit and crosses his arms over his chest. Looking at where I can see his broad shoulders slightly straining against the fabric, I can see he has tiny little tacos all over his shirt. The idea that this giant man is passionate about science and wears shirts with little prints all over them just makes him all the more adorable. He closes the distance just a little bit more between us, "Hey would you want to go grab a drink after this--"

I interrupt before he can finish that sentence, "Liam, I don't know if that's such a good idea." *Oh, yes, it is,* the irrational part of my brain thinks.

His eyes go wide, and his words come out quickly, like if he doesn't say them all right now that I'll get upset, "Oh no, not like that! A bunch of us are going to a pub down the street called Crenshaws. We all like to go hang out there sometimes because the drinks are cheap, and the pool tables are free. Kind of a dive but... it's cozy."

I feel the heat of embarrassment stain my cheeks. *That's what you get for interrupting Ella. Why would he be asking you out? You told him you should just be coworkers and it's not like he disagreed or anything.* "Oh, um, that sounds like fun. I'd love to! I've been meaning to get to know everyone more anyway."

He blows out a small, even breath, looking relieved that I no longer think this is a date. "Cool, we're meeting there in twenty. See you in a bit." He gives me a half wave and then turns to leave the room while I clean up the last remaining mess left over and try not facepalm myself.

*

After I type Crenshaw's into my GPS, I'm pulling into a gravel parking lot about five minutes later. I park the Prius and walk toward the door to a small building surrounded by siding. Through the windows I can see the glow of neon signs and a brightly lit open sign blinking on and off in the doorway.

As I open the door, I hear the scrape of metal against the scratchy green carpet. *Carpet in a bar? That's a bold choice...*

I walk into a small dimly lit room with a large oak pool table in the middle and wood paneling surrounding the room. The walls are covered in various neon signs for different beers, and I can see a Joe Camel poster advertising cigarettes that has to be at least thirty years old behind a karaoke machine. The poster seems on brand because the bar still has that old cigarette smell that seems to be baked into the insulation of this place.

Indiana outlawed smoking indoors twenty years ago, but some smells linger, like a time stamp of when this bar was in its hay day. It's oddly comforting in this dimly lit place, like what I would imagine staying at grandma's house would've been like. If grandma was a chain smoking, beer drinking, biker. Not like I would know if she was or not, considering my grandma and grandpa disowned my mom for getting pregnant out of wedlock and not knowing who the father was, but I can imagine all the same.

Behind the bar is an elderly woman, with dark eyes crinkling at the corner, curly salt and pepper hair, and ebony skin. This may be the first time in history that I've ever seen an elderly woman in a leather vest, but something about this woman tells me that it's a staple in her wardrobe. She looks tough as nails, and I'm immediately under the impression that this woman takes shit from no one. I love her.

I see a table of some familiar faces under a Natural Ice sign, and wave to them before walking up to the bar to order a drink.

As I get closer, I see that the name Lola Crenshaw etched on the lapel of the leather vest. She's polishing a glass and looks up when I sit on the stool in front of the bar. "Let me guess, white claw?"

My face must look completely perplexed because as basic as I feel when I order them, I do love a good claw. "I'm sorry... how did you know that?"

She smirks a little, "Call it a gift I suppose. Forty years of tending bar makes you really good at reading people. When someone new walks in I like to guess what they're going to order. I'm almost never wrong." I look above her head to see a sign that reads, Crenshaw's Est. 1983, while she reaches into a small fridge to grab out a mango white claw before popping the tab.

"Glass?" She asks while tilting the can toward me.

"No, the can is fine. Thank you!" I hand Lola my card and leave a generous tip before going over to the table.

As I'm walking away, I hear Lola call after me, "Hey big tipper what's your name?"

Her bluntness makes me laugh and turn around to shout, "Ella!"

"Nice to meet you Ella," she says, her red lipstick-stained lips curling into a smile that makes her eyes crinkle at the edges.

I look to see Josie waving me over to the open seat next to her, and I plop down into the wooden chair. I recognize some of these teachers from the school, but the only ones I've talked to so far are Josie and Liam. I haven't been super great about getting to know everyone just yet, but they all look like they're in a passionate discussion.

Mrs. Corinth the art teacher, or Stella around coworkers, sticks her maroon-painted fingernail on the table and taps passionately. I'm guessing she loves the color maroon because she's wearing lipstick in the same shade as her nails and is wearing a pashmina that is almost identical in color. It suits her though, offsetting the deep wrinkles in her dark skin and wild black curls sprinkled with silver that are being held back by a thin gold scarf.

She peers through the glasses on the tip of her nose, "All I know is that I'm not doing it! I'm a year away from retirement and I'm too old for this shit! I've made it decades without getting suckered into the activities committee and I'm not about to start now!"

Coach Gutierrez, who is both the football coach and health teacher, also known as Sergio, rubs his face in an exhausted manner. His dark brown eyes and perfectly gelled hair reflect the glare of the neon Natural Ice sign. Even though he looks completely exhausted, he's still handsome.

He lets out a deep sigh before saying, "It's football season. I know it's only middle school but I'm really trying to get these guys ready to play at the high school level, and I can't be two places at once. Practice three nights a week and games on Friday nights doesn't really leave a ton of time for anything else."

"It's really not that bad guys," I hear Liam say has he moves the swizzle stick in his rum and coke before taking a sip.

I watch everyone at the table roll their eyes and groan. I'm sufficiently confused so I ask, "I'm sorry, what are we talking about?"

Senora Segovia the Spanish teacher, or Nadia, ruffles her red brown hair. She seems shy at first, but then brings her eyes to meet mine, a beautiful hazel color, and smiles at me warmly. "Jenna, Mrs. Clark, just had her baby and went on maternity leave. She was actually the social studies teacher you took over for since she decided to stay at home. She was on the activities committee and Bledsoe is trying to find someone to replace her."

"What's the activities committee?" I ask the table.

Liam quirks his head up, his amber eyes meeting mine. "Basically, we're in charge of fundraising and chaperoning the 8th grade trip. We try and make it as inclusive as possible so we spend all year raising the funds so every student that wants to go can go. We also help plan the end of year dance, but that's a lot less work than the trip to D.C."

The idea that the whole school works so hard to make sure every child feels included warms my heart. "That doesn't sound so bad," I reply.

I hear a snort come from across the table and Stella's face is full of mirth, "Yeah, if you don't mind a bunch of hormonal fourteen-year old's running amuck in a hotel for three days trying to make out with each other and confiscating vapes!"

Josie giggles, "Oh, Stella stop, it's hardly that riddled with debauchery." I vaguely remember Josie saying that she was part of the committee now that they were explaining it. She always made it seem like it was fun.

Stella grunts, and I decide then and there that I want to do it, if nothing else because it'll keep my mind busy on work and less busy on sexy science teachers that refuse to roll down the sleeves of their button ups. "I'll do it!" I say brightly.

I can feel all the eyes at the table turn to stare at me questioningly, as if they're astonished that after everything they just said that I would still want to do this.

"What? I really don't mind! It'll keep me busy." They all look amongst each other awkwardly, so I say, "Plus, I've really been wanting a new vape, so now it sounds like I won't have to buy one!"

The table laughs, and I hear Mr. Lennox the choir teacher,

or Jack, yell jokingly, "God speed bitch!"

That sends us all into a laughing fit as Jack, clearly impressed with himself, runs violet nails through his blonde hair, while his bright blue eyes try to conceal the fact that he's internally laughing at his own joke.

The scraping sound of the metal door dragging on the green carpet cuts through our laughter as everyone suddenly freezes. The eyes of everyone at the table watch as nurse Blair walks through the door with a person that looks very familiar holding her perfectly manicured hand.

I hear Jack whisper shout, "Oh, my god is that Superintendent Bronson?" He's about as good at whispering as Josie is.

Of course, that's why he looks familiar! He's quite literally everyone in our school's boss. I look over to see what Liam's reaction is, but he just seems frozen. Not sad, mad, or even trying to blow it all off as no big deal. Just frozen. That just tells me he's clearly not over his ex-quite yet. I try not to dig too deeply into why exactly disappoints me.

Blair throws her glossy brown hair over her shoulder and coyly looks back at Liam as she places a hand on Bronson's shoulder. Oh, she's petty and not even remotely subtle.

I watch as Blair turns to Lola, who is looking back at her with narrowed eyes that say she can smell bullshit from a mile away. I can't tell if Blair takes the hint or not, but she orders a vodka tonic before sitting at a small high-top table off to the side of the bar.

Stella gets visibly irate at this display, "That hussy. She knew you'd be here and came in just to rub it in your face. They're fancy enough they could've gone to wherever they wanted. I'm sorry honey," she says, her voice changing to a loving grandmotherly tone as she pats Liam's hand.

"Stella, it's 2022, you can't just call another woman a hussy." Josie scolds, even though she's visibly trying to hold back her laughter.

"I'll call her a hussy if I damn well please! She broke my poor baby's heart," Stella says loudly, and with the confidence of someone who is elderly and therefore doesn't give a shit about what she says or who might hear it.

Liam's face unfreezes and he takes Stella's hand lovingly, as if he's trying to talk his very angry grandmother out of dualling someone at dawn. "It's fine Stell, really. I'm over it now."

You didn't look very over it when your face just became frozen like a facetime screen with bad reception, I grumble internally. I take a big gulp of mango white claw hoping that it'll quell the irrational jealousy building inside me.

I hear Stella grunt, mumbling to herself, "Still a hussy…"

The table chuckles despite themselves, and I can't help but realize that Stella is the grandma I always wished I had.

Chapter Nine
Liam

It's early the next day and I'm still trying to wrap my head around how exactly I thought staying out at Crenshaws until all hours of the night when I had to be up for work at six a.m. the next morning was a good idea. Yet here I am, slightly hungover, with eyes so dry that I had to wear my glasses instead of my contacts today. *Coffee. I need coffee.*

I make the five-minute walk to the teachers' lounge in search of caffeine, hoping that it will help ease the dull ache in my right temple. I have twenty minutes before I have to get my shit together and talk about neutrons for seven hours, so if the coffee doesn't help it's going to be an extremely long day.

As I open the door to the lounge, I'm greeted by the smell of fresh coffee, thank Jesus, Mary, Joseph, and the camel someone already started a pot.

The lounge isn't exactly the fanciest place in the school, but something about the mismatched couches and scuffed linoleum brings me a sense of peace. Quite possibly because it's the only place here where the loud anarchy that is a middle school full of teenagers can be hushed to a dull roar. One thing I've learned these last five years is that when you're a teacher you can't be picky with how and when you get a moment of peace.

I open the cabinet above the coffee pot and grab my favorite Garfield mug that says 'I hate Mondays' and fill it up to the top. My brother Eric on more than one occasion has called me a psychopath for drinking my coffee black, but I can't fight the efficiency of it.

The bitterness sometimes feels like a balm, and what once was a move purely to save money in college, because cream and sugar cost money, now has just become another part of my morning ritual. I enjoy routines enough that I tend not to deviate from them, so my morning cup of cheap ass black Folger's coffee in a Garfield mug is just as much about the comfort of the ritual as it is getting the caffeine.

I lean against the old and slightly peeling countertop, smelling my coffee and breathing it in before I take a sip. My mind drifts back to last night when I saw Blair with Superintendent Bronson. I was shocked at first, more so just because I didn't know they were together. I can't tell if it's a good or a bad thing that it didn't even actually bother me.

Had I really considered marrying her only a few months ago? That seemed like another life, another Liam. I'm genuinely happy for her though; it seems like everything is going in the direction she wants it to.

Although Stella did have a point, it did seem like she was rubbing the relationship in my face for some unknown reason. I couldn't even begin to guess why, we both knew why she dumped me, it's not like she had to belabor the point.

I hear the door to the lounge squeak open and look up from my coffee cup to see Ella standing in the doorway. *Beautiful,* my brain sighs.

She's wearing hot pink flats, her thighs and hips perfectly hugged by a pair of black jeans paired with a Fleetwood Mac t-shirt and a hot pink blazer. Her strawberry blond hair is pulled back from her face in a ponytail and her gray eyes are shining, she looks like a fucking dream. A dream that is currently smiling at me in a way that makes me go dumb and struggle for words, the same one that I am physically unable to help but smile back at.

Because this woman must get off on torturing me, her wide smile turns into a smirk, "Mr. Scott," she says like she knows how in awe I am of her, either that or she just genuinely finds me amusing.

I clear my throat and look directly into her eyes, "Ms. Jacobs," I say and then proceed to wink at her.

Did I just wink at her? Jesus Liam. I attempt to change the subject, "So you're really going to join the committee?"

I watch her walk toward the cabinet that houses the coffee cups, and she pulls out a blue mug that says 'Teacher Fuel' in white script and fills it halfway. "Yeah, why? Are you afraid that Stella talked me out of it?"

I chuckle at that, "Yeah well, I'm sure you saw how passionate she can be. I'm pretty sure that woman could convince anyone to do anything, if she didn't make it as middle school art teacher, she could've had a career as a cult leader."

She walks to the fridge and pulls out the creamer, filling her cup with what looks to be almost an equal amount to the coffee inside of it, "I'm tired of men acting like women can't have it all. We can be art teachers and cult leaders, it's 2022!" She deadpans for as long as she can before she starts smiling at her own joke. It's not long. Probably like five seconds, and it just makes her even cuter.

"Forgive me, for I know not my own misogyny," I say sarcastically while placing my hand to my heart.

I watch her put four sugar packets into her mug and stir. "I'm sorry but dear God is there even any coffee in that?"

She stares at me with her mouth agape, "Are you judging

how I drink my coffee Mr. Scott?"

"I would be if I even considered that to be coffee." I deadpan.

I know I shouldn't be watching her lips as they purse against the edge of the cup, but I can't help but stare. Her eyes are amused, and then she does probably the cutest thing I've ever seen and scrunches her nose at me. *I want to kiss the place where her nose crinkle meets her eyebrows so badly it's alarming.*

"Let me guess, you drink your coffee black," she muses.

"And how could you possibly know that?" I retort.

She leans against the counter by me, and I feel my skin begin to warm at the sheer nearness of her. "Well A. I can see the coffee in your mug, and it's black. B. I'm pretty sure it's physically impossible for a black coffee drinker to be one and not talk about it. It's like how people that go to Harvard always find a way to bring up how they graduated from Harvard. Black coffee drinkers always bring up how they drink their coffee black."

As she says this, I'm mid-swallow on a gulp of coffee, and I laugh so hard that I can feel the liquid go down the wrong way and a strange mixture of a coughing laugh comes out as I choke.

Just when I think the coughing has subsided, one last one comes that is so strong I jerk forward spilling the hot coffee on my hand, making me drop the Garfield mug on the linoleum and shattering it. "Shit!"

Ella immediately sets down her mug and hurries over to take my hand in hers to look at it closely. "Oh my God! Are you okay? Did you burn yourself?"

Her hands are so soft... She's close enough that I can smell lemon, and the very thought of her touching me has my heart pumping wildly.

"It was just a little hot I'm fine," I try and reassure her, but she's already rushing over to the first aid kit attached to the wall and pulling out burn cream.

"It's red! Let me put some ointment on it." She closes the metal door to the kit and walks back over to where I'm standing, dodging glass shards and coffee as she does.

"I'm really fine Ella," but she isn't listening, she's too focused on taking care of me. I wonder if something like this is just second nature to her, caring for others, like she didn't even think twice about grabbing the ointment and taking care of me.

She puts a dab of ointment on her index finger and gingerly places my hand back on top of hers. I watch as she gently rubs the burn cream into the red part of my skin, but even though I can feel it soothing, I feel heat beneath her touch. The cream has already been rubbed in, but she's still holding my hand.

I look up from where our hands are holding one another's and see her eyes boring back into mine, like churning molten steel. My whole body is burning now, aching to touch her, kiss her, lick her, feel her against the hard ridge straining against my zipper. The energy between us feels static, like hundreds of tiny zaps forming in the now very little distance between us. *Am I into being burned and shit now? Or am I just so attracted to her that I could care less that I just burned the mess out of my hand?*

Just as I can feel us pulling closer together, the loud creak of the door breaks the silence and Sergio walks in. Quickly we jump apart, the moment over like we were doused with ice water. I immediately see Sergio's face and I know, he's about to give me shit for this.

"What happened here?" He asks while smiling and raising a dark eyebrow. His eyes quickly glance between Ella and I and then down to the floor, looking at us like we had been fucking passionately in the teachers' lounge and knocked over a bunch of coffee cups while doing so. *What I wouldn't give...*

I lightly clear my throat, "Oh, I, uh, burned my hand on my coffee and dropped the mug. Hence the glass."

A knowing smile ticks the left side of his mouth up, "And you two were holding hands because... you were checking his pulse?"

A red blush creeps up Ella's neck and pools at her cheeks, "Oh, um, no I was helping him apply burn cream."

Sergio fiddles with the whistle around his neck playfully, "A truly difficult task to do on one's own to be sure."

I can feel my face getting hot, and I'm sure my head looks like it's transformed into a tomato by now. As I look over at Ella, I see her eyes quickly dart away from mine before she says, "Oh would you look at that, first period starts soon. Better get going. See you for the first meeting tonight?"

I grab the paper towels off the sink and crouch down to start picking up the shards of glass on the floor. "Definitely," I say and smile back at her.

She stops in the doorway, "Crap sorry I'm not thinking straight, do you need help cleaning up?"

I lightly wave the hand not currently holding a Garfield mug graveyard in it, gesturing for her to go ahead and go. "Nah we've got it. Serg will help me. Won't you Serg?"

Sergio's eyes narrow back at me before he takes a few sheets off of the paper towel roll and starts to soak up the remaining coffee. "Yeah sure. Why not."

Ella's eyes dart between Sergio and I, and a small smile begins on her lips, "Awesome, okay bye guys!"

Ella is barely out the door before Sergio starts fucking with me, "I saw the way you looked at her, she made you so nervous that you dropped your mug, huh?"

I glare at him as I pick up the last piece of glass from the floor, "Shut the fuck up Serg."

He laughs as he gets up to throw the remaining coffee-soaked paper towels away, "So that's a yes then. It smells like pheromones and coffee in here."

I roll my eyes very visibly at him, but I know there's no denying what he saw. Even though Ella and I will never be together, there's no doubt in my mind that if we were it would be electric.

Chapter Ten
Ella

When I woke up this morning, I was having a good brain day. I put on my favorite hot pink blazer and flats to match along with my favorite Fleetwood Mac t-shirt and my confidence was in full swing for the first time in a long time.

I've struggled all my life with loving the person that reflects back at me in the mirror, of not being overly critical or worried about what people might think. Some days the battle is harder than others, but I just got so tired of always feeling like I was never good enough, and I knew I had to make a change, for my own sanity.

It's not that I think I'm ugly by any means, but more like I set extremely high standards for myself and then would get anxious when I didn't meet them: too many stretch marks, my boobs aren't perky enough, my bottom lip is bigger than my top lip, my stomach is squishy. The thoughts became exhausting, overwhelming, and who wants to live their life this way? Sometimes it would feel like I was drowning in my own thoughts, my brain has always been my worst enemy.

After everything that happened at my last school, I did a major life overhaul. I finished out the year, talked to my doctor, got put on anxiety medication, and worked on my relationship with myself.

My mom always recommends that any time I look in the mirror I say something kind to myself, and I actually started doing it. It was difficult at first.

When I used to look at myself, sometimes I would feel like I didn't belong in my own body, like a snake waiting to shed its flesh. However, months later I'm realizing with each day that I'm feeling more and more at home in my own skin.

Do I have bad days still? Yes, but they are fewer and farther between, and even though nothing can happen between us, the way Liam looked at me that night made me feel all the more confident.

So here I am, walking down the now silent hallways that feel as if they have negative sound without hundreds of students among them, walking with the confidence of a woman I always wished I could be. Thank God for modern medicine and my looney tune pills.

I finally arrive at my destination, Josie's office, and lightly tap on the door before opening it. I can only see the top of Josie's face from behind her giant computer before she pops up and gives me a giant smile. "Hey El!"

"Hey Jos, how goes the world of guidance counseling today? Mediate any love triangles of note?" Since Josie is the school counselor she's always up to date on the latest gossip, or tea depending on what age group is being referenced, and there's never a shortage of stories to tell. She can never actually tell me who it is, but the anecdotes of teenagers are amusing all the same.

Josie heaves a dramatic sigh, "No none today unfortunately, it was all very above board, which meant I spent half the day waiting for something to pop off and the other half working on I.E.P.'s."

In addition to mediation and counseling, Josie is also responsible for managing students' I.E.P.'s, which are the documents we have on file for accommodations for our students with disabilities. She's such an incredible advocate for our students and is always making sure they have all the tools that they need to succeed. I know I'm probably biased, but she's incredible. "How about you?"

I put my right hand on my temple and gently massage while closing my eyes, collecting my thoughts. "Oh, you know, a little bit of pre-American Revolution, a little bit of basically holding hands with Liam and embarrassing myself." I open my eyes to see her reaction, it's as expected.

Her dark brown eyes go wide, and she stands up from her rollie chair, "I'm sorry, I must be confused, what did you say?"

My mouth kicks up at the side ruefully, "It was all very innocent at first! Basically, Liam burned his hand on his coffee, and I decided to put burn cream on it even though he's literally a full grow adult, and when a regular human being would've released said very big, strong, hand I just held onto it while we stared at each other. It was all very fuck me eyes and I wish you could take me on the back of this couch from the '70s right here right now. It all escalated very quickly."

Josie's mouth dropped open, "Oh my God, you like him, don't you?"

My face burns red, because, of course I do, he's fucking hot. He's sweet, he's smart, he's funny, he has arms like a damn Greek God, and the glasses he was wearing this morning were the cutest fucking thing I've ever seen. I wanted to rip that collared shirt off so hard that every single button popped off, but that doesn't mean I'm going to. "How I feel doesn't really matter, you know that nothing can happen between us."

She narrows her eyes at me in an annoyed manner, "Only because you won't let it!" She's walking around the edge of her desk now so that she can tower over me and make her disagreement with me all the more palpable.

"Jos, I've said it a thousand times..." She's so much taller than me that I have to look up at her to meet her eyes, which she rolls dramatically.

"I know, I know, you've sworn off dating coworkers," she's very clearly exasperated with me, but I know that she just wants me to be happy, and I do too. Which is why I won't let myself be fooled into putting myself in another situation where I'm the butt of everyone else's jokes.

I link my arm with hers and start pulling her toward the door, "Good so you do listen to me. Now come on I don't want to be late for my first meeting!"

Josie closes the door to her office and locks it behind her before we walk back down to the auditorium together. Technically, I'm back tracking because my classroom is closer to the auditorium than it is to Josie's office, but I didn't want to walk into my first meeting by myself. It wouldn't be the first time I've used Josie as my social anxiety ShamWow, and it won't be the last.

We walk into the auditorium and the familiar smell of polished wood emanates from the decades old room. The auditorium just seems to be one of those places where no matter how well it's cleaned it still has the faint smell of aged velvet. It reminds me of hiding in my mom's old steamer trunk full of vintage dresses when we would play hide and seek together.

As I walk down the aisle, I can see faint dust motes glittering in the spotlights pointed at the stage before Josie and I slide into the front row with the rest of the group.

Principal Bledsoe is sitting on the edge of the stage with his long legs hanging over the side. He seems relaxed, and even though he's my boss and that's still slightly intimidating, I relax as well.

As Josie and I fold down the old velvet maroon theater chairs I look up right as Liam walks in and sits next to Josie. "Hey Jos!" He peers at me through his glasses and gives me a playful smile, "Ms. Jacobs."

"Mr. Scott," I smile back and hear a small snort escape from Josie.

I throw a small glare her way before I continue, "Great glasses by the way. They give you a real Clark Kent at the Daily Planet vibe."

I can't help myself, I take a quick glance at his arms, and follow his corded muscles all the way to where they disappear underneath his dark blue button down with banana print on it where his sleeves are rolled up. I say quick, but in all honesty, I don't know how long I've been looking at him. I've entered a parallel universe where time is irrelevant and the only word that's spoken is arms, and truly, I'm okay with that.

He clears his throat, *shit I've definitely been staring a long time and am in fact, not in a parallel universe,* "Thanks, I normally wear contacts, but those were a no go this morning."

"I like them. They suit you," I say while looking into those melty amber eyes. *Jesus Ella get a fucking grip.*

"Ohhhhh hey Liam," Josie says all elongated and without a trace of shits given about how obvious she's being.

I cut my eyes to her, pleading with her not to egg herself on, but thankfully as I do so Mr. Bledsoe announces he's about to start the meeting. Josie leans in and whispers in my ear, which it should be mentioned once again that she is in fact a terrible whisperer, and says, "You can cut the sexual tension with a knife."

I take my hand and lightly smack Josie on the shoulder, "Oh

my God the only thing that's going to be cut around here is you if you don't shut the fuck up," and because I know how to actually whisper, she's the only one who hears it. Unfortunately for myself I'm about as intimidating as a bunny rabbit with a shank made from a carrot, so Josie just laughs even harder at me, which then proceeds to make me laugh in turn.

"Excuse me ladies, but if it's all the same to you I'd like to get started," I hear Bledsoe's voice cut through our laughter.

We mumble our apologies before he continues. I feel like one of my students, how embarrassing. "Hello everyone! If you're a returning member, thank you all for once again volunteering for the Activities Committee. If you're new to the committee, welcome, we're so thankful you're here. Each year this committee works tirelessly to make sure that each and every student has the opportunity to attend the 8th grade trip to Washington D.C. if they want to. For some students, this will be the first time that they ever experience leaving the state, and for all of them it will create memories that they'll cherish for a lifetime. Since the 8th graders spend all year learning about American history in their social studies class, it is a great way for them to actually see some of what they're learning firsthand."

Bledsoe, who is very clearly an expert public speaker, pauses momentarily to allow for applause before continuing. "Now last year, Liam had the fantastic idea of creating a safe trick-or-treat at the school and inviting all of the Elementary schools in the township to attend. I think we should expand on this, sell tickets and allow our students to either purchase tickets to trick-or-treat themselves or participate in the event. What do we think?"

"I think that'd be a great idea," Liam replies. "That way it will feel like the students are able to help earn the money for the trip themselves. I think a lot of them would really enjoy it."

"Perfect," Bledsoe says before jumping off the edge of the stage, which is really just putting his feet down because of how tall he is. "Liam, do you mind taking care of the volunteer sign up for the students?"

"Yes, of course."

"Wonderful, now you'll need someone working with you on the teacher sign up side of things. Without enough of them volunteering their classrooms the safe trick-or-treat won't even be able to happen. Is there someone willing to volunteer?" He looks at the group, waiting for someone to respond.

Before my brain can actually form a rational thought my hand shoots up in the air, "I can do that."

"Ella, wonderful, thank you for that. Liam's a pro with recruiting volunteers, and I'm sure he'd be more than happy to help if you need it." My cheeks flush slightly because I think my body is secretly working against my brain and it's wanting all the help that Liam is willing to give.

Chapter Eleven
Liam

In the last weeks since the planning meeting it seems like everything started moving fairly quickly. Having Ella for a partner worked out even better than I thought it would, not only because it meant that I had more of an excuse to see her, but also because she has an extremely persuasive personality. She had convinced a little over twenty teachers to participate in the event. A majority of them even looked excited to be decorating their classrooms and getting set up.

She has this way with people that honestly kind of blows my mind. Ella approaches everything with such genuine kindness and excitement that it makes you feel the same way just being around her.

These past few weeks planning with Ella I've gotten to know her even better, and what I thought was going to be a crush that would go away just keeps getting more and more intense. She compels me to feel happier, full of joy, and more carefree than I have in so long.

Not that I've been depressed my whole life, but that all the joy that I've felt up to this point was the equivalent to the opening act and now I'm finally experiencing the headliner. All she has to do is flash me that smile, the one that warms me like the first spring day after a long Indiana winter, and it feels like I snorted a line of serotonin directly into my bloodstream.

I've never been a guy that was super outgoing, but I'm not

really an introvert either. It's like I'm somewhere in the middle between the two. I'm never the most fun guy in the room, but I'm not the most boring either.

All of my life I've been surrounded by big personalities: my dad is the director for a local dinner theater, my pop owns an art gallery downtown, my older brother Eric is in the army but was always that typical popular football player, Max is always the most outgoing person in any room, and then there's me, the guy who likes science.

My dads were always supportive, and they really tried their best, but they were never able to relate to my interests. With Eric it was easier because they could go to his games and learn about football to understand, but when your kid wants to read books written by Neil DeGrasse Tyson and study covalent bonds it's a bit harder.

Even though I was adopted so young I have no memory of my birth parents, whether they meant to or not I always felt brushed to the side. It's not like it was Eric's fault that he was a result of a sperm cocktail medically turkey basted into his surrogate, and I was adopted. They started the surrogate process after they were wait listed for adoption. They wanted a baby so bad, and surrogacy was the faster option. To their surprise they got a call six months after Eric was born that they had a baby that needed emergency placement and they had twelve hours to decide. They figured they already had the baby supplies so might as well, and they brought me home.

I couldn't help but slightly resent him for it. Not like he didn't love rubbing it in. One time when we were little Eric had actually convinced me that I was an alien that had been sent from another planet. That was a traumatic day in my five-year-old life.

I spent a lot of my time growing up feeling like I was living in my brother's shadow, even though we're completely different people. Not just from my dads, it wasn't like they compared us necessarily, but it felt like pretty much everyone did. Such is the plight of being the younger brother I guess, always feeling like people compare you to the one that came first, even if it was only a school year before you. As a result, it felt like I've spent my entire life trying to make up for being the bonus kid. It feels like I always blend into the background and as a result I care more than anyone else around me, but my dad's always say that's not the case.

Being around Ella makes me feel like I am that outgoing guy, like for once I could be Steven Tyler and not just the scarf tied to the microphone that he sings into. Something I didn't know I wanted until I had it, and now I find myself wanting to dig deeper.

The rush of putting together a trick-or-treating event a month and a half before didn't seem even remotely stressful with all the extra help that Ella provided. We're a great team, and I was able to get fifty students to volunteer along with the teachers she got to participate. Although, a third of the volunteers really came from Sergio and his football team, he seems to have developed a soft spot for Ella.

They've only known each other for a few months now but I can tell he sees her like a little sister. Some people you can know for just a short time but develop a bond like you've known each other for a lifetime. It seems that Ella has that effect on a lot of people, me included.

Now the night of the event is finally here, and I have my mad scientist room set up with spilled beakers of blood, which is just ketchup, and jars filled with fake eyeballs and various other body parts.

I go to the mirror above the eyewash station in the corner of my room in the attempt to fix my hair that was messed up in my attempt to put on my cape. I wet my fingers and run them through my hair to tame the longer curls on the top of my head into submission. I adjust my glasses, a habit I may or may not have gotten into after wearing them regularly since Ella noticed them, I decide to go check on her and see how her classroom is coming along.

As I walk in, I see a few of the football players surrounding Ella and Sergio with zombie makeup coating their faces. Sergio is sitting on top of one of the desks facing away from me, and Ella has her full concentration on his face. She's gingerly holding a sponge coated in red paint and dabbing it in random areas all over him.

She looks absolutely beautiful, albeit I have no idea what or who she's dressed as, maybe a witch or someone from Harry Potter? Her long blonde hair is curled and pinned up in a bun, with random curls pulled out to frame her face. It looks like some sort of green lizard stuffed animal is attached to her shoulder, and a midnight blue dress covered in planets pulls out a bluish hue in her gray eyes.

I can't help but let my eyes rove over her legs, covered in tights that lead into black heels. *Fuck, what I wouldn't give to have those tight covered legs wrapped around my head.* The thought of her in thigh highs threatens to undo me, but I have to remind myself that I am literally working right now, and also in spandex. I start thinking about kittens in pajamas in an attempt to diffuse the current hard on threatening to bulge, and it works. For now, anyway.

As I picture an orange kitten in duck print footie pajamas Ellas eyes peer to the side of Sergios head, and she sees me. A huge grin spreads across her face and she puts the finishing touches on the fake blood dripping from his mouth.

"Hey Liam!" She waves after putting the sponge back down on the pallet. "Okay Serg, you're ready to make your debut as football coach of the undead."

Sergio holds his phone up in selfie mode so he can see his makeup, "Dang El! This looks crazy realistic. I'm going to be the sexiest zombie in the game. *Dawn of the Dead* eat your heart out."

Ella lets a slight smile cross her lips, like she isn't sure how to respond when someone compliments her, almost like it makes her feel awkward. "I think you're overselling it a little bit but thank you none the less." Ella grabs the paper towel next to her and uses it to wipe the excess paint off of her hands.

"Your costume looks great El," I say as my eyes dip slightly downward before I can stop myself. Clearing my throat, I ask, "and you're someone from... *Harry Potter?*"

She scoffs, "What? No! I'm Ms. Frizzle!"

"Ms. Who?"

Her mouth hangs open in surprise, "Ms. Frizzle! From the magic school bus?"

"Is that like a stoner movie?" I ask, even more confused than I was before.

"What?" she laughs loudly, "No! I wouldn't wear something from a stoner movie to a school event."

She points to the stuffed lizard on her shoulder, "It's a cartoon about a teacher who has a lizard for a pet and a magic school bus that can transform into basically anything. She takes her students on crazy outlandish field trips like to outer space or shrinks them down to go into another student's body."

"That doesn't do much to convince me it wasn't made by a

high person. And the parents were totally chill with this teacher taking their kids into space?" I ask jokingly.

She giggles before putting both hands on her hips, "It's not meant to be something you split hairs over."

"Well, I've never seen it," I say as I watch Sergio smirk at me behind Ella when she's not looking, making a heart with his hands. Jesus he just loves to fuck with me.

Once again, her mouth drops open, and I really wish she would stop doing that because it's lowering my kitten in pajama defenses. "Tell me you had a bad childhood without telling me you had a bad childhood."

"I had a very good childhood thank you very much, I wasn't much of a tv kid, but I did watch a lot of Bill Nye the Science Guy." As previously mentioned, I've been a science nerd even at a very early age. Even now I still love Bill Nye and watch his Netflix show.

"Of course, you were. For the life of me I can't understand how a science teacher has never seen *The Magic School Bus*," she smiles and crinkles her nose at me, "Why are you dressed up like a neon green booger with a cape?"

Okay, now it's my turn to scoff, "What? I'm not a booger, I'm Kryptonite. See the KR on my chest? It's the periodic symbol for Krypton, the planet that Superman is from."

Her nose crinkles up again as the corner of her lip quirks up, and it's so fucking cute I can't stand it. "Seems like a bit of a stretch."

Sergio looks at me pityingly, "Yeah, man I don't think Halloween costumes should take that much work to understand."

I roll my eyes dramatically, "You two have no appreciation for a good pun. It's funny!"

I watch as Ella takes her arms and folds them across her

chest, and the movement pushes her breasts upward as they rest there. "I don't know about funny, but what you lack in humor you sure make up for in spandex..."

Her eyes very visibly rake down my body, whether she's conscious of it or not. She subtly bites her bottom lip, her gray eyes flashing up at me before she seems to realize what she's doing and snaps out of it. I can literally feel my insides heating in response to her gaze.

Suddenly, I hear a throat clear from behind Ella, "Well on that note I should be getting back to the rest of my zombie football players. They're probably wondering where their leader of the undead has gone."

Ella turns quickly to reply to Sergio, "Thanks for helping out and convincing the team to participate. The kids are going to love the zombie football team."

Sergio nods at Ella, "Of course, El, no problem. Happy to help!"

The remaining football players follow Sergio out of the room, but not before he catches my eye and silently urges me to make a move on Ella. As if I'd do that in her classroom of all places. Have I thought about it before? Obviously, but I'm not that reckless.

Ella wraps her arms behind her back and gives me a small smile, "How do you feel about hanging cobwebs?"

"Can't say I have a strong opinion about it either way."

"Are you opposed to helping a friend," she places very strong emphasis on that last word, "hang cobwebs all over a bunch of dead presidents?"

"Oh, we're friends, are we?" I'm teasing now, but it doesn't hurt to hear either. If I can't be with Ella, then her friendship is the next best thing.

"I mean I can't say many of my friends have had my nipple in their mouth before, so that would be a friendship first, but one doesn't simply ask for her cobwebs to be hung by just anyone." She walks over to her desk and grabs the packages of fake web, tearing open the package.

I chuckle as I walk over and grab my own bag, ripping it open and pulling the cotton out. "I can't say I've ever had one of my friend's nipples in my mouth either, but I'm open to new adventures."

I start pulling apart the threads of the cobwebs, thinning them out so they look more realistic and less like a giant cotton ball. "However, I'm flattered to be chosen to perform such an important task."

Ella gathers the stretched-out fabric and hangs it over her desk and computer, "I think this needs more spiders." She opens her desk drawer and pulls out a giant bag of spiders of all different shapes and sizes.

"I think that might be the first time that phrase has ever be said in human history."

She giggles, "Accurate."

Gently she places plastic spiders over the top of the desk. "How does it look?"

"Terrifying." I grin.

She dusts off her hands and places them on her hips, "Perfect. That's exactly what I was going for."

I watch her walk toward a desk at the front of the room and push it toward the whiteboard. "Can you hand me some web?"

I grab a chunk and hand it to her after she climbs to the top. "You do realize that a perk of having a tall friend help you hang web is so that they can actually reach the places you can't. Therefor lessening your chances of falling to your death and giving the kids a real haunted house they'll never forget."

"I think falling to my death is a bit dramatic, it's a desk a few feet off of the ground," she says as she stretches up on her tip toes to hang web on the picture of James Madison. "I'm an independent woman that can hang her own webs."

"She says after literally asking me to help her," I muse.

She looks down from the desk to glare at me. "Not the same."

"I beg to differ," I reply as, I hand her more webbing.

She stretches toward Andrew Jackson, but her right heel slips on the corner of the desk. I watch her wobble and quickly lift my arms to catch her in case she falls.

Unfortunately, or fortunately depending on how you look at it, when my arm shoots up to catch her it goes under her dress. I must've thrown her off even more because she really does fall backwards then, and I catch her in my arms.

As she's cradled in my arms, her gray eyes get big and then dart downward to where my hand is still under her dress. For a brief moment before I realize what's happening and move my hand, I can feel her plush ass against my firm hand. Even when we were in Jamaica we got interrupted before I could feel the bare skin of her gorgeous backside. She must be wearing a thong because I can feel the soft warm skin there and I realize then that she is definitely wearing thigh highs. *Damn it, this is not how a friend thinks. Picture the kitten wearing a monocle and a smoking jacket, a pipe dangling from beneath his whiskers. Think of literally anything other than the way the soft skin of her ass feels gripped in my palm.*

I control myself and lower her back onto her feet. When I look at her face, she is beet red, "Maybe next time take me up on my height when I offer it," I chuckle.

She covers her hands over her face, "Oh my God that is so embarrassing." She separates her fingers to peep at me through them, "I guess this can be added to my list of friendship firsts considering I've never had a friend's hand go up my dress before."

"That's actually not a first for me," I deadpan.

Her eyes go wide, "What?"

I chuckle, "I'm just kidding. That's never happened to me before, but one thing I've come to realize is that this friendship is probably going to be full of firsts."

I lower my eyes so I can look directly into hers. "I should probably go get ready for the trick or treaters before I mortify myself any further."

The redness in her face is starting to fade, "Yeah same here. Thanks for catching me and preventing all the kids from being traumatized and needing years of therapy."

I laugh, "Anytime El." Then I walk back toward my classroom and try very hard to think about a back story for the kitten in a smoking jacket and not about how Ella's perfectly round ass would look with my handprint on it.

Chapter Twelve
Ella

Cleaning up the aftermath of a school wide haunted house is exactly as exhausting as it sounds. Thank the lord for the volunteers that helped out because I would be up to my elbows in cornstarch blood and cotton spider webs.

My classroom alone is already taking more energy to clean up than I seem to have left in my body, but it was worth it. Ticket sales were massive, and it put us over halfway to our fundraising goal. Plus seeing all of the cute little pirates, princesses, dinosaurs, and the other adorable costumes alone would've been worth it.

I move a desk to the front of the room to remove the cobwebs that just a few hours ago Liam helped me put up. I climb on top of the tan-colored desk because I apparently didn't learn my lesson the first time, but at least this time I'm careful to not let my black bootie slip over the side like it did previously.

As I begin the tedious task of removing all of the bits of the cotton webbing from multiple dead presidents, I can't help but think about Liam's large firm hands on my body.

When he caught me against his chest, I felt warm all over. The heat of him caressing every inch of me, his spandex was thin enough that I could feel his firm chest beneath it, giving me flashbacks from when just a couple months ago I was running my hands up and down it, reveling in just how fucking sexy the man is.

And oh, my god the smell of him. It's different than before, replacing the smell of rum, smoke, and salt air with a cologne that invoked something primal in me. What I can only describe as a clean soapy smell that was equal parts citrus, musk, and pheromones.

As I pick off the leftover cotton threads from the picture of James A. Garfield, I realize that refraining from throwing myself at Liam is getting harder and harder to do. I thought I could be a professional and easily squash the ever apparent need I have to lick every inch of the man's body, but apparently, I'm not as mature as I think I am.

Ella, it doesn't matter what you want damn it, it can't happen. I've been telling myself this over and over enough that I hope it actually convinces my brain to move past the man, something that's not easily done when his classroom is right across the hall from mine, and I can hear his deep voice drift into my room all day long.

I've never been in a situation like this before, being so viscerally attracted to a man that I can't have. I've dated a few guys before, but nothing serious enough to last longer than a few months. I've had a longer relationship with my vibrator, Ol' Reliable, than I ever have with any of the men I've dated.

I'm sure a therapist would tell me it has something to do with the fact that most of my childhood was spent tagging along with my mom as she hopped from place to place, boyfriend to boyfriend.

Like mother like daughter, I guess... I say to myself as I climb down from the desk and push it away from the wall. One good thing about having a Mom who gets pregnant with you at a Grateful Dead concert by a man she doesn't know? You grow up in a super sex positive household.

As I'm throwing the last of the remaining trash away, I hear a light tap on the door and turn to see the very man I was just daydreaming about at the threshold.

My God that spandex should be illegal. They contour every delicious inch of him, and I'm trying not to think about the hoops he has to jump through to keep his dick in check. I never got to see it, but from what I could feel through the barrier of his shorts and my panties a couple of months ago, it'd be no easy feat.

Shit. I'm staring. My eyes trail up to meet his amber ones, and I feel my skin heat with embarrassment, because behind them is a knowing look. His lips quirk, enjoying my perusal. *Clearly, I'm not as subtle as I think...*

I watch him walk into the room and lift up his hands, "Don't worry, I'm keeping them to myself this time." He jokes, even though there's an irrational part of me that wishes he wouldn't and would touch the aching center of me instead.

I lean my hips against my desk and cross one foot over the other, smiling at him, "Good to know."

He shifts his weight back and forth between his legs while reaching a hand up to rake through his inky black curls. "Listen, I was wondering if you wanted to go to Crenshaw's?"

My heart begins to palpitate. "Typically, I like to buy a lady dinner before I try and grope her."

His cheeks color slightly, and I cock my head to the side sarcastically, "I don't recall you ever buying me dinner when we were in Jamaica?" I say as a smile plays on my lips.

"Fair enough," he laughs. A deep sound that comes from the bottom of his throat. The fact that even this man's laugh is sexy is extremely unfair.

I shift off of my desk anxiously and cradle my arms across my chest, something I've always done to help me feel centered and in control, something I've noticed that seems to slip whenever this man is around. "Liam, I'm not sure that's a good idea..."

He once again holds up his hands and takes a small step forward as he does so. "I get you don't want to date, believe me. We can just go as friends if you want. Unless you think I'm so good looking you don't think you'll be able to keep your hands to yourself?" He says, satirically waggling his eyebrows at me. *Yes, actually that is exactly what I'm afraid of...*

Rationally I know that going to dinner as friends with a man I was just moments ago thinking of biting the neck of is not a wise decision, but this isn't the first time I've done something that was less than wise with this man. Namely dry humping him in public with my tits out where anyone could see.

Am I actually mulling this over? Treading a line that I should know better than to balance on? Yes. Yes, I am. "Okay fine. As friends, but friends that pay for our own food in a very platonic way."

I watch the cutest grin spread across his face, "Awesome. Do you like cheese curds? Because if you do, Crenshaws has the best room temperature curds I've ever had."

I lift an eyebrow questioningly, "Has there been another place you've gone that serves room temperature cheese curds?"

"Nope," he deadpans.

I giggle at that, "Okay sold."

*

Hearing the crumble of the gravel drive beneath my tires and seeing the reflective glow of neon signs against my windshield comforts me, signaling that I'm in the parking lot of Crenshaws.

While I sometimes still feel new in a school with so many tight knit staff members, it became the first place where I got to know them all. I've grown attached to its creaky metal door, baked in cigarette smell, aged green carpet, and most of all, Lola.

As I walk in through the threshold I'm greeted by the now familiar scrape of metal against the carpet. I see Lola behind the bar, polishing a whiskey glass, seeming very focused on her task.

When I reach the old oak bar top, I give it a little knock, startling her. "Ella, what the fuck? Jesus, you scared me." Her big brown eyes are wide, and her breathing has become slightly more audible.

Her surprise makes me giggle, "Sorry, Lola! I didn't mean to make you pee your pants."

Lola sets down the whiskey glass on the counter and narrows her eyes at me, "Whatever incontinence may or may not have taken place stays between us."

I snort while placing a hand over my heart, "Your secret is safe with me, I promise. That whiskey glass must have a nasty stain on it because you sure were polishing the crap out of it. Normally the metal door acts as its own bell."

She shrugs her shoulders, rustling her leather vest as she does so, and clears her throat. "That's true yes, that sound is how I know someone is here, but I just have a lot on my mind."

I've never seen Lola vulnerable before, granted it would probably go against her tough dive bar owner persona, but it worries me. "Do you want to talk about it?" I hedge.

I don't want to pressure her, I've gotten the impression talking about her feelings isn't something she thoroughly enjoys, but if I can be there for her, I want to be.

"Not a lot to say really. My wife and I have a big decision to make by the end of next year, and one option might result in me selling the bar." Her eyes take on a different look to them now, like she aged fifty years just saying that sentence.

"Oh, Lola no! You love this bar. We love this bar." I watch her feel the bar beneath her hands absentmindedly, a small smile crinkling the corners of her eyes.

"I do. I love my regulars, but I love my wife more and she retires in a few months. She wants to sell the bar and use the money to get an RV so we can travel across the country, but I don't want to use my bar as collateral. We've been arguing about it, and it just feels like I'm talking to a brick wall." She sighs and rubs her eyes, looking thoroughly defeated.

I reach my hand across the bar top and pat her arm, "I'm sure you'll both think of something that doesn't involve giving up something you love. We might just have to get creative. There's got to be a solution that can involve both the bar and the RV." I look around this place that I've grown to love and feel so sad that Lola feels like she has to make an impossible decision.

Lola reaches down into the fridge behind her and grabs out a mango white claw, cracking the top before setting it down on the bar top. "Yeah well, if I think of something I'll let you know."

I give her a small smile as I hear the door scrape against the carpet. I turn to see Liam in jeans and a black Henley, what has to be the opposite of green spandex, stride through the door. His inky curls are mussed perfectly, and his glasses make him look the perfect balance of sexy and adorable. "Hey Lola!" he says warmly, and the looks at me, lowering his voice an octave, "Ms. Jacobs."

I'm sorry, but do friends drop their voices in a sexy demeanor? No, they don't. *Jesus this man...* I can't help it; it makes me smile. "Mr. Scott," I say coyly.

Lola's eyes go wide and toggle back and forth between us

skeptically while grabbing a whiskey bottle and pouring the liquid into a glass. If I wasn't feeling so self-conscious right now, I'd admire her ability to literally pour drinks without looking.

"Hey Liam," she says smugly. She adds ice and coke to the whiskey and puts it on the bar. I'm awed that she can memorize people's drinks this way, she was meant for this place.

Liam gives Lola a megawatt smile, "Any chance we can get some cheese curds?"

Her eyes roll dramatically before she smiles, "Will do," she says before disappearing into the back where I can only imagine is where the kitchen is located.

Liam grabs his drink off the bar and heads toward a small table in the corner under the Joe Camel cigarette sign, and he pulls out a chair for me.

I sit down on the wood backed seat and take a sip of my white claw, letting the bubbles burn my throat all the way down. "So, you weren't going to relay the message that we were supposed to change into normal clothes before we got here?" I say as I lift an eyebrow in amusement.

He begins to lift his whiskey to his lips but pauses and smiles at me. I'm trying not to think about those lips on me, but it's becoming increasingly difficult.

"I'm not an idiot, I know full well that if I came in this bar with spandex on Lola would never let me live it down." He parts his lips and takes a sip of his drink, the ice clinking as he does.

The thought makes me laugh, "Okay, fair enough."

"Plus, I like that outfit on you," his eyes dip down briefly, and when they come back up to meet mine, they're heated gaze is something I've become all too familiar with. I can feel that look all the way down my body, heating me from the inside out.

Because there's a merciful God somewhere taking pity on

me, Lola shows up with our cheese curds and drops them on the table without a word, breaking the tension between us. He smirks then, "Even if it looks like that thing's eyes are following me everywhere I go."

I scoff dramatically, "How dare you? This 'thing' is a lizard, and she has a name, it's Liz Ard."

"Are you telling me the lizard's name is lizard? For someone who has notoriously creative field trips that's a very lackluster name," he chuckles.

My mouth opens in mock irritation, "No! Her government name is Liz Ard. First name Liz, last name Ard." I say as I point to the stuffed Liz on my shoulder.

He holds up his hands in defeat, "Oh yes, sorry my mistake. That's *much* more creative." His emphasis on the word much is clearly sarcastic.

I narrow my eyes at him before popping a cheese curd. It's so hot it burns my tongue and I have to open my mouth and suck in air to cool it down, exposing Liam to what I'm sure is a perfect view of half-chewed up curd.

My powers of seduction know no bounds. "I thought you said these were room temperature!"

"They usually are! Lola must've made them fresh this time or something," he smirks.

I swallow the cheese curd and take a gulp of my white claw, hoping the bubbles will slightly soothe the burn. "I want you to know that in this moment, burning my mouth on a cheese curd with a stuffed lizard attached to my shoulder is the sexiest I've ever been. This is peak. I'll never be hotter than this."

He chuckles, "Well good thing we're just friends, right? Otherwise, I might be lured in by this siren song of yours."

He grabs a curd and pops it in his mouth, completely unfazed by the temperature. *Is it just me, or was there maybe, a little too much emphasis on the word friends in that sentence?*

"I've led many men into shipwrecks that's for sure," I respond with mock smugness. The way the corner of his mouth tips up tells me he's remembering our conversation from the first night we met, just like I am.

"Something to be proud of definitely," he pauses for a second, looking a little nervous. He looks like he wants to say something but is unsure if he should.

"So, I know you don't love this topic, but I'm curious. If you don't want to answer it feel free to tell me to shove a curd in it, but why did you leave your last school?"

My stomach instantly flip flops. *Do I tell him?* If we really are friends, then this topic was bound to come up at some point. I sigh and dust the crumbs from my hands, "It's a long sordid story, but the short version is that I left due to the aftermath of a man's very fragile masculinity."

Liam's eyes go wide, "How so?"

Well, looks like I'm telling him the whole story. I take a long swig of my white claw and begin, "Well the principal at my last school really disliked taking no for an answer. He seemed like a nice guy at first. He offered to help with lesson plans and seemed to be really hands on. All of the students and faculty loved him." I look to see Liam making a cringe face, showing that he can tell where this story was going.

I blow out a slow breath, trying to calm my stomach that currently feels like it's full of jumping beans. Telling this story always puts me in knots, I never know what people's reactions will be, or if they'll even believe me.

I continue, "Yeah, so I thought it would be fun for the students if we did a club like model U.N. Principal Phaser was immediately supportive of the idea and wanted to be involved. He even offered to secure the funds we needed to organize meetings, transportation, and field trips."

I clear my throat, "One day a few months after the club started, he came into my classroom after the students had all left for the day and I was grading papers. He told me I looked beautiful, I felt awkward, but I didn't want him to get upset so I told him thank you. I thought it would end there, but he walked behind my desk and leaned over me. I can still smell the disgusting cologne he was wearing. He ran his hand up my thigh, and I jumped up from my desk immediately. I told him that I wasn't interested in him and that he was being extremely inappropriate. He got angry with me then, and said he was doing everything I wanted and that I couldn't possibly expect him to do that for nothing." I look down at my drink that I had been absentmindedly twisting, unsure of what Liam's reaction will be.

When I get the courage to look back at him, his face is full of rage. "What the actual fuck. What a slimy asshole. Did you file a complaint?"

My stomach is more at ease now, he believes me, I sigh with relief. "I tried. I really did, but he had gotten to the admin staff first. He said that I had thrown myself at him and that he wasn't interested. He told them that I was bitter because he turned me down and lashed out. He said that I threatened I would lie and file a report against him. He told them that he felt sorry for me and didn't want me to get fired."

I watch Liam's nostrils flare; I've never seen him angry before. "So basically, it was your word vs. his?"

I finish the last of my white claw and move it to the side of the table, letting the bubbles of the drink take the tense feeling out of my shoulders. "Yep. After that the rumors and gossip amongst the staff was unbearable. You would think that they were the middle schoolers. Any time I walked into a room it would get quiet, like they had just stopped talking about me. None of the other teachers or staff would speak to me. All I had were my students, and as much as I loved them, I couldn't stay there anymore."

I clear my throat, silently begging the burning feeling behind my eyes to go away. "Jos told me that the school she worked at had an opening for a Social Studies teacher, so I applied. We've always wanted to be in the same school since we were younger, so in a twisted way I guess it worked out."

Liam's eyes soften, and he reaches out to cover my hand with his. It feels warm and comforting. Like a balm soothing the aftershocks of my anxiety high, calming me down. "That's so fucked up Ella, I'm so sorry. I'm glad you came to Valley when you did, the students and faculty love you there."

I stare at him then, feeling a tear prick at the corners of my eye by how sweet this man's words are, "Thank you. I'm trying to move past it, but that's the reason I've been so adamant about not dating anyone I work with. I can't go through that again."

As if my words brought recognition to his touch he removes his hand from mine, "I understand completely."

Even though his hand is no longer on mine, I feel the heat lingering on my skin. I want to grab his hand back and keep it there, but that would just make not being with him even harder. As much as I know I can't have him, I crave him, and because of my fucked-up brain that just makes me want him even more. I'm in a constant battle with myself, wanting his touch, but in the same breath terrified of what would happen if we didn't work out. I love Valley, and mentally I can't move schools again.

I speak softly, looking into his face that seems to be just as conflicted as mine, "I should probably go. I have essays on the Louisianna Purchase to grade."

Liam finishes off his drink, "Yeah definitely, I've got seventy-three labs I still have to grade too. Let me walk you to your car."

We wave goodbye to Lola and walk across the parking lot, the sound of gravel crunching beneath our feet accompanying our footsteps. I unlock the Prius and turn to look at Liam. I smirk playfully, "Thanks for the ass grope and the cheese curds forged from the fires of hell."

Liam's face turns bright red with embarrassment, "Again, very sorry about that. Especially, knowing what you went through I feel even more terrible, if that's even possible."

I don't know what possesses me to want to say this. Maybe, it's seeing how tortured his face looks, and how I just want to make him feel better. Maybe, I want him to know that not being with him, especially after tonight, is hard for me too. Maybe, it's all the unearned confidence from the white claw and the aftershocks of bearing it all to him.

Before I can think better of it, I take a step closer to him and look at him straight in those beautiful eyes, "Well if it's any consolation I liked when you touched me. Believe me, if it wasn't for the fact that you taught across the hall from me, I would've fucked you already."

I watch his mouth drop open and his eyes fill with longing. I give him my best devilish smile, climb into my car, and shut the door, waving goodbye to him through the windshield.

That's where I leave him, mouth agape in a gravel parking lot, and I can't help but think to myself, *now why the fuck did I just do that?*

Chapter Thirteen
Liam

This whole week I feel like I've been measuring time differently. Instead of the usual numbers on a clock the rest of the world goes by I've been using Ella. Namely, is it time for me to see her or is it not?

Seven a.m. is when we meet in the teachers' lounge for coffee, when we both get to the school and we get to talk for a bit before the first period bell rings at seven fifteen a.m. Between third and fourth period I know I'll get to see her because we both have hall duty during the passing period, and on Wednesdays we have lunchroom duty together. We get assigned a lot of the same responsibilities because our classrooms are right across from each other. In fact, the only exception is our dismissal assignments. Not that I'm complaining by any means, it just gives me more chances to see her.

I know we're friends, albeit there's obviously tension there that we both feel, something she made abundantly clear a few days ago. *'Well, if it's any consolation I liked when you touched me. Believe me, if it wasn't for the fact that you taught across the hall from me, I would've fucked you already.'* I hear those words rattling around in my brain all day long, unshakeable, like she could tell I felt embarrassed, and she couldn't bear for me to feel that way and she'd do anything to reassure me. As if I needed any more reason to want to fuck her more than I already do. I don't think I'll ever be able to forget how she smells, the taste of her skin, the feel of her perfect ass in my hands.

It's not even just about how badly I want to bend her over her desk, wrap her perfect blonde hair around my hand and use it as leverage while I rapidly pump my dick in and out of her. *Although, I definitely do want that.* It's her personality too. She's so incredibly fun to be around. She's charismatic, funny, kind, and a genuine person. It's not just about physical attraction with her. I'm mentally attracted to her too. Especially after she opened up to me a few days ago.

She bared her soul. I could see it, the hurt in her eyes. When she told me about what that asshole did to her, my first reaction was rage. How dare that fucking prick try and abuse his power that way? Just looking at her I could tell that reliving the experience was still painful because she couldn't help but fidget with her can on the table, she had to frequently try and control her breathing, and she couldn't even look me in the eye. Like she was ashamed, as if I could ever think she had anything to do with how that dick treated her, but I guess in the past when she told people they didn't exactly believe her either.

When I covered her hand with mine, I knew that it wouldn't absorb any of the pain she felt, but I wish it could've. In that moment I would've done anything within my power to unburden her, but unfortunately that's not how this stuff works. As much as I wanted to be an emotional sponge that soaks up every last inch of her hurt, I couldn't. The pain of not only being tricked by someone you trusted, but also rejected by an entire school of people, that shit has to cut deep.

Even after reliving all of that, the moment I felt even a shred of embarrassment or shame she still tried to do anything she could to make me feel better, even if her words also made me rock hard.

It's not like I'm going to act on it or anything though. I respected Ella's decision to not date coworkers before I knew what happened, although, I disliked it greatly, but now I know there's no way I could try and convince her otherwise.

Dating Ella would trigger her, and I couldn't live with myself if I knew that I caused her any pain, even if it was unintentional. If we can't be together, I'll still take being friends with her over nothing at all. Hell, after these last few months one thing I know for sure is I would do just about anything to make her happy.

Somehow, I've managed to make it to Friday without completely losing my mind, although, I guess that could be argued considering what I agreed to let the students do today.

We've been learning about acids and bases this week, and my dumb ass thought it would be a great idea to let them make exploding baggies. I paired them off with their lab partners and let them create a chemical reaction with vinegar, baking soda, and water. It went everywhere, and what was ten minutes of fun turned into a shit ton of cleaning for everyone involved.

After we all finished cleaning, I let the students use whatever time remained as a free period. The hilarious part is that I had to do this six different times, realizing after first period just how big of a mess was going to be made every time, but I was powerless to stop it. If the first period students got to do it and not the other classes, there would be hell to pay. They loved it though, and despite the mess I'd do it again because I can guarantee they understand chemical reactions better after today.

By the time sixth period arrived, the last one of the day, I decide my classroom is going to smell like vinegar for what I assume will be eons. Even if a nuclear war ensued, the space that my classroom previously occupied would still carry an odor. All that would remain of this world would be cockroaches, twinkies, and the smell of vinegar.

As I finish cleaning up what would be my sixth round of splatter on my desk a hand shoots up from a lab table and Luke, one of my students, asks for a hall pass to use the restroom. I quickly grab the notepad, fill out the slip, and tear it off to hand it to him.

I'm not sure how much time has passed, but it feels like only a minute before the sound of sneakers screeching on freshly polished floor and the rattle of lockers echoes throughout the room. The sound of thrashing and yelling makes me realize what's happening, a fight. *Oh, good Lord.*

I run out of the classroom quickly, hearing my students' chairs scrape against the floor as they run to the doorway behind me to watch.

"Guys go sit down and finish your homework!" I yell back at them, to the surprise of no one they don't listen and crowd the doorway, but I don't have time to waste on chastising them anymore. At the end of the hallway near the bathrooms I see Luke has a boy from my fourth period class named Eddie in a headlock.

"Stop!" I yell, picking up speed.

It's not until those words leave my mouth that I see long red blonde hair swaying back and forth farther ahead of me. Ella's running toward the fight.

I watch in horror as she yells, "Knock it off! Get away from each other!" and wedges herself in between the two of them.

Eddie, now out of the headlock, tries to reach around Ella and punch Luke in the face. The force of the movement knocks Ella to the ground, and a sharp yelp escapes from her mouth and she cradles her ankle. *Oh, fuck.* "Ella! Are you ok?" I yell as I run down what has to be the longest hallway in existence.

I've almost reached her now, and I watch as she seizes her opportunity and lunges forward to grab Luke's ankle in an attempt to stop him. *Well, she's a scrappy little thing, isn't she?* I think as I finally reach her.

"I'm fine! Help me separate them!" She yells back at me as she's laying fully flat on the floor holding onto his ankle with all her might.

I rush to pull Eddie away and as I pry him from Luke's hands I see Jack, Mr. Lennox, turn the corner of the hallway and run to grab Luke to keep him farther away from Eddie.

Now that she doesn't have to hold onto Luke's ankle anymore, she scoots back and rests against the lockers, inspecting her ankle.

Jack locks his arms around Luke so he can't move, "What in God's name are you two thinking? You both were in choir this morning and seemed perfectly fine!"

Luke strains against Jack's grip and lunges for Eddie again, who I have firmly gripped and am currently preventing from retaliating. "He knows what the fuck he did!" Luke snarls, attempting to wiggle out of the hold. *Where the fuck are the security guards?*

Eddie chooses this moment to lurch forward, but thankfully I'm about three times the size of him so it doesn't do much. "She's not interested in your sound cloud rapping ass anymore!" Eddie spits back.

Okay, I'm not waiting for security anymore. "Okay you two enough!" I bellow. "Bledsoe's office, now!"

I look over at Ella sitting on the floor inspecting her ankle, the image fills me with rage. I grit my teeth and as calmly as I can muster, I speak, "Jack, can you help me take them down to the office?"

I look at Ella then, only to realize that her gray eyes are already peering back at me. "I'm going to bring them down to the office and then I'll be right back to help you get to Blair…"

She gives me a small smile, "Okay, I'll be here. Mostly because I can't move very well right now anyways."

Just then I finally see the security guards, along with Sergio, rushing down the hallway. "Sorry! We thought it was in a different hallway," one of them says, "We'll take them now." The security guards each grab a boy and escort them around the corner and down the hallway, Jack following close behind, toward the front office and out of view.

I reach down to Ella and put my shoulder beneath her arm, so I can help support the weight she would otherwise be putting on her ankle. I watch as Sergio's face slowly grows more and more panicked, "What happened?" He yells.

Ella smirks, "Oh you know, a fight broke out and I tried to stop it with my ankle."

I roll my eyes and look at Sergio, "A fight broke out and she tried to stop it but got knocked down and landed on her ankle instead," I correct.

"Jesus Ella!" Sergio remarks, and it's then that I remember all the students crowding the classroom doorways watching everything unfold.

"Serg, I need to take her to Bl—the nurses office to get her looked at. Can you round up the students and watch them until dismissal?"

As I say this, I already know he'll say yes, "Yeah, no problem," he grunts and looks around the hallway at all of the students in the doorways.

"Okay guys we're walking laps around the gym until the bell

rings!" There's a collective groan from the onlookers.

I look toward Ella then, and I can feel the warmth of her body on mine as she leans on me for support. I'm in no way happy that she was hurt, but I'd be lying if I said that I didn't revel in the way her body was pressed against my side. "El, are you okay to walk down to the office if I help you?"

She smiles up at me like she's not in any pain at all, "Yeah, I think I can manage." She shifts her weight then and wraps her arm around mine. We wait until Sergio has rounded up all the students and they're on their way to the gym before we attempt walking down the hall.

As we descend the long hallway toward the nurse's office, the halls are basically empty. The fluorescent lighting shines where it can on floors that have been scuffed from hundreds of students all day long.

My vision is bouncing back and forth between where we're headed and frequently looking down to check how Ella's ankle is doing. I'm supporting pretty much all the weight on her right side so that way she has to put minimal pressure on it. An image of me carrying her cradled in my arms while walking down the hallway crosses my mind, *Should I do that, or would it freak her out?*

I rationalize with myself that it would be much more efficient to just scoop her up and walk her down to the office than go at the current pace that we are because at this rate Blair will be retired by the time we get to her.

Without thinking twice, I stop walking, which inadvertently makes Ella stop with me, and she gives me a puzzled look. I return it with a sly smile, which only makes her question more, "Liam...?" she says as her eyes grow wide.

It's then that I make my move. I bend down and scoop my

arm underneath her legs to cradle her against my chest. A yelp escapes her mouth as I pull her up, and she begins to giggle.

A southern belle accent overtakes her voice then, "My hero!" she exclaims while clutching her invisible pearls. "Oh, my stars thank the good Lord a big strappin' man was here to rescue me in my hour of need."

Her performance makes me laugh as I carry her down the hallway. I look down at her then, her gray eyes looking almost silver against the fluorescent lights and amusement dancing in them. "Don't worry killer. I'm sure you would've made it down here all by yourself. Although by the time you made it everyone would be gone for the day."

She clearly doesn't miss the sarcasm in my voice because she narrows her eyes at me and scoffs, "I would've figured it out thank you very much!"

As we finally approach the door to Blair's office, I give her a small smile and knock on the door that's already slightly ajar before walking in, "I have no doubt."

I see Blair at her desk, and when she looks up to see me holding Ella her eyes get big and she rushes toward me, "Liam? Is everything okay?" Her eyes grow wide with worry.

Before I can answer Ella interrupts, "I fell on my ankle, can you look at it?" She gives Blair a friendly smile, and if she feels awkward at all by our current situation, she doesn't show it.

I move Ella to one of the brown pleather day beds and Blair crouches down to inspect her further. "I'm sure it's fine. It probably looks worse than it is." She says this like she's trying to convince herself that it's true, despite the fact that her ankle is already turning yellow and purple.

Blair holds up the ankle gingerly, "Can you move it?" She asks.

Ella gently rotates her ankle and winces. "It looks like you rolled your ankle. It's definitely going to swell so make sure you put some ice on it and stay off it as much as you can, but you should be fine."

Ella smiles at Blair, "Will do, thank you."

"Lucky for you it's Friday so you can stay off it for a couple days. Hopefully you don't have any big dates planned." As she says this she very obviously looks back and forth between Ella and I. Smooth Blair, smooth.

Ella laughs humorlessly, "Hah. Not quite."

"Well, I guess we can't all have reservations at Griffins tonight," Blair remarks. Something I didn't notice about Blair until after the breakup is that she can't help but make most conversations about herself, and if she can brag about something, well then that's bonus points for her.

"Fancy," Ella deadpans.

But because she can't take a hint, Blair keeps talking, almost like she wants to see if she can make me jealous. Unfortunately for her I think Ella has officially cured me of any jealousy I could have toward her.

"Oh yeah, Dean had to make the reservations weeks in advance, but he said it was worth it so he can show me off." She looks at me then, assuming she wants to see what my reaction will be.

Of course, she's going to refer to Superintendent Bronson as Dean... I say to myself while internally rolling my eyes. This is her way of saying 'he can give me all the things you couldn't.'

Ella interrupts and smiles at me from the day bed, cutting the tension in the air that I'm sure she can sense. "Liam, can you help me to my car?" She says this in a pleading tone that I don't recognize.

"I don't think I can make it all on my own." Her voice has developed a sultry tone, making my blood buzz against the surface of my skin.

I smile back at her; thankful she was able to end the conversation. "Yeah, sure thing."

I scoop Ella up to cradle her in my arms once more, and she makes a show of wrapping her arms around my neck. Holding her there I can smell the scent of her skin wrapped around me, like lemon and spun sugar.

How the fuck does she still smell this good... My God and her soft skin against mine... I can feel the heat of her touch down my spine, and I know that the longer I hold her the more unraveled I'll become.

This woman will be my undoing, and at this rate I'd gladly let her if it meant just being able to be near her. Clearly the whole being friend's thing is going super well for me.

As I walk toward the door with Ella cradled against me, she peeks her head over my shoulder and waves at Blair. "Thanks again!" Giving her the biggest smile imaginable with an added overindulgent amount of enthusiasm, and it's in this moment I know for sure what she's doing, putting on a show to make Blair jealous of her.

I know she doesn't actually have feelings for me, and that she's doing this for my benefit more than anything else, but I lean into all the same. I'm starting to realize that I have it so bad for her that I'm more excited about the idea of a pretend version of Ella and I than I am about making Blair jealous. I'm not a petty person by nature, but I do enjoy the quiet guffaw that comes out of Blair's mouth as we leave the nurse's office.

As I walk down the empty hallway, I give Ella a side eye and smile, "You didn't have to do that you know."

Her beautiful gray eyes shine as she looks back up at me with a wry smile and feigned innocence, "I'm not sure what you mean?"

"Come on El, you were putting on a show in front of Blair for my benefit. I know full well you would never actually say 'I don't think I can make it all on my own'." I say in the best impression of her sultry voice I can muster without laughing. *Yeah, Liam pretend like it was funny and not that her tone of voice alone gave you a semi.*

She lets out a cackle, a deep guttural sound that just makes her even more cute, "Okay yeah you caught me," she says as I open the door to the parking lot. "You know I can walk fine, right? This whole you carrying me thing seems a bit overdramatic."

"As if I would let you walk. You heard what Blair said, you need to stay off it, so the swelling goes down." I spot her Prius toward the back of the lot and head toward it.

She rolls her eyes at me dramatically, "You do realize that I have to drive home and at home I'll have to walk on it correct?"

As we approach the Prius, I lean her gingerly against the side of it while she fishes her keys out of her wristlet. "I could drive you home you know?"

That earns me yet another eye roll, "Liam, I appreciate the concern but I'm fine!"

The Prius chirps as she unlocks the door and I watch her face contort into a wince as she leans down into the car to climb into the driver seat. She sucks in a deep breath of air, "See! Totally fine and not at all incapable."

I narrow my eyes and frown at the fact that she is clearly lying to me, "Okay enough with the bravado. I'm taking you home. We'll worry about picking up my car later."

I quickly help her out of the driver's side and walk her over to the passenger before shutting the door and adjusting the seat farther back. Like a lot farther back, she's significantly shorter than I am.

I look over to see Ella wringing her hands together, a motion that I've seen her do before, "Everything okay El?"

She glances at me from the side of her eyes, "Yeah, um, I just feel guilty is all. I'm completely inconveniencing you right now."

I go to put the car in reverse and my eyes quickly find hers. I can see the guilt there already forming like storm clouds behind her eyes, "Ella. You are not inconveniencing me. I want to do this."

"That can't possibly be true."

"It is."

"Okay," she says quietly.

It's then that I notice what's playing over the Bluetooth speaker, Elton John's 'Benny and the Jets.' I smile as I pull out of the parking space, "I didn't realize you were a fan of Sir Elton John."

I see her smile return, vanishing the lingering guilt, "I mean who isn't a fan of Elton John? He has an amazing voice, plays piano, and wears funky glasses and sparkly suits. What's not to love?"

She types her address into her phone and points it at me so I can see the directions. "Sorry," she giggles, "I do actually know where I live obviously, but it's easier than me trying to tell you every turn and then inevitably getting distracted and forgetting to tell you where to go and ending up in Ohio."

"I mean I would hope we would figure it out before we ended up in an entirely different state," I reply wryly.

"Don't hold your breath on that one, my lack of directional capabilities knows no bounds," she responds.

I snort, "That's fair, unfortunately I've become really reliant on GPS, so it works better for me too. My dads tried teaching me how to read a map, but by that point GPS was already invented so I didn't really pay attention to what they said." I hesitate, waiting to see if she notices that I said 'Dads' plural and not Mom and Dad.

She smiles, "How admirable of them. My mom tried teaching me once too. We moved around a lot when I was little and therefore did a lot of road tripping, but none of it stuck because, well, MapQuest and GPS."

As we pull into her driveway, I can't help but smile, because she didn't even react, like it wasn't something shocking or different to her. I guess the lack of reaction makes me happy because it would be the same treatment someone would get if they mentioned their mom and dad.

Growing up I was always nervous to tell people I had two Dads, not because I was embarrassed, but because I never knew how they would react. I was the only person I knew who had two Dads and I would always wait with bated breath on what they would say or the questions they would ask. 'But how were you born if you don't have a mommy?' 'Do you wish you had a mommy?'

It was all too much, and each and every time I never knew the reaction I would get. Thankfully as time has gone on having two parents of the same gender has become a lot more normalized.

I remember when the show 'Modern Family' came out and how excited we all were that there was another family that looked like ours on TV. We would all pile on the couch under a ton of blankets and watch the new episode that would air each week. It was one of the only shows all four of us could agree on, and it led to some of my favorite memories.

I park the car and turn off the ignition before getting out and opening Ella's door. I offer her my hand and she takes it, letting me lead her to the front door of her house.

It's small, but pretty much exactly where I would envision Ella living. The house is white with blue shutters, a few bushes that have already lost their leaves to the chilly November air, and a small porch with a rocking chair in the front.

As we stand on the porch a chilly Autumn wind whips through, tossing around leaves and blowing loose strands of Ella's hair around her face. The wind has a bite to it, and I can see the cold flush grow across her cheeks, reddening her nose. She smiles at me as she brushes the hair from her face, "This really wasn't necessary, but thank you."

Standing on this porch I know we're both freezing, but I'm realizing that I'm not ready to say goodbye yet. "You know… I don't have any plans tonight, so if you need someone to help you out, I don't mind staying."

I can see it already, the guilt clouding her eyes again. "Liam, I couldn't possibly ask you to do that."

"Why not?" I reply as the wind whips through once again. "Aren't we friend's Ms. Jacobs?"

I watch as her eyes dart, like she's at war with herself, deciding if she can let me help her without feeling guilty. Watching this I wonder who in her life made her feel as if everything she did was inconvenient, like she was a burden.

I take my index finger and tilt her chin up, so she's forced to look at me, "Hey. Question, would you do this for me?"

She tilts her head slightly, "Huh?"

I keep my voice steady and reassuring, "If this situation was reversed, would you do the same for me? Drive me home, help me around the house?" I know the answer before she even says it.

Her reply comes as a whisper, "Of course." As if she can't bear to look in my eyes any longer, hers flit away, looking out toward the lawn.

I refocus her again, urging her to look at me, "Okay then let me help you. That's what friends are for." I drop my finger from her chin and hand her the keys. Even as I say this, I know the heat I feel between us isn't exactly friend territory right now, but I can't help but touch her. I need her to know that she's not an inconvenience. That I want to do this for her because I care about her.

A big smile spreads across her face, "Okay Mr. Scott, I guess you have a point." She puts the key in the lock and turns, opening the door. "Go ahead and come in, but no funny business!"

Believe me, if I had it my way nothing about this would be funny, it would be nothing short of carnal, but I put those thoughts aside, because this is about me taking care of Ella, not the absurd amount of need I feel toward her.

I press my right hand over my heart and raise my left hand, "I wouldn't dream of being even remotely funny."

She turns around to look at me and smirks, "Something that comes naturally to you obviously."

I scoff at her with mock offense and shut the door behind me, before leading Ella to a spot on her living room couch.

Chapter Fourteen
Ella

Well... what the fuck? Liam is here. As in Liam, the very hot Chemistry teacher that works across the hall from me, the one that I am very much still trying to forget the taste of his tongue tangling with mine, is in my living room.

What exactly am I supposed to do with this information? Am I just supposed to pretend that this man didn't just carry me up and down the hallways of the school like I weighed nothing? That the scent of him didn't paralyze my senses from how good he smelled? That I didn't feel the warm hard muscles of his chest ripple underneath his pineapple printed collared shirt? Damn him and those adorable shirts, amber eyes behind thin wire-framed glasses, inky black curls, and sharp stubbled jaw line!

Putting on a show in front of Blair was far too easy. Mainly, because I did in fact want to fling my arms around his neck and be cradled into his chest. Which is one hundred percent not conducive to the friendship that we're shooting for, and when he grabbed my chin, forcing me to look into his eyes, I could've melted onto my front porch.

Now he's taking care of me? I know I can't forget why I made the decision not to date him, but does he have to make it so fucking difficult to remember? I'm only human.

When Liam helps guide me to the couch is around the time that I realize I still have water bottles scattered all over my coffee table, along with a large stack of quizzes I have yet to grade, and the lacy black bra I was wearing yesterday. Wonderful.

My cheeks heat slightly with embarrassment and Liam quirks up his eyebrow as he watches me grab the bra off the coffee table and sling shot it across the room. "Sorry the place is kind of a wreck right now. If I would've known that I was going to have a knight in shining armor take time out of his busy schedule from catching randomly fainting women, I would've picked up a bit more."

He smiles wide, exposing perfect teeth because, of course, they're perfect, "I decided to expand my horizons from solely fainting women to incorporate women with twisted ankles."

As he says this, I watch him grab two yellow pillows from the end of the couch and carefully lift my ankle on top of them.

"Ah yes, well in today's economy it's important to diversify," I reply while trying not to think about how his hand is caressing my ankle. Lord, has it really been so long that I've been with someone that I'm into ankle-play now? What am I, a puritan? I guess this is my life now, one touch of his hand against my ankle feels like sin in the best way possible.

As he looks at me from the other side of the couch he grins, before pulling off my pink Toms to inspect the damage. "Do you happen to have any ice packs?"

I look down to see my already swelling ankle turning purple, and it feels like it has its own pulse "Umm... No, I don't."

He begins to stand to walk toward the kitchen, "Frozen peas?"

"I think I have a bag of freezer burnt pizza rolls in there somewhere?" I reply with a question, because I'm not entirely sure there's even anything in my freezer. I don't remember the last time I even went grocery shopping.

I watch him walk through the doorway into the kitchen,

"Good enough," he replies before finding the bag and bringing it back into the living room to rest on my ankle. The shock of the cold makes me flinch before I ease against the pillows and try to let the pizza rolls numb the swelling.

Once Liam decides that my ankle is sufficiently propped up, he sits on the opposite side of the couch, making himself right at home. I grab the remote off the coffee table and point it toward the TV, "Well since we're apparently in this for the long haul should we watch a movie?"

Liam smirks at me, his eyes dancing with amusement, "Why Ms. Jacobs, are you propositioning me to Netflix and chill?"

"Ha, only in your wet dreams Mr. Scott," I retort as I scroll through the movie options on Netflix.

"I'd be lying if I said I hadn't dreamt of that," he looks at me then, and I can't tell if he's joking and deadpanning or if he's serious.

I'm going to go ahead and pretend he's joking. I roll my eyes at him and try and act as if the idea of him dreaming of me doesn't make me feel a pressure at the bottom of my stomach when I scroll past 'Mean Girls.'

"What about 'Mean Girls'? That's always a classic." I ask.

"Never seen it."

I look at him, shaking my head, "I'm sorry that was weird, it sounded like you just said you've never seen 'Mean Girls' before."

"That's because that's what I said."

My mouth hangs open in astonishment, "Okay well it's not an option, we have to watch it now." I press play and grab a blanket from the back of the couch to ensure supreme movie watching comfort.

As we watch Cady Herron navigate through her first day of

school, I can't help but look over at Liam to watch him when he laughs, and he does that thing where he laughs hard enough that his eyes crinkle to the point of nearly disappearing behind his glasses. I'm very much trying not to find it adorable.

"Wait, she's giving her friend protein bars that are making her gain weight, but is telling her they'll make her skinnier?" He asks around halfway through the movie.

"Well, they aren't really friends, more like rivals pretending to be friends, but yep." I reply, popping the p at the end.

He chuckles, "Diabolical."

I laugh in response as he takes the pizza rolls off my ankle and sets them to the side.

As time passes, I'm starting to notice that the farther we get into the movie, the closer Liam and I get to one another on the couch. Around the time that Regina George starts making copies of the burn book, I realize that my ankle is now propped up on Liam's lap.

"Damn the teacher gets accused of being a drug dealer? That's fucked up."

"Um, sir, I think you mean a drug pusher, but it hits a little too close to home huh?" I laugh.

I'm so caught up in the warmth of Liam underneath my leg that before I know it the movie is over, and I realize I'm not ready for him to leave just yet. As the credits roll, a slow clap emerges from beside me, "Wow. A true cinematic masterpiece."

"I told you! It's a classic!"

Just as I think he's going to come up with an excuse to leave, he adjusts farther into the couch, leaving my leg draped across his lap, settling in. "Okay, so even though those pizza rolls I pulled out of the freezer are now thawed and gray I'm currently hungry enough to consider eating them. Want to order food?"

I try not to let a big obvious smile spread across my face at the idea of him staying later, you know, a normal friend response! "Chinese?" I ask.

His face lights up, "That would be so fetch!"

"Stop trying to make fetch happen Liam. It's not going to happen!" I cackle as he pulls out his phone to order what I know is far too much food for two people before getting up to put the questionable pizza rolls back in the freezer. I'll need my makeshift ice pack for later after all.

He walks back into the living room with two bottles of water in hand and sets them on the coffee table. "Okay so I ordered us crab Rangoon's, egg rolls, dumplings, lo Mein, general Tso, and mushu pork. Is that good?"

I unscrew the cap to the water bottle and take a sip before responding sarcastically, "No I think we'll need at least three more orders of crab Rangoon."

"Ah, a fan of crab Rangoon, are we?"

"Um, yeah, I would do a lot of unspeakable things for a crab Rangoon," I answer wryly.

"Noted," he replies with a sharp nod before taking a sip of water himself. "I'm more of an egg roll guy myself."

I narrow my eyes at him, "As in you like egg rolls better than crab Rangoon?"

"Correct," he nods, clearly unaware of the atrocities he's spewing.

I pull out my phone to check the time, "Well, friendship time of death, 5.43 p.m. It was fun while it lasted Liam."

"Why? Because I like egg rolls better than crab Rangoon?" he scoffs.

"I said what I said," I deadpan while he picks up my leg to place it back on the pillows on his lap.

His eyes meet mine playfully, "Well if I'm getting kicked out, I'm taking the food with me."

"Fine, but leave the crab Rangoon when you do," I tease.

He rolls his eyes at me dramatically, "So are we going to watch another movie, or just argue about Chinese food for the foreseeable future?"

I pick up the remote to scroll through Netflix once again, "Fine, but this isn't over." I find a movie that catches my eye, one of Josie and I's all-time favorites, 'Bridesmaids.'

I look quizzically at Liam, "I'm afraid to ask this after the last movie, but have you seen 'Bridesmaids'?"

I watch as Liam pulls awkwardly at the back of his neck while a flush creeps up it, "*Ummm...* I've seen the first ten minutes of it."

"How in the hell…?" I trail off before finishing the sentence.

Liam tilts his face up to the ceiling and clears his throat, "Well, um, Blair and I watched it on our second date, but got distracted about ten minutes in…" His cheeks flush bright red.

I give him a smirk, "*Ohhh* I see…"

I press play to start the movie and pretend that thinking of Liam and Blair together doesn't make me feel the tiniest pang of jealousy deep in my stomach. "Well not seeing this movie at least once should be a crime. Kristen Wiig and Maya Rudolph are in peak comedic form."

"Well then thank God you're here to educate me," he laughs.

Shortly after the movie begins the food arrives and we have to pause it. Despite my protests that I am more than capable of helping, Liam clears off the coffee table and sets out our veritable buffet of food. "Fork or chopsticks?" he asks while reaching into the bag.

"Chopsticks," I reply and grab them from his hand before

resuming the movie and biting a crab Rangoon in half.

"*Mmmm...* so delicious." I say loudly.

He studies me for a moment before saying, "I've never seen anyone so close to achieving orgasm from a food before."

"That's because eating a crab Rangoon is an out of body experience for me," I laugh.

He picks up an egg roll, taking a giant bite, "Wow this is amazing," he moans with the egg roll still in his mouth.

"*Oooh* I'll have what he's having," I laugh.

His mouth breaks into a wide grin, "Was that a 'When Harry Met Sally' reference?"

"Oh my God a movie he's actually seen!" I retort while popping the remaining half of my Rangoon in my mouth.

As the movie goes on, I can't help but constantly look over at Liam. Even though there are two pillows separating my leg from his lap and we aren't actually touching, this is probably one of the most intimate moments of my life.

I've had sex before sure, but I don't think I've ever had a guy actually take care of me like this. Even though I know this isn't a date, if it was it would probably be the best date I've ever been on. Usually on dates I'm anxious, worried that I'll slip up and say the wrong thing, or that I'm not pretty or funny or interesting enough, but with Liam it's easy. I can just be me without panicking for once.

I hear a loud laugh come from right next to me, "Oh, my God is she shitting in the street?"

Realizing that I was zoning out and not paying attention to the movie, I adjust quickly to look at the screen, "Yes she is in fact shitting in the street."

"That's fucking hilarious," he says while still laughing.

I grab the container of noodles and fish around in it with my chopsticks, "Indeed."

As the movie continues, and we've eaten an ungodly amount of food, I watch Liam point at the TV, "That giant cookie was dumb. I'm glad she punched it," he remarks, and I respond with a truly heinous cackle.

I can't help but think to myself that I could stay this way forever, laughing on my tattered blue couch, wrapped in blankets, eating Chinese food, and watching movies, with Liam. The concept is confusing for my brain because men that I find attractive, and friends, have always been in two separate parts of a Vinn diagram for me, but I think Liam might be the first person to ever fall in the category of both. All the more reason that this entire situation is so unnerving.

I'm not even close to paying attention to the movie at this stage because as I look over at Liam laughing, I watch the way the muscles over his throat stretch. I remember the warmth of the skin there as my lips and nose pressed against him, smelling him, tasting him. The way that he played with my body like he knew it already, like he knew all the ways he could drive me over the edge. I try not to remember the way it felt to have his hands rove over my body, grasping my hips to urge me on as I writhed helplessly on him, my skin consumed with fire fueled by lust.

I feel my cheeks heat and the sensitive skin between my legs ache. *Damn it Ella snap out of it;* I scold myself and force my eyes to look at the screen.

I'm not exactly sure how long I was engrossed in a sexual fantasy, but I look to see that the movie is basically over, and Wilson Phillips is playing. I swing my leg off of Liam's lap and start to stand when he grabs my hand, "Excuse me, ma'am what are you doing?"

I turn my head to look at him and try not to think about how warm his hand feels on mine, "I'm just cleaning up…"

He stands up and gently guides me back to the couch, "Absolutely not. I'll do it!" He then turns around and begins collecting cartons to put in the refrigerator.

"I'm not incapacitated you know!" I yell after him as he enters the kitchen.

"Christ just take the help!" He yells back from the other room.

"Fine," I say curtly while rolling my eyes even though I know he can't see me.

I hear the faucet to the kitchen sink begin to run and the clang of dishes knocking together and realize that he's literally in there doing my dishes. Knowing Liam if I told him not to do the dishes it would just earn me a tongue lashing, and not the fun kind, so I don't even bother. The sweetness of this man will probably be the death of me.

I can't for the life of me figure out why Blair would break up with him. How could someone so kind, thoughtful, and let's face it, hot, not be what you're looking for in a man? The thought keeps niggling at my brain and the curiosity gets the better of me. When I hear the faucet turn off, I yell into the kitchen, "Hey want to talk about why it's still so weird between you and Blair?"

I hear what sounds like a cabinet slamming shut before I watch Liam's tall frame come into view. He throws a dish towel on his shoulder with one hand and runs through his hair with the other, all the while I see a small sadness creep into those beautiful eyes.

"I don't know if there's much to really talk about…" he trails off while leaning against the doorway.

I give him a second to continue and he does, "We broke up months ago, but it still feels weird to be around her. It's not like

I love her anymore but being dumped by someone doesn't make being around them easy."

I watch as he moves from the doorway, taking the towel off his shoulder as he does, and sits next to me on the couch again. "Why did she break up with you?"

I know I'm probably overstepping, but I truly can't figure out why she wouldn't want to be with him. Was he secretly a weirdo that collected toenails in trash bags that he keeps underneath his bed or something? Did she watch him put milk in the bowl before the cereal one day and realized he was a psychopath? Inquiring minds need to know.

His hand goes to the back of his neck to pull on it, and he sucks in a deep breath, "We wanted different things," he shrugs before continuing. "I love teaching, but Blair wanted me to go work as a chemist for a corporation because the money is better. She didn't understand why I would ever choose teaching over making six figures, and we argued about it a lot."

I watch as he puts his hands in his lap and looks down at them, clearing his throat. "It all finally came to a head when we were arguing about it, yet again, and she told me that she didn't see a future for us if I wasn't willing to leave. She always wanted to be the stay-at-home Mom that gets to go do hot yoga in her lulu lemons and never have to worry about money."

He looks up at me then, his amber eyes looking somber. "Not her exact words, but that's the gist of it. I'm sure you know none of that is exactly possible on a teacher's salary."

I can feel my face heat with anger, my blood boiling. "That's very shitty of her."

He smiles at me, but I can tell it's fake because his eyes don't crinkle at the edges, and he shrugs. "It is what it is. I think we stayed together for so long because we kept thinking the other would change their mind but looking back on it now that's just dumb."

My anger begins to ebb and becomes sadness. I want to hold him and make all the pain go away. To make sure that he knows that he is so much more than how much money his big brain can earn.

Before I think better of it, I sit up on my knee and scoot closer to Liam, wrapping my arms around him in a hug. I didn't realize how tense he was until his shoulders visibly lower with my head resting in the crook of his neck. He relaxes his head against mine and I just sit there holding him while trying not to think about how good he smells or how warm his skin is.

I pull back slightly, my nose only inches from his and grab his face in my hands. I peer into those amber eyes, forcing him to look at me like he did earlier, and whisper. "There are so many things you do that are more important than money."

As he looks at me the air in the room begins to shift, and I become fully aware how close we are to each other. He seems to notice as well because I watch his eyes harden, no longer full of sadness but something different entirely, want.

We sit there, staring at each other, listening to one another's breathing pick up speed and feeling the air between us getting thicker and thicker by the moment. I'm reminded of that same rubber band feeling from the first night I met him, the one where it feels like all the tension between us is pulled so tight that we might snap.

However, unlike last time the rational part of my brain is currently in control, and I know that we can't be together. I know that there's a reason we said we would be just friends, and I can't back out of it now just because all I can think about is how good his lips would taste against mine.

I clear my throat to break up the tension and give him a small smile, "Well I should probably get some sleep."

His intense gaze seems to have snapped back to reality because within seconds it's gone, replaced with the sweet and easy-going look I've grown accustomed to. "Yeah, me too," he smiles back.

I begin to rise off him and stand, keeping the weight off my bad ankle so Liam doesn't scold me, and I can't help but notice how cold I feel now that I'm no longer touching him. Like he was warming me from the inside out without even trying to.

"Here I'll hobble you to the door so I can lock it," I smirk.

He chuckles as he rises off the couch, walking toward the door. He looks at me, a small smile pulling at the corner of his lips, "I had a lot of fun tonight, El."

I open the door and gaze back at him, "So did I," I reply, because I truly did, more than he could ever realize. "Goodnight Liam."

"Good night, El," he responds. He pauses then, halfway between the doorway and the porch as if he's at war with himself. I feel the same elasticity as before emerging between us, but whatever it's about he decides quickly, turning toward the driveway and walking to his car.

As I shut the door behind him, I lean my head against the cold door, hoping it brings me to my senses, because am I crazy or was he very close to kissing me? I rub my eyes, frustrated with myself, because I know that if he did, I wouldn't have been strong enough to stop myself from kissing him back.

Chapter Fifteen
Liam

It's been a little over a week since I went to Ella's, and still, I can't stop thinking about her. When I wake up, I think of gray eyes that can peer deep down to my bones. When I lay down to go to sleep at night, I think of strawberry blonde hair cascading over lush curves and the smell of lemon carried on spring air. Just the mere thought of how close I was to giving in and kissing her fills my brain with a buzzing sound. I don't know if I've ever been so consumed with the thought of another person before. Blair and I dated for a year, and I don't think my every thought was plagued by her.

It's the Sunday before pie week, the fundraiser the school does the week before thanksgiving break to raise money for the 8th grade trip, and I promised Ella I would help her with her pies tonight. Which means I'm going to Ella's house again, and it's going to take all my concentration not to kiss her. Last time I almost snapped and gave in to my desire, and I can't do that. Which means most likely I'll have to take care of myself in the shower before I go over there, not that I haven't done that basically every day since I met her anyway.

Max insisted we play basketball after our workout today, which is honestly preferred so I can hopefully burn off some of this sexual frustration that's been building up to a fever pitch inside me since I knocked Ella into the sand all those months ago. I'd say it would distract me from thinking about her in general, but I know that's a lie.

The indoor court at our gym is small with only one hoop and smells like floor polish. When Max isn't traveling for work, we end up playing here a lot.

I was never the kid that played sports, but when Max and I became friends, he taught me how to play. He whoops my ass pretty much every game we play, but at least he's not a dick about it.

I can feel the sweat drip from my disheveled hair and down the back of my old robotics t-shirt I cut the sleeves out of. Annoyingly enough my hair keeps falling into my eyes and I'm thankful I decided to put my contacts in instead of wearing my glasses today.

If I'm being honest with myself, I've been wearing my glasses more than normal recently because Ella said they were cute. I've made the mistake of playing basketball with glasses on before though and they ended up crushed under my foot. Never again.

As I dribble the ball and get ready to shoot it, I look at Max, "I don't know how much longer I can do this man."

The ball bounces off the rim and Max catches it, dribbling the ball and trying to dodge my advances. "What do you mean? Tired already old man?"

I roll my eyes as Max shoots the ball and I block it. My one advantage at this game is that I'm taller than him, and yet he still wins ninety percent of the time. "I mean yes, I am tired of you whooping my ass, but I'm talking about Ella. I know why we can't be together. I know she doesn't want me in that way, but I literally can't stop myself from trying to be around her any chance I get."

I dribble the ball as Max lunges and tries to take it from me,

"So basically you're a glutton for punishment."

I snort at his wording, before pushing my sweaty hair out of my eyes again. Annoyingly enough Max's hair looks completely unchanged due to the large amount of gel in it, and also because he's kicking my ass and not even breaking a sweat. Can't relate. "Yeah, it appears that way."

I shoot the ball and it actually makes it in the basket this time. When it falls through the net Max catches it and shoots it immediately for a lay-up, making it before looking back at me. "And you still want to be friends with her?"

I rub my eyes and sigh, "Some Ella is better than none."

Max chuckles, "Jesus man you have it worse than I thought."

My sneakers squeak against the polished floor as I swipe the ball from Max and shoot it. It bounces off the rim and flies off to the corner of the room. I groan as I walk over to retrieve the ball, "Yeah, I fucking know, and I'm supposed to go to her place tonight to help her make pies for the fundraiser."

I throw Max the ball so he can reset, but he tucks the ball in between his arm and his old Go Army t-shirt. His gaze turning serious, "Are you going to shoot your shot?"

I pinch the bridge of my nose to center myself, "Believe me I want to. Jesus I'm starting to think it's all I can think about, but she set a boundary. Unless she makes the first move, I'm not crossing it."

Max takes his hand, the one not holding the ball, and puts it over his heart, sighing dramatically, "What a guy."

I narrow my eyes at him, "It's not like that shit makes me a good guy. Respecting her boundaries is literally doing the bare fucking minimum."

Max throws me the ball, and I catch it but don't move. "Touche' good sir. Now shoot the ball already so I can finish kicking your ass."

Once again, I roll my eyes at him, and shoot the ball, trying not to take it as a metaphor for my life when I miss.

*

After I leave the gym in my little black Honda, I pull into the parking lot of my apartment complex and head up to the third floor.

When I walk in the door, I'm blasted with the heat trying to counteract the cold of the late November air. I set my gym bag in the hallway closet and make my way to the shower.

I turn the faucet on warm and take off my sweaty gym clothes while I wait for the water to heat up. Steam begins to fill my bathroom as I step into the shower, letting the warm water glide down my body. Considering my current state, I probably should've taken a cold shower, but oh well.

As I rub the shampoo through my hair my thoughts drift to Ella, and what I would do if she was in the shower with me. I can see her now, soapy, warm, and wet gliding against my body underneath the spray of the shower head. My hands roving over every inch of her with soap until she couldn't handle my teasing any longer. I'd press her against the cold shower wall, the sensation making her shiver at first before covering her body in mine.

I look down at my swollen cock, and I know, I'm going to have to take care of this before I see her tonight. If I don't then who knows what kind of embarrassment I'll endure. I spit in my hand to aid the water coming down from the shower head and coat my dick.

As I pump my hand up and down my shaft my thoughts pick

up where they left off. My body pressed against Ella's while I kiss down her neck, her wet blonde hair wrapped in one hand as my other hand slowly makes its descent down her body.

I brace myself against the shower wall while water sprays down my back and think of rolling her perfect nipples into peaks before sucking them into my mouth. I remember how sweet her moans sounded, and just the thought of it sends me right to the edge.

As I think about my fingers parting the hot flesh between her legs I come. For a moment I'm still. I lean against the shower wall, chest heaving, and my breathing begins to slow. I finish my shower and dry off, knowing all the while that jacking off just now did not a damn thing to prevent how much I still want her.

*

I pull into the driveway of the familiar white house with blue shutters and turn off the ignition. I'm in Ella's driveway, which means that at any moment I'll be in her house again. A house that smells like her in every room, the familiar scent of lemon and fresh air that I've come to recognize as her.

I rest my head against the cold steering wheel and take a deep breath before walking up to her porch and knocking. Behind the door it sounds like something clatters to the floor before Ella whips the door open in a frenzy.

A panicked look crosses her face, "Thank God you're here!" she gasps, tugging me through the doorway.

I quickly kick my leg to shut the door as she pulls me inside, "Um, hello to you too?"

Once we're in the kitchen I see what looks to be an entire orchard's worth of apples, and Ella turns around, giving me a frantic look. I know she looks like she's in the process of a meltdown, but I can't help but think that even like this, she looks adorable.

Her blonde hair is tied into a messy bun with a pink scrunchie, and she has a hot pink apron on that says 'Whatever frosts your cupcakes' accompanied by a picture of a cupcake. She has two small gold hoops dangling from her ears, a white tank top, and black leggings that contour every single inch of her curves. I can feel the zipper to my jeans begin to tighten, *I fucking knew jacking off wasn't going to make a difference.* I roll my eyes internally, I exhaust myself.

Ella rifles around in a kitchen drawer before finding a black apron and throwing it at me. When I unfold it, I realize it reads, 'I like my butt rubbed,' with a picture of a pig next to it.

I chuckle at her, "Do you have a thing for novelty aprons or something?"

I watch as she bends over into a different cabinet and pulls out an apple peeler, "I wouldn't say it's a THING, but I do feel like if you're going to wear an apron it might as well be catchy!"

Off to the side of the kitchen is a small table covered with apples and another peeler, "I'm sorry, do you own two apple peelers?"

Ella laughs as she brings the other apple peeler to the table and sits down, "No, of course, not! I borrowed one from my mom. I'm a teacher, I'm not exactly working on a two-apple peeler salary."

I smile and take the seat next to her after tying my apron, "Oh right, the two apple peelers will come once you're tenured."

She smiles at me, her gray eyes meeting mine, "Exactly."

She places an apple in the peeler and starts to move the crank. "I don't know what the fuck I was thinking volunteering to make ten pies."

I load up my apple peeler and follow suit, "Yeah that does seem extremely overconfident of you."

I glance at Ella from the side of my eye to see that she's glaring at me, "We can talk about all the dumb shit my overconfidence has gotten me into later, namely you, now less talking and more peeling!"

A snort escapes me as I watch the green peel curl off the apple, "Yes ma'am," I retort.

Ella turns on her Spotify and we work together in comfortable silence listening to music. Once it looks like we're nearing the end I watch Ella get up from the table and momentarily disappear around the corner. To my utter horror, she returns with two giant sacks full of apples.

I feel my eyes physically widen, "Jesus Christ Ella, how many apples did you get?"

She sets the apples on the table with a loud thud and gestures wildly, "I don't know! Like five hundred? It said to use ten per pie!"

"Ella, that's literally one hundred apples!" I yell.

Ella lowers her voice and puts her hands on her hips, mocking me, "Oh, my name's Liam and I know how to do math. Thank God I don't have a vagina that keeps me from understanding numbers."

"El, you literally just said five hundred apples, you have to make ten pies and each one needs ten apples. That's one hundred," I deadpan.

"Don't mansplain apples to me!" She yells.

"Oh my God fine," I say exasperated, "But if we personally created a shortage in the state of Indiana on apples, you only have yourself to blame."

Ella looks solemnly down at the table, "I'm just yet another statistic of the American education system." I can see her trying desperately to keep herself from laughing.

I roll my eyes, "Says a teacher in the American education system."

She smirks at me and crosses her arms, "There's nothing wrong with being self-aware. Oh, and also, there are actually one hundred apples. When I went and got them, I actually did do the math, thank you very much!"

I hold my hands up in defense, "Let the record show I not once said you didn't know how to do math. You know what, I'm just going to go ahead and keep peeling," I say while loading up the peeler once more.

When I look at her from the corner of my eye, I see her grinning. Clearly, she's entertained with herself.

Once we've made it a little over halfway through the apples, I watch Ella take her hands off the crank and shake them out. "I've peeled so many apples I don't know where my hand ends and the apple begins."

I hold up my peeler as if on display, pieces of apple skin falling off as I do, "This is my peeler. There are many like it, but this one is mine."

I watch as Ella laughs uncontrollably, "Was that a 'Full Metal Jacket' reference?"

"That it was."

"Truly inspired," she says while still laughing.

I could kick myself, because I'm realizing that I would do just about anything to make her laugh. I can't help but look over at her and revel in how beautiful she is.

Her blond hair escaping her bun, gray eyes sparkling with laughter, rosy, pink lips elongated with her smile, it's enough to make me physically incapable of focusing. Peeling apples is clearly the least of my concerns.

An unknown amount of time passes because at this stage it feels like I've entered another universe in which time is measured in apples instead of minutes, and I see Ella grab the last remaining apple and peel it.

When she finishes, I see a giant smile grace her face and watch her flex her fingers. "Oh my God I can't believe we're done peeling. I thought I was going to have to leave those apples to my least favorite grandchild in my will."

"So, in this scenario, the apples are going to live with you for the remainder of your life?" I question while grabbing the trash can to throw the leftover peels in.

She grins at me when she gets up from the table to wipe down the prep counter, "Yes, unfortunately it would end up being a common law marriage. It's not the torrid love affair I always dreamed of, but at that point, would I even know how to live without them?"

How in the hell does she come up with this stuff? The idea makes me laugh, "This really went off the rails, didn't it?"

She giggles then, grabbing flour and spreading it over the counter tops, "Yes I suppose so."

While Ella starts rolling out the dough from the night before for the crusts, I start on the pie filling as Stevie Nicks' voice crowds the room, and she starts to sing along.

"I love Stevie," she smiles. "When I listen to her, it reminds me of my mom."

"Are you and your mom close?" I ask while measuring out the sugar.

Ella starts portioning out more flour onto the countertop, preparing to roll out the dough. "Definitely, she's one of my favorite people in the universe. For a long time, it was just her and I. She used to say it was the two of us against the world."

"Used to say?" I ask while grabbing the apple pie spice.

"Yeah, I don't know my dad, and actually neither does my mom. She was a Dead Head and followed them around wherever they went. According to her my dad was a hot guy that she met at a show that offered her weed. They smoked together and two months later she found out she was pregnant."

"A love story for the ages," I reply while adding the last of the ingredients and stirring the apple mixture.

She chuckles lightly while spraying down the disposable pie tins with cooking spray, "Yeah, my grandparents are super conservative and when they found out about me, they disowned her. I've never even met them, so until my mom met Hank it really was just us two of us."

"Hank is your stepdad?" I ask while stirring.

"Yeah, he's the closest I've ever had to a dad. He's a good guy, and he loves my mom so much. He's more than I could ever ask for, even if I was a teenager by the time he came into the picture." I turn to look at her and I can see that she really does care for him, and if she's sad about not knowing her biological dad, she doesn't show it.

I smile at her then, "Well, I have two Dads and no Mom so we can share if you want."

Her face lights up at that, "Are you and your dads close?"

I see the mixture begin to bubble and I turn off the burner, "Yeah, we are, they adopted me when I was a baby shortly after my brother was born, so I don't even have any memories before them."

She bends down into a cabinet and pulls out a rolling pin, "Are you and your brother biologically related at all?"

"No, we aren't. My dads wanted a baby really badly, but adoption takes a long time, so they went the surrogacy route with my brother. Six months later they got a call, they were still in the system apparently, and they said they had a placement for them, and the next day I was theirs. Personality-wise I don't think my brother and I could be any more different. I was a nerd, he was a jock, tale as old as time you know?"

She looks over at me then and chuckles, "Oh, yeah I can definitely see you being a nerd."

I scoff at her, reach into the bag of flour next to me and throw some at her. "You did not just throw flour at me!" She gasps while trying and failing to get the flour off her apron.

"Oh, but I did," I laugh. Her eyes narrow, and in a flash, I see her walk over to me and grab a hand full of flour, holding it up menacingly.

"You're going to regret this Mr. Scott," she declares before opening my shirt and throwing flour down it.

The shock registers on my face, "Oh hell no! Down the shirt? This is a declaration of war Ms. Jacobs!" I snatch the bag of flour so she can't grab more and gear up to throw.

Ella's eyes go wide, and she holds up her hands in defense, "Oh God Liam, no… no… no… please no!" She squeals before turning to run away.

As she runs, I catch her by the waist and pin her against me so that flour gets all over her back and butt, and I realize that her ass is currently pinned against my dick, forcing a wave of heat to flow through my body.

She turns her head to look back at me and our eyes lock. We sit there for a moment staring at one another, and I feel that familiar tension I've become all too familiar with before she clears her throat, "Um, I should probably finish rolling out the crust."

I release her then, lightly shaking my head, "Yeah definitely," I reply while going to preheat the oven.

She walks over to the counter and begins spreading the dough and rolling it out with the rolling pin. I notice that the dough isn't thin enough, so I walk toward her.

"Here let me help you," I whisper from behind her, my mouth near the shell of her ear.

Her breath hitches then, "Thank you," she says while my arms cage hers and guides the rolling pin.

"You want the dough to be just a bit thinner, so the crust cooks the same throughout," I whisper in her ear, my arms still guiding her.

She relaxes into my touch, bringing her body flush with mine, and my senses are flooded with lemon and fresh air and apple spice.

As we roll the dough together our bodies move as one, and it's a hypnotic form of tension that overwhelms me. Her ass is pressed against my cock and it's getting harder and harder by the second.

I can't help it, when the hard ridge of me rubs against the plushness of her ass I let out a soft groan, and I know she hears it. My mouth is still next to her ear. She stills then and turns around to face me. Before she can say anything, I reach around her and take the dough off the counter and mold it to the pie tins.

"See! Perfect!" I say all too enthusiastically.

I can't tell what she's thinking, but she must decide to move past it because she grabs another hunk of dough and rolls it out. We work like that for what seems like an hour, in silence, and I want to smack myself because I'm a fucking moron and probably just ruined everything.

We find a rhythm, swapping pies in the oven and prepping the others until all the pies are ready to bake and there's flour coating nearly every surface of her kitchen.

"I think there's going to be flour in my lungs for a while," I say jokingly, trying to break the silence. *Maybe, if I just keep talking, I'll distract her from the fact that I just moaned in her ear like a teenager that can't control himself...*

She grabs a towel and smirks before throwing it at me, "Make yourself useful and help me wipe up the aftermath of this flour inspired dust bowl?"

"Yes ma'am!" I say saluting her before turning to the sink and wetting the towel.

"You know we wouldn't be in this predicament if you hadn't started a flour war in my kitchen," she says in a matter-of-fact tone as she wipes down the gray laminate countertop on the other side of the kitchen.

I ring out the towel in the sink before continuing, "Excuse me ma'am, but I recall you're the one who called me a nerd. Justice had to be served."

I look over my shoulder at her to find that she's smirking back at me, "Mr. Scott you've now called me ma'am twice within the last five minutes."

"Ah, yes, Ms. Jacobs, well, my dads did teach me the importance of manners. Just because we're at war doesn't mean I've forgotten all my social graces."

I watch as she walks over to the sink to rinse the towel in her hands. We're in closer proximity now, our shoulders nearly touching. "I didn't realize we were still at war."

"I may or may not have considered making a trojan horse out of dough before realizing I actually have zero capabilities of doing that." I say while I watch her dry her hands and linger next to me.

She giggles while turning to the refrigerator a few feet away and pulling out a beer, "I propose a truce."

She walks back toward me and hands me the beer, a white claw in her other hand. For someone whose extremely unpredictable some things about her are extremely so.

"Buying my truce? This will work just fine," I reply while we clink our cans together and followed by the hiss of the popped tabs.

We stand in silence for a while, both of us now leaning against the island countertop still coated in flour. Not that it would really make any difference to either of us because we're both already covered in it.

I look at Ella out of the corner of my eye and watch as she takes a gulp of her white claw and I watch it travel down her throat. Her head is tilted back slightly and the blonde hair that's escaped her bun flows down her back. *Even like this she's absolutely stunning,* I think to myself.

I try and attempt to make myself think of literally anything other than how much I wish those perfect pink lips were wrapped around mine instead of that can. "I don't know how you drink those things. They taste like TV static."

If she's offended, she doesn't show it, and laughs instead. "Josie says the same thing. She calls me basic, which I am, and I don't care who knows it."

I take a sip of my beer and let the froth coat my throat on the way down, "Way to conform to societal standards and yet also not conform?" I say with a teasing tone.

She laughs again, "That's me. A constant conundrum."

She's closer somehow, our shoulders mere centimeters apart. In height I feel like I tower over her, and looking down at her from this angle I'm reminded of just how short she is. While looking at her, I notice a smear of flour near her hairline and laugh.

She looks up at me, her mouth agape, "Excuse me sir are you laughing at me?"

"Sir? Now who's using formalities?" I question before taking another swig of my beer.

"Don't change the subject!" She says narrowing her eyes at me playfully.

"I'm laughing because you've got flour smeared on your face," I say glancing down at her while a smug grin spreads across my face.

She lightly shoves my arm and scoffs, "Well then get it!"

"Okay, okay one second," I laugh while grabbing a paper towel and wetting it at the sink.

I walk back to her and gently unfold the paper towel. I bend down so I'm eye level, and that's when her gray eyes accost me. I can't help but stare back at her as I move my hand gently up to the flour residue on her head. When my hand touches her face, I could be making it up, but I swear I hear her slightly gasp.

I wipe the last of it from her head, but I don't move. I remember this tension well, it's the same one that I've felt from the moment I met her months earlier. That feeling of a rubber band being stretched as far as it can go before it snaps.

I want her. This. Us. I want to take her on this counter right now, the smell of apple pie spice and her scent encompassing the air around me, but I know I can't.

I clear my throat and my voice comes out gravelly, "All good."

"Thank you," she replies breathlessly. Still neither of us move, we stand so close we're almost touching, so there is almost no room between us.

The air grows thicker by the second, and I watch as her chest begins to rise and fall more rapidly as what could be seconds or minutes tick by. I feel like I can sense her want for me, but there's also the jabbing thought of how I can't be the one to make the first move. This has to be her decision. She made her rules clear, and I promised myself I would respect her wishes, no matter how difficult that's proven to be.

Her gray eyes seem clouded with indecision, and my eyes dip down to her bottom lip which she's tugging at with her teeth. I can't take it; I have to know what she's thinking. I have to know what she's clearly so at war with in her mind.

Still bending down so that my eyes are level with hers, I use my arms to cage her on either side. Enough to show that I'm here to comfort her, but also with enough room that if she needed me to give her space I could step away.

"El, everything ok?" I ask.

In that moment I see a spark ignite in her eyes, turning them to melted steel, and the rubber band snaps. She flings herself at me then, wrapping her arms around my neck and her lips possess mine.

A groan comes from the bottom of my throat as her pillow soft lips mesh with mine. In this moment I wish I could put my hands on every inch of her. Our kiss is desperate, needy. Like we've both been wanting this for so long and are tired of fighting it.

I lift her up onto the counter and she moans, her perfect mouth meshing with mine. That sound is just kerosene on a body already on fire, and I snake my hand into her hair and grab tight, using it as leverage to open her mouth wider. She started this, but now I'm in control, and she's handing it over to me so willingly it makes me shiver.

My tongue meets her own through parted lips and massages possessively against hers. She moans again, and I know then that this is the only instance in which she likes to lose control.

I can feel my dick grow even harder in my jeans just thinking of all the ways I could possess her beautiful body. I pull my mouth from hers slightly, her lip lightly caught between my teeth as I do so before moving to her ear.

I remember how she preened under my praise from our night together that ended far too soon. My lips meet the shell of her ear, "You're so beautiful El. You taste like fucking sin." I whisper.

She whimpers and I feel her arms leave my neck to untie my apron and reach beneath my shirt. She quickly removes it and her eyes rove over me. "God damn it Liam, you're so fucking hot," she pants before pulling me back toward her, so our bodies are flush with one another.

My lips find hers once more, the push and pull of our tongues tangling, the taste of her has become my drug of choice. "A shirt for a shirt El," I say as I undo the knot at her lower back where her apron is tied, my voice comes out like I swallowed gravel.

She lifts her arms up and I pull it over her head. Beneath is a black lacey bra that looks like it's straight out of a wet dream.

I use my finger to play with the hem of the cup and stare into eyes full of heat, "If I pull these beautiful tits out will your nipples show me just how badly you want me? How you've wanted this just as much as I have ever since we almost fucked all those months ago?"

Her back arches slightly, offering me easier access to her perfect breasts. "Yes," she says with a hiss.

I unhook the front clasp and her beautiful breasts spill out and they're even better than I remember, her rosy nipples already pulled into a tight point.

"My God you're beautiful," I say as I catch her mouth with mine once more and use the hand that isn't steadying her against the countertop to gently cup her breast. When I lightly roll her nipple between my fingers she inhales sharply, and I know that I need her in my mouth.

My lips leave hers and trace her jaw, down her soft as silk neck, and I use my tongue to lick along her collarbone before finally reaching her nipple. I part my lips and take the bud into my mouth, gently sucking.

My eyes never leave hers, and the sensation has her writhing in pleasure as she wraps her legs around my hips attempting to bring me closer.

"You're such a good girl El, letting me know what you want," I respond before bringing her to the edge of the counter.

While she dwindles on the edge, I use the arm supporting her against the counter as leverage and pull her toward me, so my rock-hard cock is pressed against the heat between her legs. The sensation threatens to undo us, and we moan in tandem. She feels so good, too good, and half of her clothes are still on.

Our mouths meet once more, lips parting and tongues joining as we seek the friction we both crave. I grab her ass and use it to up the pressure against me as she grinds against my dick. I remember this well, the feel of her body moving against mine, her scent filling every particle in the air until I'm paralyzed by the heat and smell and feel of her.

I reach the hem of her leggings, realizing that we'll finally make it past where we had to abruptly end in Jamaica. As I begin to toy with the place where the hem of her leggings meets the flesh of her hip, a loud buzzing noise fills the room.

As if knocked from a trance Ella pulls away, her eyes wide, "Shit! The pies!" She yells as she hops off the counter and runs to put on an oven mitt to pull out the pies.

I shake my head, feeling like I just woke up from a trance, "Right. Yeah. The pies."

Ella turns to look at me, her face clouded with worry. I feel like I know what's coming, and I feel dread pool in the pit of my stomach.

She rings her hands together anxiously, "Shit. Shit. Shit. We shouldn't have done that!" She quickly grabs her discarded apron and wraps it around herself.

I walk over to comfort her, placing my hand on her arm, but she shrugs away from my touch. "El, what do you mean? That was incredible. I've been wanting to do that for so long…"

I can tell I've said the wrong thing somehow, and I watch as she clams up even more and the wringing of her hands picks up speed. "Liam, I'm sorry. I can't. I shouldn't have done that; we're supposed to be friends."

"Friends? El, we're more than that and you know it." The dread in my stomach leeches into the rest of my body, feeling like it's paralyzing my limbs.

"We shouldn't be though. I've told you why…" she says, her eyes pinching together, like saying these words are painful even to her.

I feel a lump forming in my throat, and I try and swallow past it. "El, I don't know if I can do this… I thought having you as a friend was better than nothing, but this… this is too painful."

I grab my shirt off the floor and quickly pull it over my head, not even bothering to see if it's inside out or not.

She unclenches her hands then, her eyes filling with worry, "Liam, wait no…"

I walk toward the door then, "I... I need space. I'm sorry." The lump in my throat gets bigger, and there's a burning behind my eyes. Moments ago, I was at the highest of highs, and just as quickly I'm at the lowest of lows. The rollercoaster of emotions is raging through me.

"I understand," She replies softly.

I look at her and see sadness behind her eyes. I know now that she's genuinely choosing to prevent herself from being happy, and I can't for the life of me understand how both of us together aren't worth the risk.

She leaves the door open and watches me walk to my car and drive away, the burn in my eyes never leaving me, even when I get home.

As I take the keys out of the ignition, I realize I'm cursed to live a life of never knowing what it will feel like to move past dry humping Ella.

Chapter Sixteen
Ella

What the fuck is wrong with me? I've asked myself that question so many times in the last twenty minutes I should have an answer by now. Hence the reason I'm eating leftover pie filling with a wooden spoon while my tits threaten to fall out the side of my apron. Apparently, I never put my shirt back on. In my haste to try and smooth things over with Liam I decided that apparently my shirt was optional, and a hot pink apron would suffice. My neighbors must've gotten quite the show.

Stupid horny vagina. I literally couldn't take the tension between us any longer. It was physically painful not having his hands on me, his lips caressing mine, his tongue in my mouth.

Tasting him was euphoric. It was like I was a woman possessed, and flashbacks from the first night we met overtook any and all sense of rationality. Like any anxiety, fear, or concern for social decency is expelled from my brain and replaced only with my need for him anytime he's around.

Stopping him was a gut reaction to the realization that I had so clearly lost my sense of control over the situation, and loss of control is not something I deal with well. My brain automatically hit the panic button and before I knew what was happening, I slammed on the brakes.

Of course, he would leave. Who would blame him? I threw myself at him like a fucking feral animal. If the oven timer hadn't gone off and triggered me out of my lust-induced hallucination,

I would've fucked him. Hell, it took all my willpower not to keep going even after being interrupted. The buzzer was the equivalent of a gallon of ice water getting dumped on my head, waking me up from my stupor.

I finish baking the last of the pies and clean up the remaining flour residue from the floor and counters. A feeling I'm all too familiar with begins to spread through my body, the one that feels like my blood is solidifying into pure iron. It's the same one that feels like someone put a boulder on my chest. The spiral is starting. I quickly grab my phone and text my mom the tornado emoji, our signal for an incoming panic attack, and try to steady my breathing.

I do everything I know to do. I've had enough guilt induced anxiety attacks in my life that if they gave out awards for it, I'd have two gold medals and an honorary doctorate degree from Yale.

I sit on the cold linoleum floor, my back against a cabinet, and hug my legs to my chest, making myself as small as possible. I focus on slow breaths and try not to listen to the words hammering into my head.

You ruined everything. He'll never forgive you. You deserve to feel nothing but shame. On the floor again? Pathetic. You couldn't even make it six months before fucking up again. Classic Ella.

I don't know how long I end up sitting there. It could be five minutes or five hours, but I hear my mom turn her key into the lock and rush through the door with Hank in tow.

"Sweet girl," she coos. Her long blond curls are pushed off of her face with a bandana, and when she sinks to the floor beside me and wraps me up in her bangle-covered arms she smells of patchouli and tea leaves.

Hank grabs my tea pot and fills it with water before putting it on the stove, "I'm working on some chamomile tea, that should help." His long gray hair is pulled back into a ponytail, and a long feather earring dangles from his ear, not for the first time I realize how thankful I am for my makeshift dad, you would never know I wasn't his.

"I fucked up mom. He hates me, I know he does." I say in between staccato breaths.

She smooths her hand over my hair and peers at me with my same gray eyes, "I'm sure whatever it is, you can fix it. Whatever it is won't break you."

I fling my arms wide, exasperated. "Look at me! It already has! I'm fucking twenty-eight years old, and my mom and dad had to come over at midnight and coddle me."

A small smile spreads on Hank's weather-worn face, "I know this isn't the time, but being called Dad never gets old."

My mom gives me a stern look, "Hey! There is nothing wrong with needing your mom. We're in this together, you and me against the world no matter how old you are. Hank, why don't you go get the stuff from the other room so I can do a cleanse."

He leans over to kiss the top of her head, "Of course my love," and walks into the living room. The 'Shoshana Jacobs Cleansing Ritual' has been with me since childhood. She nudges me to get up and we go into the living room to sit on the couch while she and Hank burn sage and palo-santo through the house while I hold a Hematite crystal. If it wasn't already midnight, it would be followed by a Molly Ringwald movie marathon.

Once she determines that the space is sufficiently cleansed and my aura is a better color she kisses the top of my head, her bangles clacking together with the movement. "Just remember, everything can be fixed. I know it took me a long time, and meeting Hank, to realize that, but at your age I wish I would've known it."

I wish it was that easy. I want to be able to convince my brain that's the case, but my critical thoughts like to leak through no matter how good of a resolve I've mustered. "Thanks mom."

When they leave, I begrudgingly walk to my bedroom. I pull on an old worn-out SpongeBob t-shirt and crawl into my bed, not even bothering to wash my face or comb my hair. I feel so mentally and physically drained that the thought of walking the ten steps to the bathroom might as well be climbing Mt. Everest.

The subsequent acne and matted hair will be my punishment for fucking up, and if Liam sees me like this then all the better. My humiliation is the least of what I owe him after I threw away our chance to be friends because I couldn't reign in my feelings for him.

Chapter Seventeen
Ella

Almost four months to the day after I shame spiraled in my hot pink apron; I find myself now funneling what feels like a hundred 8th graders through airport security while being severely under-caffeinated.

Thinking of that night, even after all this time, still leaves me feeling raw. I miss him, and I had no idea how big the space that he created in my life was until it was left hollow and empty. I can feel it there, the void left behind, like a missing tooth.

I attempt to shake off the memories from a few months ago and drag my tired butt through the line at security. Even though I wake up at the ass crack of dawn every morning for work and see these same 8th graders every day, there's something about seeing them all at once, and then also trying to get them safely to an entirely different state that adds another layer of anxiety and exhaustion to this.

I watch as a female security guard tells one of the students for the fortieth time to take their shoes off and audibly groans, saying she doesn't get paid enough for this. My sentiments exactly ma'am. We're clearly going to be here a while.

Near the back of the line, I see Liam talking to a few of the students and I can't help but feel that same pain in my chest I haven't been able to shake since he left my house months ago.

We've been as cordial as you can be with someone who was your almost one-night stand and then friend and then the person you almost had sex with again but stopped. Aka, we give each other awkward smiles and small waves and talk strictly about work or the school trip. It's been awful.

I've wanted to talk to him so many times about that night, but any time I try my guilt gets the best of me, and I can't bring myself to do it. He said he needed space and I have to respect that, even if I miss talking to him. Not just because he was great to look at, because good lord he is, but I miss him making me laugh in between classes, the way that he'd smile and I swear I could melt, how I felt like we could talk about anything.

I think about that night in my little kitchen more often than is probably healthy, and I'd be lying if I said reliving it wasn't Ol' Reliable fuel. My brain is constantly at war between feeling guilty that it happened, and replaying the moments over and over again in my head that made my skin feel like it was on fire.

When it's just me, alone in my bed with my rabbit vibrator, I remember the way his skin smelled lightly like cologne and soap, how his tongue tasted as it tangled with mine, and how his hands felt caressing my body. The intoxicating mixture helps me fill in the blanks of where things would've gone if I didn't stop it. The thought sends me over the edge every time, envisioning what it would've been like if I hadn't panicked.

I keep telling myself that I made the right decision, but did I? I'm starting to question whether anything could've been worth losing Liam, even if it ended with my subsequent humiliation. When I spent Christmas with my mom and Hank, they both said that they could tell something was still bothering me.

Also, when Josie and I had our typical Galantines Day, the day before Valentine's Day, celebration with M^3 and peanut butter M&M's it felt wrong. It felt like I was doing everything that I normally do during the Holidays, but in a body that was half asleep.

"Ma'am! I said I need your ID and boarding passes!" The security guard yells, removing me from my thoughts.

"Crap! Sorry about that. I'm just zoning out over here," I say hurriedly while flinging my purse to the front of my body and rifling through it. Quickly I hand over my ID while the security guard sighs impatiently before giving it back and calling next.

After finishing my run through security, I go to the other side and wait for the twelve girls I'm responsible for to make it through and meet me. Each teacher or chaperone is in charge of twelve students, and I try not to let the fact that there's twelve of them and only one of me intimidate me. I think Stella and her warnings are starting to hammer in more than I'd care to admit.

"Okay girls! Don't forget buddy system. We're going to go to our gate now. I have all your boarding passes. Don't wander off and stay together and we'll be good, capiche?" I attempt to yell over the girls all talking over one another.

"Capiche Ms. Jacobs," they all say back.

When we get to the gate, I spot Josie and she waves me over, so the girls and I go sit with her and her group.

"El, I'm so excited you decided to join!" She squeals and leans over to give me a hug.

"Yeah, me too, except for the part where Stella got in my head and now, I'm terrified that I'm responsible for twelve other humans in a state I've never been to!" I say erratically while wringing my hands in my lap.

Josie chuckles at me, "It's a lot, but these are good kids! Plus, you know their parent or guardian signed the waiver so…"

I lightly smack her arm and laugh, "Josie! Not funny!"

"In all seriousness though, you've got to chill, it'll be fine. They'll be able to smell the fear on you if you don't. We've done this for a really long time and the closest we've ever gotten to losing a kid was when two years ago one of the boys got lost in the hotel trying to find the ice machine. It was across the hall from him," she says while rolling her eyes.

I blow out a slow breath, "Okay that's good. Hopefully I'm not the first one to mess up the record."

"You won't be," Josie reassures me and hands me one of her ear buds, "Want to listen to the audiobook I just downloaded? The main character is a grumpy CEO and he just found out his receptionist booked him and his very bubbly publicist in the same room with only one bed," she says with a smirk.

"Are all of the rooms in the hotel booked up and it's the only place to stay for miles?" I ask while looking at her from the side of my eye.

She snorts, "You know it is."

"Hand it over," I chuckle while sticking my hand out.

We sit side by side listening to the narration of the audio book until they make the announcement to start boarding the plane. I quickly gather up the girls so we can all board together.

Once I make sure they're all settled I find my seat and pull out my kindle. I hear a throat clear and look up to see Liam standing in the row I'm seated in. "Uh, hey El. Looks like our seats are next to each other."

I feel the blood drain from my face, "Oh! Cool!" I say in a pitch that alludes to the fact that it is most definitely not cool and actually terrifying.

He gives me a funny look before putting his bag in the compartment above us and settling in next to me. I haven't been this close to him since pie night and I'm hyper aware of how good he smells and that the seats are so small his shoulder is touching mine.

Oh, good. So, Liam and I will be touching for an hour and a half? Wonderful. Splendid. Everything's going so well.

Once the plane takes off, I spend a good portion of the flight attempting to read the book on my kindle and restrain myself from forcing him to talk to me. About midway through the flight, I feel Liam shift in the seat next to me, and when I look over at him, he quickly looks away.

I try and angle myself as close to the window as I can and return back to my book only to get the sinking feeling I'm being watched. I hear a throat clear from the seat next to me, and once again I look over to see Liam with a smug grin on his face. *Oh, my god... is looking at what I'm reading...?*

I feel heat pool in my cheeks and look down at the scene I was just reading, and well... it's raunchy to say the least. The mafia Don and the female main character just realized that their marriage of convenience has turned into more, and well. Fill in the blanks.

I flip the cover over my kindle and shove it in my bag hastily, and I can both feel and hear the chuckle from the seat next to me. "You don't need to be embarrassed El, you like what you like, but just so you know, I could do better." Then proceeds to wink. WINK.

I think that wink just got me pregnant.

I go rigid and feel my eyes grow wide, while I feel heat pool between my legs. I have literally no response to that, and I'm sure as hell not going to talk to him about my preferred reading materials after we haven't talked about anything but work for four months. He's clearly taunting me, which I guess is the least of what I deserve. I quickly turn toward the window so he can't see the flush crawling up my neck and try and suppress the urge to talk to him about what happened on pie night.

I figure he'll talk when he's ready to, I'm not sure how much space he needs. I guess you can't really put a time limit on that sort of thing, so I don't talk for the rest of the flight and neither does he. I'm afraid at this point I may never get to be friends with him again.

*

When the plane lands at Ronald Regan National Airport it's a virtual mele. All the teachers and chaperones collect their kids and board them on a shuttle service that will take us to the hotel. Even with all the fundraisers, donations, and grants it blows my mind that we're able to do this for our students. Truly, I'm in awe.

A lot of them have never even been out of the state of Indiana, let alone on an airplane. Liam had mentioned this had become a passion project of Bledsoe's, and up until the last few years they would take buses to D.C.

Bledsoe wanted them to be able to have more time learning and less time on a bus, so he worked out flight arrangements with an airline that was willing to help make it more affordable. The dedication that these teachers have toward their students is exactly what makes me love working for Valley so much. I'm amazed at all the work that went into this, and I'm so glad I decided to be a part of it.

I load the girls into the shuttle, and we head to the hotel. On the way they're all a flurry of energy, full of excitement, and talking over each other at once. When we finally get to the hotel, I'm surprised by how nice it is. It's not fancy or anything, but it's not a place that looks like they rent by the hour either.

In attempt to not overwhelm the woman at the front desk Bledsoe goes to get all the room keys to divvy out to the teachers and chaperones. Naturally the students are all restless and groaning, because they're teenagers, and they hate waiting.

Finally, Bledsoe hands me the pack of key cards and I have the girls follow me up to the third floor where our rooms are.

When we get to our floor, I show the girls their rooms and give them the key cards along with a rundown of the rules. Basically, the rules at school apply here, and if they're broken, I'll have to be a buzzkill and I don't want to do that so please don't make me etc....

After all the girls have dispersed into their rooms, I get settled into mine and unpack my suitcase. The room is pretty standard for a mid-grade hotel, with crisp white bedding and nondescript art hanging on the walls.

I realize then that I should probably find the ice machine just in case one of the girls goes wandering and gets lost. Though I'm sure it wasn't intentional, Josie's story made me paranoid that I'd have the first student to actually get lost finding the ice machine and then cause an international incident, so I open the door only to hear the beep of a keycard come from beside me.

I look over and who do I see? Liam. We look at each other, and both of our eyes go wide. Like the mature adult I am, my first instinct is to panic and flee so I quickly turn back around into my room and shut the door.

God damn it Bledsoe I'm starting to think you want us to fuck each other...

*

After I've paced a virtual hole into the oddly patterned carpet of my hotel room, Bledsoe sends out an email with the floor assignments and our partner for hallway duty.

In addition to Liam, Mrs. Port the librarian, and Mr. Brown, one of the parent volunteers, are on our floor as well. When I see that Liam and I are partners and have hallway duty together tonight I realize I can't even be shocked. The amount of times that I get thrown together with this man... I'm starting to question if maybe I'm ignoring some giant sign from the universe that's telling me to climb him like a tree.

I look at my phone to check the time and realize we have to be down in the lobby in fifteen minutes. When I open my door, I get a random whiff of something that smells strongly like cotton candy and see two of the girls huddled together at the end of the hallway.

"Mia and Raquel are you guy's vaping?" I say loud enough to startle them.

They jump apart and I see their eyes go wide, "No Ms. Jacobs! We don't do that stuff." She says while shuffling her feet, not remotely suspicious at all.

I tap my chin and give them a confused expression, "*Hmmm*... that is so weird because it smells like cotton candy down here and not at all like old hotel carpet and cleaning supplies like the rest of the hallway..."

I watch as they both shift awkwardly, "That is weird..." Mia says as her voice goes up an octave. These girls have got to get better at lying, I mean honestly.

I fold my arms over my chest and give them a reassuring smile, "I tell you what. If you do have a vape, which I'm not saying that you do, and you happen to slide it under my door later, I wouldn't know how it got there. If I don't know how it got there then well, I can't do anything about it, but if you do get caught with a vape then I'll have to call your parents. I hate having to call parents, makes me feel like a snitch."

Raquel and Mia look at each other and then look at me, "Got it Ms. Jacobs," Raquel says before pulling Mia toward their door.

"And girls, if you're trying to not get caught doing something, a communal hallway isn't the best place to be discreet!" I yell after them.

A low husky voice bends down behind me and whispers in my ear, "Are you sure you aren't just trying to get a free vape out of them?"

I turn around to see Liam smirking down at me. His dark curls are tussled perfectly, and his amber eyes are glowing behind the wire-framed glasses I'm a sucker for. I look at the perfect jaw line I've licked and try to maintain composure. He's wearing one of his classic collared shirts, but this one has The Bill from *School House Rock* in small print all over it. *Damn this man and how fucking cute he is! It's infuriating!*

"You caught me," I say while returning a smirk back at him.

He shuffles slightly then, and a black curl falls into his eyes, I watch him intently as he pushes it away, "So… your room is next to mine…"

I look down at my favorite black Toms with constellations printed all over them, as if they'll make me feel any less awkward in this current moment, "That it is." I reply before meeting his eyes once more.

A small smile crosses his face, "And we're also on hallway duty tonight together…"

I chuckle, "God does have a sense of humor."

I watch as he looks off to the side awkwardly, "It does seem that way."

I swallow the lump in my throat that makes me feel nervous

to say what I'm about to, "This is weird right? I mean I hate this. Not talking to you." I can't believe I actually just admitted that. I must be desperate.

I watch as Liam visibly relaxes and exhales a breath, "Yeah me too."

The fact that he didn't say he was loving not being around me like I thought he would relaxes me, "I don't want you to feel like I'm pressuring you into being friends, but I do miss you."

He smiles at me then, a huge one that spreads from ear to ear, and it feels like I've been exposed to direct sunlight with how beautiful it is. "Yeah, I've missed you too," he says while nudging my arm. "I watched *Mean Girls* the other day and it wasn't as funny without you."

The thought of him watching *Mean Girls* alone makes me laugh, "You watched *Mean Girls* again?"

"Is butter a carb?" He says in the same way that my stepdad Hank used to say, 'Does a bear shit in the woods?' to me when I asked a too obvious question.

"I'm so proud," I giggle while placing my hand on my chest.

"I knew you would be," he smirks at me. I feel the familiar tension I've come to know well in the time I've met Liam. The one that feels like the air is getting thinner and my breathing picks up.

I snap myself out of it and nudge his arm. "Let's round up the troops. The Washington Monument awaits!" I announce before turning back down the hallway and telling the girls it's almost time to leave.

*

When the shuttles pull up to the Washington Monument the

parent volunteers and teachers collect their groups, and I find my girls quickly enough to pull them aside. We're in the group that gets to do the Washington Monument and Lincoln Memorial on day one and then the Smithsonian the following day, the same as Josie's thank God.

Once I've double and triple checked my head count and remind them for the hundredth time to stay with their buddies, we're on the move.

It takes a lot of energy not to geek out over the amount of history that permeates this entire city. Being the history buff that I am, and the fact that this is the first time I've been to D.C. myself, I'm in awe of the massive building.

I hear a snicker come from beside me, "It looks like my dick," one of my third period students, Lewis, remarks.

I hear the rumble of a familiar voice come from the same side and see Liam walking behind Lewis. "Someone's a bit overconfident aren't we Lewis?"

Lewis turns around with wide eyes and blanches, clearly not realizing Liam was behind him. His friends in the group find the entire interaction hilarious, and it takes every ounce of restraint I have not to bust out laughing too. Without a word Lewis runs slightly ahead with his friends in tow and joins the girls in my group.

I look at Liam from the side of my eye and smirk, "To be fair he isn't completely wrong. It does look like a penis."

Liam stops walking and feigns surprise, "Well Ms. Jacobs I guess I'm glad that we never got that far. I'd hate to disappoint."

My jaw drops and Liam walks toward our groups that have now merged together while laughing at his own joke. *Well thank God no one else was around to hear him say that...*

I do a quick jog to catch up along the stone path and yell at them to stop when they get to the reflecting pool so I can give them the educational spiel on the building.

Once, they've stopped and gathered, I give them the rundown. "Okay everyone this is the Washington Monument. It was built in honor of the first president of the United States, George Washington. Upon its completion in 1884 it was the tallest building in the world. That being said, we're going to ride the elevators to the top so we can see the beautiful view. If I've said it once I've said it a thousand times, please please please stay with your buddy and let me know if for some reason you have to branch off from the group." After my spiel I lead our groups toward the long line awaiting the elevators to the top of the monument.

Once we're in line Liam comes to stand beside me and I watch as Josie and Mrs. Port have their students shuffle in together. Josie's eyes catch mine and she waves so wildly at me that her curls bounce around her face and the tie-dye on her shirt blurs together. I smile and wave back frantically before the doors close in front of them.

I feel when Liam leans in toward me. The electricity of him being in such close proximity potent against my skin. "It's cool how close you two are," he says.

He nods toward the elevator doors that Josie just went up, "I don't think you ever told me how you two met."

A smile breaks across my face at the thought of my best friend and how lost I would be without her. "Yeah, Jos and I have been best friends since high school. We took a class together that was meant for people interested in education and our teacher had an Elmo puppet that she would talk through. Jos sat next to me, and we always laughed together at everything Elmo said. I knew at that point that we had the same sense of humor, and it was meant to be."

The line moves a bit and we're next up. When we come to a stop, I see Liam's eyebrow quirk up. "I didn't realize Josie wanted to be a teacher."

A laugh full of mirth escapes me, "Oh yeah, all the way until our junior year when we shadowed in an elementary school classroom. A kid came up and told her that he had a booger collection behind his bed, and he just found number thirteen. After that she changed tactics."

"I don't blame her I guess," he chuckles.

I watch as the elevator doors open back up and Josie's group files out. She walks toward me smiling ear to ear. "The view is breathtaking," she sighs.

My excitement can no longer be contained, and a squeal escapes me, "Ah I'm so excited! I've wanted to go to the top of the monument since I was little. I mean the historical significance alone…"

"Nerd," Josie deadpans. She can't stay serious long, and she starts to laugh while gathering her students to the side to get them ready for lunch.

As I load the girls onto the elevator, Liam's group joins us, and I glare at Josie until the elevator door closes in front of us. In the confined space Liam is pressed against me, and I try not to revel in the feel of my body against him and maintain composure.

I feel him bend down slightly behind me so his mouth is close enough that I'm the only one who can hear him whisper. "I think it's cute how hot for phallic monuments you are."

Even as he rights himself and he's no longer near I can feel the tingle of his breath against my ear lingering, and my face heats. I narrow my eyes at him and whisper back, "Says the guy who gets a boner every time he sees a periodic table."

"That only happened twice and I'm sure it was just a coincidence," he deadpans. I can't help but gawk at him. "I'm just kidding," he chuckles.

I laugh as the elevator doors open and we all begin to file out. My laughter peters out as I look and see the view from the top of the monument. Collective gasps come from the students, and it warms my heart to know that I'm not alone.

The attendant waves us through, "You have five minutes before you'll need to head back down for the next group."

I immediately press against the glass to get the best look at the view that I can. I marvel at the sight. "You can see Virginia from here. It's more beautiful than I imagined."

I feel Liam walk up beside me and gives me a look I can't quite figure out before taking in the view, "I know what you mean."

*

I went from barely saying two words to Liam for months to spending an entire day with him. The realization that our groups have been virtually glued together the entire time doesn't surprise me, considering it's common knowledge that Lewis has a huge crush on Mia and both friend groups are trying to get them together, not that I'm complaining. I wasn't being dramatic when I said that I truly missed Liam, and I think we're making up for lost time today.

What I did not plan on however is that the pull I have toward him physically hasn't gone away in his absence, but it's gotten even stronger. Any time he's near me I find myself begging whatever God will listen that he comes closer.

That's me. A total professional. Even my perpetual

excitement over all the monuments and historical information is being overshadowed by the fact that all I seem to think about is how Liam's tongue would feel between my legs.

It's not even just the fact that the man is the hot nerd of my wet dreams, but he's funny and sweet and thoughtful and so good with the kids, and oh my god this crush is getting out of hand. I literally have hallway duty with him tonight. What the fuck am I going to do if I can't get my body to cooperate with the very strategic plans that my brain has for my life?

All of this to say, I'm getting ready to go out in the hall now and I'm bringing my kindle with me in an attempt to read and distract myself. I tug on my favorite linen pants and a black Queen t-shirt before tossing my hair up into a banana clip and leaving the room.

When I go to the door, I find a Juul pod was slid underneath it, and I can't help but laugh hysterically and knock on the door that attaches my room to Liams.

He opens the door and my brain fumbles because there he is in front of me in a black T-shirt that contours all the muscles on his chest, and gray sweatpants that grip him in all the right places. I swallow a lump that's caught in my throat and try to recover while he looks down at me with a smirk. *Oh, so he knows I think he's hot. Splendid.*

"Hey big guy, want to vape?" I say in a mock sultry voice while waving the Juul pod.

He flashes me a smile, "No thank you ma'am my dads told me smoking is bad."

I tuck my fist under my chin in a pensive way, "Well golly gee I sure hope you don't break your ankle."

I watch as the expression on his face turns into one of complete confusion, "What?"

I lean what I think is casually against the door frame, but is probably in fact not graceful at all, "I just figured when you were climbing down off of such a high horse you might fall and break something."

He narrows his eyes at me, "Ha. Fucking. Ha." he deadpans.

I nudge his shoulder with my hand and Jesus it's so solid and I can feel everything underneath that thin t-shirt, "Come on. It was funny."

He rolls his amber eyes dramatically behind his glasses, trying not to smile. "I thought you had a stroke at first. I was about to ask you if you smelled burnt toast." He's teasing me obviously because that grin is fully breaking through.

I flail my arms in mock exasperation, "Ugh you and Josie and your burnt toast stroke references, is it too much to ask to be told I'm funny? It's the attention I crave. I need it for survival."

His eyebrow cocks up and he folds his arms over his broad chest, "Survival? Well, I didn't realize this was a matter of life and death. In that case," he bends down at eye level to look at me directly and I feel like those eyes are melting me from the inside, his voice becoming very serious, "El you are so funny. I don't know if anyone has ever made me laugh as much as you have. You're beautiful and kind and everything about you is perfect."

I feel my cheeks heat at his praise, "Thank you," I whisper and try not to let the giant smile threatening to escape spread across my face.

I realize we've been staring at each other and before I do something I regret I clear my throat. "Are you ready for our hallway duty?"

He looks at me like he's going to say something, but then changes his mind. "Yeah, meet me out there in ten. I've got to do something first."

I give him a thumbs up, "No teens sneaking out on our watch!" I say before shutting the door behind me.

"Narc!" I hear him yell through the door, making me cackle.

I've never been super good at waiting, so I check my phone about once every minute until I know that ten minutes have passed. If I was still lying to myself, I'd say it was because I just wanted to get this over with, but either fortunately or unfortunately, I'm not sure which, I've become more self-aware. I know that the real reason is because I can't stop thinking about that black T-shirt clinging to the same broad chest that I ran my hands along months ago. My fingers twitch at the muscle memory of the way his skin felt underneath mine before I shake them out and open the door.

For a slight moment, I'm confused because there's a giant blanket in the middle of the hallway, but after a moment my brain seems to register what's happening. Amongst the oddly detailed carpet with random lime green squares is Liam, sitting on a giant white blanket and leaning against a pile of pillows on the wall. In the middle of the blanket is a pile of snacks and his phone positioned with the kickstand up.

I can't help it; a giant smile takes over my face. It's been a while since I've dated someone, so maybe my opinion is skewed, but this is so fucking cute. A pang in my chest develops at this man that I've gotten to know over the last seven months.

There's always been attraction, hell from the moment he ran into me and I fell on my ass I wanted to cling to him like a spider monkey, but it's getting harder and harder to deny that my feelings for him are just mere attraction. In the seven months that I've known him he's done more for me than any guy I've ever dated, and we were just friends.

I internally roll my eyes at myself, because I know that the tight rope I've been walking on under the guise of friendship has been one I've fallen off several times. This man that caught me from falling from a desk, that carried me down the hallways of Valley after I twisted my ankle and took care of me, that helped peel a hundred apples and then possessed my body in a way that I've never felt before.

Fuck, I think it's safe to admit that this is more than a crush. I'm questioning everything. Are my convictions even worth losing this feeling? A chance for something more? Honestly, would he even still want me after all this time? After I pushed him away? Probably not. I'm sure I fucked up any chance we ever had of being more than friends. *God I am so stupid.* My heart squeezes in my chest at the thought.

I strain to keep the smile on my face after realizing just how badly I blew it, "What's all this?"

A smile so beautiful it makes my heart ache crosses his face, "I figured a stake out wouldn't be complete without snacks."

Well, since I ruined any chance of us being more than friends, settling for friendship with Liam is still a good deal, and I need to make the most of it.

I sit down on the blanket next to him and fluff the pillows behind me until they reach a peak comfort level. I'm sitting close enough to touch, but not, and the small space between us feels physically painful. I try to put the thoughts of how badly I want to touch him out of my brain.

"Is this stakeout a month long?" I ask while quirking up an eyebrow.

I watch as those beautiful amber eyes look down at the floor and he shifts self-consciously, "I wasn't sure what you would be in the mood for, so I got a variety of stuff. If it's too much though…"

I wave my hands to reassure him, hating to see the self-conscious look across his face, "No, no, no this is so sweet. Thank you." I say interrupting him.

I spot a pack of peanut butter M&Ms in the junk food pile and tear into them while I watch Liam grab a pack of Reese's. "So, what movie will we be watching this evening?" I ask as the crunchy chocolate and peanut butter mixture coats my tongue.

A cocky smile plays along his lips, and I fight the urge to lick it off. *Jesus Ella calm the fuck down;* I internally scold myself. "Well, I know *Moulin Rouge* is your favorite movie, and they just added it to Netflix…"

I can't help it, a squeal escapes me in excitement, "Oh my God yes! You've never seen it before, right?"

I watch as he bites a Reese cup in half, "No, but I've heard the soundtrack. It's good."

I roll my eyes dramatically at him, "My God did you live under a pop culture rock before we met?"

He deadpans, "Actually. This is really uncomfortable for me to talk about, but I feel like I can trust you. When I knocked you over in Jamaica I was actually running because it was my first time ever seeing another human being. Before then I was raised by gorillas and swung from vines in only a loin cloth."

"I'd almost believe it, but we both know you were trying to catch that frisbee like your life depended on it. Though I'd be lying if I said that seeing you in a loin cloth wouldn't pique my interest," I snort.

He waggles his eyebrows at me, "Ah, so you're into rugged jungle men, are you?"

"When I watch *George of the Jungle* and see Brendan Frasier oiled up and wearing a loincloth it makes me tingly," I say with a laugh.

"Honestly, who wouldn't get tingly seeing Brendan Frasier

in a loin cloth?" He remarks while picking up his phone to press play.

"Someone lying to themselves."

"Truer words have never been spoken," he says, and presses play.

I stop him then, realizing we should probably call lights out before we have to interrupt a legendary *Moulin Rouge* ballad. When I mention this to him, we both stand up quickly and tap on all the doors to let them know big brother is watching before returning to our makeshift picnic in the middle of the hallway.

We return back to our spots on the blanket, almost close enough to touch, and I swear I feel the heat of his skin so close to mine we might as well be touching. I clamp my teeth down on my bottom lip, hoping the pain focuses me enough to not let my mind drift down the endless rabbit hole of erotic thoughts about him that it's prone to do. *Don't think about how good he smells. Don't think about how good he tastes. Don't think about how his teeth nibbled on your neck. Don't think about how his hands gripped your ass so hard it was close to bruising.*

To my horror, I can't imagine what must be showing plainly on my face as Liam waves his hand in front of me to get my attention. "El, I said are you ready?"

I shake my head lightly and let out a laugh to play it off. I didn't play it off. I sounded like a jackal that got its foot stuck in a bear trap. I don't even know if jackals live in a place where bear traps would be, but I'm clearly spiraling.

"Yep!" Cool. Totally played off the fact that I was just thinking about his teeth grazing against my skin. Super chill.

He gives me an odd look and smirks before pressing play. We sit in companionable silence, watching as Nicole Kidman sings and dances to 'Diamonds are a girl's best friend,' and laugh at the perfect balance between the serious and corny acting that this movie does so flawlessly. I find myself looking over at Liam every so often, enjoying his reactions as much as the movie itself.

About halfway through, I feel the scratchy dry feeling behind my eyes as they begin to get heavy. This day has been nothing short of exhausting. "I feel like it's cruel and unusual punishment to make us go through a whole morning of traveling, walking around the Washington Monument and Lincoln Memorial, taking a bunch of fourteen-year-old's to a restaurant, and then making us stay up to do hall duty."

He quirks an eyebrow up at me, a gesture I've become accustomed to and yet it still sends a shiver through me each time I see it. "Are you suggesting that we leave the fourteen-year-olds to police themselves?"

I yawn dramatically, "Yeah sure. Night one could be like the middle school version of the purge, except instead of murder they raid the vending machines and probably make out with each other."

He leans over and grabs a package out of the pile, "Exhaustion is making you delusional. Here, have some sugar," he says while handing me a yellow starburst.

I narrow my eyes at the offending candy, "Yellow? Absolutely not. Pink and red or die."

He rolls his eyes at me while the sound of Ewen McGregor singing 'Your song' plays in the background. "You're one of those people that they make the special starburst packs for, aren't you?"

I give him a smug grin and pop the pink starburst into my mouth, the flavor bursting on my tongue, "Proudly."

We turn our attention back to the movie, and I get comfy on the pillows laying against the wall. The last thing I remember is vaguely hearing the song 'Roxanne,' before waking up the next morning in my hotel room with no idea of how I got there.

Chapter Eighteen
Ella

I shoot up out of my bed, the digital clock on the nightstand next to me showing the time as eight a.m. Shit, I'm supposed to have the girls up and ready to go down to breakfast by nine a.m. I look down at the Queen shirt and linen pants I was wearing last night, my shoes taken off and sitting next to the bed and my banana clip resting on the nightstand.

I panic and go to the door adjoining Liam and I's rooms, knocking rapidly. A few minutes later Liam comes to the door, gray sweatpants hanging low enough on his hips that I can see the V shape of his muscles filing downward. I try and swallow the lump in my throat as I note the scruff of his face and the sleepy look in his eyes. *Even when he's half asleep, he's still fucking hot,* I groan internally.

"Did I fall asleep last night? The last thing I remember is the 'Roxanne' dance." I say erratically.

He lifts his sleepy eyes to mine and chuckles lightly, "Yeah, I'm not sure how one falls asleep during that particular number, it's quite intense, but you definitely did. I have the drool stain on my shoulder to prove it." He says while tapping a white mark on his shirt.

My face floods with heat, complete embarrassment washing over me. "Oh my god. No, I didn't," I say while pinching the bridge of my nose.

"Oh, but you did," he smirks lazily, pointing to his shoulder again.

I crinkle my nose at him, "Ew, you're still wearing my drool shirt?"

He scratches lightly at the scruff on his face, "I figured there were worse things than having your saliva on me."

"Be careful Mr. Scott, flattery will get you everywhere." I say, pretending like I'm not absolutely mortified that I not only fell asleep on him last night, but also slept hard enough that I drooled on him.

I see a spark in his eye, that smirk once again playing on his lips as he leans against the doorway, his shirt lifting higher to show off more of his skin. It takes all of my strength to not let my gaze linger there.

"Well, I think we both know that if that was the case all I would do is talk about how beautiful you are. I'd tell you how your eyes change different shades of gray depending on your mood, but my personal favorite is the lust filled stormy dark gray they turn when my lips are on yours. How your hair is the softest thing I've ever touched, and that you smell like lemons and warm skin. I'd tell you that I can't even be near you without wanting to inhale you and see how dark I can make your eyes get."

My jaw goes slack, need burning through every inch of my skin. The place between my legs going both leaden and molten at the same time. My entire body has got to be covered in a flush. I feel his words unfurling over every inch of me, caressing me like a gentle wind picking up a spark before the start of a wildfire. *Maybe, I didn't ruin things after all...?*

"Yeah, just like that." he says with a cocky smirk.

I don't know how long I stand there speechless, but before an actual thought can form in my brain, he looks at me with those amber eyes full of want. "See, but I know better than that. We're just friends after all." He says before winking at me and closing door.

I stand there still speechless, gawking at the gray door that attaches my room to his. My defenses have faltered. The very flimsy wall that I had built to try and protect my heart from falling for this man has all but crumbled.

I was right last night; I can't pretend any more. I can't act like I have the strength to fight whatever this is. I want him. All of him. Mind, body, soul. Everything. I want to let him possess me like before, but instead of running away from my feelings this time, I'm going toward them. Potential shame spiral be damned, whatever may happen next can't possibly be as painful as not being with him.

*

Walking along the glossy floors of the Smithsonian, my arm is linked with Josie's while our girls walk in front of us in the rotunda. We give them enough space so we can talk without them hearing what we're saying, but the fact that they're teenage girls and can't stop laughing and talking over one another helps drown out the sound around them anyway.

As we walk around the rotunda the girls marvel at the giant elephant, their laughter echoing in the space all the way to the high ceilings above. Are we the loudest people in the entire Smithsonian? Yes. Do I care? No, because these girls are having the time of their life.

Josie's wearing her favorite neon mystery machine shirt, our combined love of graphic t-shirts makes me smile as I look down at my black acid-wash Van Halen t-shirt. We're not technically at school so all the teachers have gone a lot less "business casual" and a lot more "wearing what we'd wear in our everyday lives" on the trip.

I watch as Josie leans down toward me and whispers, "Sorry, so he said, once again, that he thinks you're hot and very clearly wants to play a very long game of hide the hot dog with you, and you feel nothing?"

I snort, "No Jos, that's the problem, all I can think about is all the places I want to hide that man's hot dog." Josie laughs so hard her curls shake around her, clearly pleased with herself.

"Are we married to the hot dog metaphor? I feel like we can do better," I say as we walk arm and arm.

She taps a black painted nail to her chin in contemplation, "*Hmm...* how about becoming the one-eyed snake charmer?"

I cackle in amusement and all the seriousness of the delivery melts away quickly as Josie can't help but laugh at her own joke. The epitome of our friendship, laughing back and forth until our sides hurt, and tears come out of the corner of her eyes.

As I laugh, I feel the tears glossing over my eyes, "Fishing for snatch with the world's biggest worm?" I say with a cackle.

That one undoes her; she starts laughing so hard we have to stop walking and she has to brace her hands on her jean clad knees. Seeing her this way makes me laugh so hard that I throw my head back and smack my leg repeatedly.

It's about then that I realize that we're no better than the fourteen-year-old girls we're supposed to be looking after when the elderly security guard narrows his eyes at us. I nudge Josie and incline my head toward security, and she grabs the bottom of her t-shirt to wipe her eyes.

We collect ourselves, straightening our faces enough to at least pretend like we're a vital part of the American education system, and keep on walking.

"This went off the rails fast," I say, feeling my still sore sides.

Josie's chocolate brown eyes meet mine, and her tone becomes more serious, "I'm just failing to see how having a smart, hot, and super sweet guy wanting to be with you is a bad thing."

"Jos, you know…"

She doesn't even let me finish my sentence as she rolls her eyes and throws the arm that's not linked with mine in exasperation, "You don't date coworkers. I know, I know. El, when are you going to realize that this situation is completely different? That prick at your old school was your boss. He used a position of power to manipulate you, and Liam is nothing like that walking human garbage can."

She's not wrong; I know she's not. The same thoughts have been plaguing me since yesterday. "Okay, that's a valid point," I say past the lump in my throat.

Josie's voice gets soft as we stop at an exhibit that the girls are idling at, "El, I can't tell you how to live your life, but I do know that you can't let what happened last year ruin a chance for you to be happy. You like him, right?"

"I really do," I whisper.

"Then focus on that. Everything else after that is secondary." What would I do without this woman? Truly I don't know.

"Jos, your wisdom knows no bounds."

She smirks at me then, "Well I'm not the guidance counselor because I think paperwork is fun. Now if we don't focus these girls won't give Lincoln's top hat the appreciation it deserves."

"A crime to be sure," I deadpan as we walk out of the rotunda into the next room.

*

I haven't seen Liam more than in passing all day, and it's given me time to think. Really think. We both have the night off since our turn for hallway duty was last night, and I could use the opportunity to talk to him; to see if earlier this morning was just flirting, or if I maybe really do still have a chance with him. Maybe I didn't ruin it with my stupid anxiety and fear of the unknown, or maybe it's insane to think that after what happened in my kitchen and four months of barely speaking, he would still have feelings for me.

We take the students to dinner at a local Chinese restaurant for dinner, and because this is an educational trip, of course, I have to tell the class about all of the influential figures that have eaten here.

Once the buffet style plates are laid out in front of us, I grab an embarrassing amount of crab Rangoon and walk toward Liam. It's only then that I realize Liam is walking toward me with an egg roll in his hand.

He smirks, "I figured you'd want a reminder of what the superior Chinese food side is."

How did he know I was going to do the same thing?

"I would never admit such an atrocity," I say smugly.

"Oh yeah, well how about a wager? We ask everyone in the restaurant which one is better, and whoever wins has to buy the other dinner when we get home?" His amber eyes spark, and there's not a doubt in my mind that in our bizarre world this is our version of flirting.

"Fine, but whoever loses can't order their preferred fried delicacy when we go out," I fire back.

He smirks at me, "I'll take that bet. Believe me, I like my

odds."

I scoff before yelling out to all the students gathered in the restaurant, "Hey everyone, settle a bet with Mr. Scott and me. If you think egg rolls are better than crab Rangoon's, raise your hand."

As I look out to the crowd, maybe, only a third raise their hand. I give Liam a cocky smile before continuing, "And if you think crab Rangoon's are better, raise your hand." I watch as significantly more students raise their hands, and yell "Victory is mine!"

Liam rolls his eyes, adjusting his wire framed glasses, "And those of you who couldn't care less about any of this raise your hand." Roughly ten students raise their hands.

"Sore loser," I fire at him.

He bends down, and I already know he's going to do that thing where he whispers in my ear that makes me weak, "I wouldn't consider me getting to take you out to dinner losing."

I stand there, realizing that somehow, I played right into his hand, and I love every second of it.

*

I could've worn a hole in the carpet with the number of times I've paced back and forth, trying to decide my next move. The familiar feeling of a boulder in my stomach surfaces, and my breathing constricts because I know what I need to do. The part of me that is feeling absolute terror at the thought of confessing my feelings to Liam is trying to win, so I decide to do what I always do when I'm terrified of something, plunge headfirst.

Before I can think better of what exactly I'm doing I walk to the adjoining door and knock on it rapidly. I stand there staring at it for what feels like forever. I feel the anxiety in the pit of my stomach begin to spread throughout the rest of my body and I fiddle with my hands trying to soothe the parts of me that feel like they're being pricked with hundreds of tiny needles.

Oh fuck, this was a mistake. I shouldn't be doing this. What the fuck am I thinking? Just as the anxious thoughts begin to sink their teeth into my mind the door opens.

I feel all the moisture in my mouth disappear, like I stuffed it with cotton balls, because this man is so fucking beautiful. Every inch of him. His inky black curls slightly mussed like he'd been running his hands through it. His amber eyes full of confusion behind his glasses, and a black Neil DeGrasse Tyson shirt tight against his broad chest while his jeans cling to muscular thighs.

"El?" he asks, his face riddled with confusion.

I feel out of breath looking at him, but I let the words come out before I can think twice about it. "What if I told you sometimes the flattery takes a second to get you everywhere?"

His face contorts slightly, riddled with more confusion than before. *Do it Ella. Now. Go.*

I quickly close the gap between us and fling my arms around his neck, my lips pressing against his. *Well so much for talking...* a small part of my brain scolds me before getting drowned out by the blood surging through my veins.

I feel his body seize up, and it must be from the initial shock. The fear that I've made a terrible mistake and misread everything floods my gut. I'm about to pull away with the sheer terror of what I've done when what's happening seems to click with him. In the moments I'm about to pull away he grabs my face with both hands and crushes my mouth to his.

The familiar smell of his clean soap and cologne scent floods my senses, urging me onward. My lips yield to his as his soft yet firm grip on them takes the lead.

I whimper as his tongue tangles with mine, a dance we've done before. The sound spurs him on, and he moans as his hands leave the sides of my face and travel down my back to the curve of my ass. He grips me there before lifting me up and wraps my legs around his waist, the pressure behind his zipper meets the aching parts of me. It's not enough. I don't know if anything this man does could ever be enough.

He presses me against the wall, and I feel liquid fire in my veins as his mouth never leaves mine, devouring it. Pressed here with my legs wrapped around his waist I can feel just how hard he is beneath me, and I grind myself against his bulge, needing friction to ease the pain of the need already pooling between my legs. The sensation is too good, and my moan is met with a grunt. *More. I still need more of him.*

As his hips pin me to the wall, his strong arms bracketing either side of me, I use the leverage to move my hands underneath his shirt before pulling it over his head. The only pause between kisses being when his shirt briefly separates our mouths.

I run my hands over the warm skin on his chest and I feel his breath hitch as I graze over the lean muscle there. One hand rests against the wall as his other lightly traces the side of my jaw, down my throat, underneath my shirt, until he's slowly palming my breast, my nipple already peaked from the instant attention he's giving it.

The rapidness of our kisses slows slightly until he moves his lips to the shell of my ear. The sensation of his heaving chest against mine and the feeling of his breath against that sensitive part of me sends delicious shivers down my spine.

His teeth graze my earlobe before he whispers, "El, what's

going on?"

I moan at how good his words feel against my ear and I can barely form words, "I can't. Take it. Anymore."

A low growl comes from his throat as he kisses down my neck, his words spoken against the sensitive skin trailing downward, "If this can't be more than just this once, stop me now."

He nibbles the place where my neck meets my collarbone, and then licks it to soothe the initial sting. I feel my pussy clench in response. His eyes meet mine and I can see the pools of lust that lay there, as if stopping is physically painful for him. Which is understandable, because there's a throbbing between my legs that feels unbearable, an ache that can only be satiated by more friction.

He rests his brow bone against mine and his lips ghost against me as he speaks. "Those months without you were unbearable. Always remembering the taste of your mouth and thinking I'd never get a chance to have it again." A light brush of his lips against mine before continuing, "I can't do this if there isn't a chance for us to be more. It hurts too bad."

My heart fractures remembering the pain I felt without him all those months too, and I know he needs reassurance that I want this. Not just now, a quick fuck, only to never be repeated again, but that I'm willing to move past my shit and acknowledge that we can be more than friends.

I hold his gaze, so he knows how serious I am, and trace his bottom lip with my thumb. "Liam, I'm tired of denying myself happiness. Happiness I know that I could have with you, because I'm too scared of history repeating itself."

I inhale a shaky breath, trying to tamp down the fear of the unknown that's threatening to swallow me whole. As much as I want to believe he feels the same way I do, this could just as easily blow up in my face.

"I want you. Not just now, but always. If you're still willing to give me a chance." I look deep into his eyes and pray to whatever God will listen that he feels the same way I do, that I didn't just completely ruin everything.

A low laugh comes out as he shakes his head, "El, that's all I've ever wanted. From the second I saw you standing on that stage."

Relief floods my senses so quickly I feel dizzy, but before the risk of me literally passing out from happiness can happen his lips are on mine once more. These kisses aren't delicate, they're hungry, like these past four months he's been starving and now he can finally eat.

He grabs my ass and lifts me off the wall, carrying me to the bed behind him. He lays me amongst the white sheets, the cool of them soothing against my burning hot skin.

Liam trails kisses down my neck, and I can't help but arch toward him. He braces me with one arm, angling me so my neck is exposed, before he nibbles once more, soothing the sting with his tongue. A pleasured gasp comes from me in response.

He smirks at me, before lifting my shirt over my head. A light hiss comes from his throat at the sight of my breasts. "Now let's see if we can actually manage to make it past me sucking on these perfect nipples this time." He says before unhooking my bra and throwing it to the side.

I giggle, "If we don't then I'm raising hell." I lay down, exposing myself fully to him as he licks his way from my collarbone to my breasts.

He sucks one nipple into his mouth, lightly licking it as he works his hand over my other, making sure they both receive his attention. My hips arch toward him involuntarily, my body craving his mouth all over me.

"You want my tongue on your pussy El?" he asks as his mouth traces down my belly, his tongue highlighting each and every curve.

"Yes," I reply with a whisper. I feel like all the air is being ripped from my lungs at the mere thought of his tongue on the sensitive skin between my thighs.

He slides my pants down over my hips slowly, so slowly. I can feel the wetness of my need for him drenching my panties, and I try to hurry him along by shoving them down with my pants. He grabs my hands and pins them to my side, his eyes burning as he looks directly into mine.

"*Mmm*... Are you trying to rush me El?" I can feel the rumble of his voice against my skin, and I truly might as well be a puddle at this rate.

"No," I lie breathlessly.

His mouth is mere inches from the apex of my thighs, and a dark chuckle rumbles from him, deep enough I can feel his breath against the soaking wet gusset of my underwear. "Good. Because I've been dreaming of how you'd taste on my tongue since the moment I laid eyes on you, and if you think for one second, I'm going to let you rush this, you're wrong."

I nod wordlessly as he slowly, torturously, kisses along the insides of my thighs. Just as I think I might lose my mind with need, I feel his knuckle ghost against my pussy as he hooks the gusset of my panties with his finger and pulls it aside, exposing my glistening flesh. He moans deeply, "I knew you'd be wet for me. Such a good girl."

His words send me reeling at the exact moment his tongue meets my pussy. Sheer pleasure shoots up my spine as he laps at me, drinking my wetness like it's the best thing he's ever tasted. He groans deeply and I feel it reverberate against my thighs, "So good. You taste so good, even better than I imagined."

He stops momentarily to quickly pull my panties down and throw them into the abyss outside the bed where the rest of my clothing currently lays. The cool air against my wet heated flesh becoming all too noticeable in his absence.

He goes back to licking me in long languid strokes, tasting me to see what I respond to the most. The pleasure of this man's tongue on me is so sweet, but he's teasing me, getting so close to my clit and then not licking it. Torture. Sweet, beautiful, torture. He knows what he's doing.

I grind my hips against his face, trying to urge him ever so slightly upwards. He grins up at me, "Should I put you out of your misery? Or should I make you wait, so you can feel the torture I felt all those months waiting for you?"

"Please," I say full of desperation. I can't even have a functional thought at this stage. All I can think of is more, more, more.

He chuckles huskily, "Well since you're so polite..." and starts from the bottom of my pussy and licks slowly all the way to my clit. The feel of his tongue there nearly shatters me in two. His licks begins to pick up speed as he slides two of his fingers inside me. *Full. So. Full. Need. More.* I grind down on his fingers, creating the friction my body craves.

I feel his fingers curl inside of me and I know I'm close to pure ecstasy. "Are you going to come for me El?"

I whimper in response, his tongue picking up speed and pressing down harder. So close... So close...

"Good girl. First you come on my tongue, then you come on my dick. Understood?"

I can't even respond because his words are my undoing. The feeling of falling over the edge of a cliff wracks through my body, my pussy clenching against his fingers with pleasure, a desperate moan wrenching from my throat.

He lifts his head from between my thighs and smiles, "I've fucked my hand so many times just thinking of doing exactly this. My tongue between your legs. Although, my imagination pales in comparison to the real thing."

I preen at his words before crooking my finger up at him, "Just imagine how good being inside me will feel," and he responds by covering his body with mine.

"Oh, believe me I have," he whispers against my throat as I wrap my legs around his waist, his rock-hard dick pressing against my still soaking pussy.

I momentarily panic realizing I don't have protection. "Shit, I don't have a condom, do you?"

He chuckles, "If you're asking if I thought, I was going to get laid on this trip, the answer is a very adamant no."

"Fuck, okay. I'm on birth control so… I'm fine if you are? It's not like I've… well… you know… recently" I want this man so bad; the thought of waiting is completely unbearable.

He lightly licks my lips so they open for him, and I groan as I taste myself on his tongue. "If you're comfortable I'm comfortable," he says in a murmur against my mouth.

"Oh, thank fuck," I whimper and pull him flush with me. His lips glide against mine once more before he lines up at my entrance and gently slides in. He's gentle, so gentle. A guttural moan rips from his throat as he takes me inch by glorious inch.

"Oh, my God, holy shit your dick feels so good," I moan as he becomes fully sheathed inside me, stretching my walls deliciously.

He begins to pulse in and out of me, and the friction gathers heat at the base of my spine. I can't believe I waited so long to feel this, feel him. Not even just the sex, but the closeness. His thumb meets the bundle of nerves at the top of my center, and I feel that feral need rip through me with more intensity.

The mood begins to shift, where he was gentle at first, waiting for me to adjust, he's now moving faster, harder. "Christ, El. You feel so good," he rasps as he pushes my legs up higher, giving me a new, deeper, angle. With this new angle, there's pressure and friction in ways I've never felt before.

The thumb resting on my clit begins to pick up pace in time with his thrusts. His mouth collides with mine once more, the hand not rubbing circles on my clit is grabbing a handful of my hair to better guide my mouth with his.

The electricity at the base of my spine is back, along with the feeling of teetering on the edge of a cliff. "So close Liam, so close. You're already going to make me come again," I rasp as my arms wrap around his neck to bring him in even closer.

That small movement sends me over the edge of the precipice, and I'm saying words and moaning and whimpering, but it's like watching myself from outside of my body. I have no control, and for once the thought doesn't terrify me. Wave after wave of pleasure wracks through me, and I can feel myself clenching around him.

"Oh fuck," he groans as he finds his release, the thought of bringing him pleasure sending aftershocks through my body.

He lowers his head to mine, and we stay like that for a moment, the only sound is the comingling of our heavy breathing against one another. Because I'm never good with silence, naturally I'm the first to speak. "That was... fucking amazing Liam."

He chuckles as he gets up to wet a washcloth and gently helps me clean up. Never. Never has a guy ever done this for me. Never cared enough after the sex was over to do anything like this. "Yes. Yes, it was."

He lays back down on the bed, and I rest my head on his chest while he draws lazy circles on my tailbone. The reality of the situation hits me like a brick in the face. Me. Liam. Together. It happened. It finally happened, and it's taking literally all my restraint not to go running down to the next floor and bang on Josie's door. Probably not the best idea since we're on a work trip.

Oh fuck... we're on a work trip... somewhere deep in the recesses of my brain I know that the anxiety is there, and that I should be freaking out about the fact that I really overcompensated on deciding to date someone I work with by in fact, hooking up with them at work. Not a super solid plan, but laying here, feeling Liam's heartbeat beneath my hand, smelling the scent of his cologne mixed lightly with sweat, and his hand now drawing uneven circles on my hip, my brain is the quietest it's been in a long time.

Chapter Nineteen
Liam

My alarm blares through the consciousness of my brain and startles me awake. For a split second, I think last night was a dream. Only to recognize the soreness in my muscles and the smell of lemon ghosting the skin on my chest and I know, it was real.

When I opened the door to her last night and saw her breathing frantically, I knew something was different. I could see in her eyes the same desperation I've felt deep in my bones since the first moment I laid eyes on her.

Those months without her were excruciating, but I knew that I couldn't handle being near her without wanting to be with her. She'd given me the space that I had asked for, but I never truly wanted it. After having Ella in your life, you don't ever actually want to be without her.

I look over to the empty space on my bed where she was only a few hours ago and wish she could've stayed. We thought it'd be best if she went back to her room in case one of the girls came and knocked on her door. The irony of the fact that this happened on a work trip isn't lost on me.

I rub the exhaustion from my eyes and get up to brush my teeth and pack up before gathering the boys and heading to the airport. We stayed up until the early morning hours making up for lost time, devouring each other. I could spend the rest of my life buried inside her, complete and utter paradise.

I've never known that kind of calm before, the kind that feels like the quality of air in my lungs is better, that the world is more colorful, that the sounds she made were the most beautiful I'd ever heard. After every time we came together, she'd curl against my chest, and I'd draw circles on her skin or play with her hair.

We talked about everything. She told me that she'd always had feelings for me, but that she was too afraid to act on them, so she buried them as deep as she could. That she feared the potential fall out and would be in the same situation she was a year ago. I told her I understood, and that my biggest priority was always her feelings. That even during those months where we barely spoke, I never stopped thinking about her. There were so many times I wanted to just say fuck it and walk across the hallway to talk to her, but it hurt too much. She told me she hoped every day that I would come see her, that we could be friends again, and that thought alone made my heart ache. She said that she still wasn't comfortable with everyone knowing about us yet, whatever we were, and I told her we could just take it a day at a time. We don't have to have it all figured out right now. We laid there for hours, until her eyes began to get heavy, and she yawned against my chest.

After I finish getting ready and pack up the last of my belongings, I walk to the adjoining door between us and knock. A few moments later I hear shuffling behind the door, and Ella opens it, her hair falling out of bun on top of her head and a sleepy smile across her face. She's so beautiful my chest aches.

"Good morning beautiful," I say while leaning against the door jamb.

Her smile widens at my compliment, making her eyes crinkle. "Good morning, Thor," her eyes skate down my body until she looks directly at my crotch. "Mjolnir."

I chuckle at that, "Wow such high praise. My dick has never been compared to a mythical hammer before."

Her laugh echoes in the doorway, "Yeah well keep wielding that thing at me like you did last night, and you can expect more rave reviews."

I can't help but smile at the thought of a next time, the idea already causes my dick to stir. "So, that means there's a next time?"

She looks at me nervously and asks, "Is that what you want?"

I could quite literally laugh at the sheer idea of her thinking I don't want to do this again and again until I die of exhaustion. "I think you know this isn't about what I want. We already talked about it last night, but if I had it my way you and I would've been together from the moment I got sand in your ass crack. I'm not going to pressure you into something you aren't ready for though."

Her steely gray eyes meet mine, "All I know for sure right now is that I'm tired of letting my fear of what happened before affect me. I'm tired of having to pretend that I don't want to be with you. Being near you, but not with you, is physically painful, and I definitely know that when we get back tonight, I want to fuck you in every single room in my house."

I feel the blood in every vein in my body surge at the thought of having her again, my cock shudders in response. I close the small distance between us and grab her hips, bending down so my mouth is pressed to the shell of her ear. "That can be arranged," I say on a groan before biting the skin of her neck beneath her ear. I hear her breath catch as she arches toward me, coaxing me for more.

She's so responsive... I fucking love it. I lightly lick the spot

I bit before pulling away and grinning at her. "Now let's go wake up the surly teenagers. We leave for the airport in an hour."

She narrows her eyes, and I feel like she could physically burn a hole through me. "Tease."

The audacity of this woman. I cross the threshold to her room and pick her up as I do, pinning her against the wall, so there's no space between us. I hear her breathing pick up as she smirks at me, clearly trying to get a rise out of me. My eyes bore into hers, and they're the color of liquid metal, my voice coming out in a rasp against her lips. "I waited eight months to sink into that soaking wet pussy, you can wait eight hours." I kiss her hard, our lips opening for our tongues to meet together, and I hear her whimper before I sit her back on the floor and pull away. I know the smile on my face is a cocky one, and I don't care.

Her face becomes flush, and her eyes narrow once more, "Oh my God you're enjoying my suffering."

I head back through the doorway to my room and grab my duffel bag, "Maybe a little. Now get dressed. If your nipples point through your shirt any harder, they'll use them for air traffic control."

I hear her scoff at me, "You're the reason they look like this!"

I turn around to wink at her before shutting the adjoining door. I can hear her voice yell at me from the other room, "Stop using your powers of seduction for evil!" I cackle at the thought and try not to enjoy the idea of her feeling just a small glimpse of the pain I've felt for the last eight months.

*

Shuffling an absurd number of teenagers through airport security is no easy feat, but now that they're all sitting at the gate and we've finished doing what has to be the tenth student check of the day, I can finally sit and relax before we board. I sit my duffel bag at my feet and plop down into a stiff-backed airport chair. My eyes quickly find Ella, who is sitting with her head on Josie's shoulder and giggling, no doubt at something Josie must've said, when I feel my phone buzz in my pocket.

El: I think Mjolnir needs to take a visit to throaten-heim

El: Get it? Like Jotunheim but it's my throat.

I chuckle before looking up to see Ella giggling at her phone, clearly very pleased with herself.

El: I'm being clever. Acknowledge me!

Me: I see we're really sticking with the Thor references.

El: Would you rather I pick a different superhero?

El: How about Hulk? Like I want you to Hulk smash this pussy?

I laugh so loudly that it eclipses the noise of all the teenagers around me talking, and they all turn around to give me a weird look before going back to their conversations.

El: Just the reaction I was looking for.

Me: You know if this is supposed to only make me laugh and not hard, it's not working.

El: Mmm... now you can be as needy and pathetic as I am.

I feel my dick get harder at the thought and I adjust in my seat.

Me: Keep talking like that and when we land I'm going to take you home and spank that ass-Gard.

I look up in time to see her reading the text while taking a drink of water. She laughs so hard that some of the water falls out of her mouth. The exact reaction I was hoping for.

*

Thank Christ, the plane has landed. I thought we'd never get home. I can't tell if it was a good thing or not that Ella wasn't sitting next to me on the flight back. On one hand, I wanted to talk and see her, but on the other, being next to her for over two hours and not touching her would've been absolute torture. Hell, just not being able to touch her for two hours was hard enough as it is.

Getting all the students off the plane and with the correct baggage was the same mele it's been every other year, complete chaos. Students flitting around hugging each other and yelling across the baggage claim, some not seeing each other for a week due to spring break, a virtual century in teenager time.

Once the last of the students had been picked up, only the teachers were left. We all said our goodbyes, and I watched Ella run over to Josie to fling her arms around her in a hug before we all went our separate ways.

Ella walks up beside me, her blonde hair twisted up in a clip and wearing a tie-dye Grateful Dead sweatshirt, and we walk toward the parking garage.

"You know, I think you're the only person I know that owns a shirt with the band they were conceived to on it," I chuckle.

She snorts, laughing so loudly that it echoes around the concrete walls of the garage. "What can I say? I have a very specific niche."

When everyone else is out of ear shot, she looks up at me, her gray eyes sparkling, "You're coming to my place." Not a question, a statement.

I can't help but smile at her directness, my blood already heating at the thought of what's in store once we get through her front door. "I am."

As we walk through the parking garage, our footsteps echo, and even though it's a cold Indiana night in early spring, it feels like I'm radiating heat as we walk up to her Prius. She leans against the car, her chin tilted up toward me, her eyes daring me to kiss her.

I hook my finger underneath her chin, before leaning down and lightly taking her bottom lip between my teeth. Her breath catches and my voice comes out husky as I say, "I'll see you there," before turning around to walk to the other side of the garage to my car.

"Monster!" She yells, the echo bouncing off the concrete walls. I chuckle as I hear the door to the Prius open and the ignition turn, fully aware that she has no idea just how bad I was tempted to take her right there against her car.

*

I've never hated a door more in my entire life. Not that the teal door to Ella's little bungalow isn't cute, it is, but when it stands between me and ripping all of Ella's clothes off it's the bane of my existence. The night is unseasonably cold for March, and I could kick myself for the lack of preparation I had as I shiver in my thin gray pullover. The cold air should be the equivalent of a cold shower, it should be, but it's not. Honestly, I don't know if there's anything at this point that could make me not want her.

I miss the taste of her on my tongue, and I need more. If it was up to me, I would've stayed buried inside her for the rest of my life with her panting in my ear, the breath of her moans caressing my throat, her thick thighs wrapped around me and coaxing me in deeper. *Damn it this is excruciating...*

I knock again and the door opens quickly, Ella looks so fucking good I want to devour her right here in the doorway. She's in a purple ABBA crop top, her nipples pebbling against the cold, and a lacy black thong, what I'm assuming are her bed clothes, her strawberry blonde hair is no longer in a clip, but cascading down her back, and her gray eyes are so sharp they could cut me right down the middle. "Sorry, I tried cleaning super-fast, and by cleaning, I mean I shoved everything in my hallway closet and its dangerously close to burying us alive like a Pompeii round two, so don't open it."

I walk through the door, barely able to register what she's saying through the static sound in my ears as I take in how fucking hot she is. "Noted, I'll just strike the hallway closet from the tour." I reply with amusement before abruptly shutting the door, the need to taste her propelling me forward.

I quickly close the small gap between us and hear her breath catch as my mouth presses against hers. Her lips are pillow soft and she tastes like heaven as she wraps her arms around my neck to pull my body flush with hers. The smell of lemon and fresh air envelops me as I bend down to better cup her ass, "You knew what you were doing answering the door like this," I moan against her mouth before her tongue licks the seam of my lips and tangles with mine.

A small giggle comes from her between kisses, "I thought you might like it."

I lightly grab her chin and tilt her head to the side while my other hand massages her ass, my voice comes out in a rasp as I kiss down her throat, "I'm now telling everyone I know that ABBA is my favorite band."

She runs a delicate hand through my curls and grabs hold, forcing me to the hollow of her throat. I bite her there and hear a sharp intake of breath, "Watching *Mamma Mia!* Will never be the same," she retorts on a breathy moan as I lick the sensitive skin I just bit.

I chuckle as I run my hands underneath her crop top and lightly roll her nipples between my fingers before pulling her shirt over her head. A low groan comes from my throat as I look at how beautiful she is standing here in nothing but a lacy black thong that I'm moments away from ripping off her.

"So beautiful El," I say as I slowly drag my fingers down her body, my hand lingering once more at her breast before continuing to move farther south. "Are you wet for me?" I ask as my fingers toy with the lace on the top of her thong.

Her hands run down my back, her body arching toward mine, trying to close the nonexistent space between us. "Yes," she cries while my nose nuzzles up and down her throat.

"*Mmm...* and what would you like me to do about that?" I say into the shell of her ear.

"*Ummm...* fix it?" she says nervously.

I chuckle darkly, my mouth still by her ear, "Don't worry baby that's a given, but I want you to tell me. Good girls ask for what they want."

I pull back slightly to see her face flush, "Uh... well I want your fingers inside me, but I've also been thinking about your dick in my mouth."

I feel my eyes darken at the thought of my dick hitting the back of her throat, "Does thinking of sucking my cock make you wet El?"

"Very," she replies, her eyes full of heat. Her hands fumble with my belt buckle, undoing the button of my pants and shoving them down to pool around my ankles along with my boxers, as my cock springs free. I watch as she removes her black lace panties, gets to her knees in the middle of her living room and licks my throbbing dick from root to tip before taking me in her mouth. The light glide of her tongue against my sensitive skin makes my legs shake and my breathing becomes erratic.

She sucks and licks and gently caresses my balls in her hands, the sensation almost too much for me to take. I sink my hand into her red-blonde hair as I feel her tongue swirl at the base of my dick and gently grab the back of her head to pulse in and out of her mouth, and I need the taste of her pussy on my tongue.

"Couch. Now." I growl at her. She stops and nods in agreement before getting up and walking toward the couch.

"Face the wall," I tell her as I have her straddle the couch on her knees while I take off the rest of my clothes. I press my length against her ass as my arm wraps around her front, my fingers deftly move to her center. My fingers find her soaking wet and warm, gently stroking her slit as her arousal coats them.

My dick is so hard it's painful, but I'm craving the taste of her. I dip my fingers inside her, her hips bucking against them, so they go farther as she moans. I pull them from her then and she whimpers, I use the hand that isn't coated in her to grab her chin and force her to look over her shoulder at me. When I know for sure she's watching me intently I lick her arousal from my fingers before sucking them clean. She tastes too good, it's unfair.

"Please," she moans, begging me to relieve her.

Luckily for her, I can't take it any more either. I need to taste more of her. Keeping her straddling the couch I bend down to the floor so I can lay my head on the seat between her beautifully thick thighs. "Ride my tongue baby. I want you to sit on my face."

She whimpers before lowering herself to my mouth, and I

flatten my tongue against her clit so she can take what she wants. The heady scent and taste of her floods my senses as she begins to lightly rock against my tongue, and I can feel her sharp gasp as she softly circles her hips. She's being too gentle.

I pry my tongue from her and look up at her, she cries out in frustration, but I need to make my point. "I told you I wanted you to sit on my face." I barely recognize my own commanding tone.

She looks down at me, puzzled, "Look at me. I'd suffocate you!"

I snake my arm around her hip so my thumb can rub against her clit. Her hips begin to rock against me, and I know she's barely coherent with her own need. "Ella. When I say sit on my face, I mean sit on it. I want to make you come on my tongue, but if you don't want to listen, I'll stop."

That gets her attention, and she looks down at me with wide eyes before I move my hands to firmly grab her ass and force her down on my tongue once more. She cries out as I use my grip on her ass to move her up and down my tongue. She's not holding back anymore, and she's fully seated on me, her hips moving in whatever direction brings her the most pleasure. She's perfection like this, and I feel my tongue coat even more with the taste of her as she moans loudly, "Oh fuck!" she yells before I taste the way she orgasms on my tongue.

My face is soaked as I move from beneath her and grip her hair from behind her, "You taste like heaven." I say against her ear.

I feel her shudder as she presses her ass back against my aching dick, "I need to feel your dick inside me. Now." she whimpers.

I grip her hair tighter, "You're such a good girl, telling me what you want. You're learning."

She leans back and grips my cock; a hiss comes from me at how good her gentle touch against my throbbing erection feels. "What can I say? You're an excellent teacher." she smirks. Always something to say this one, the thought leads a heady chuckle to escape me before I'm so desperate for her that I'm fucking her hand.

I need her now. I can't wait any longer. I line my cock up against her entrance, the beautiful view of her ass on full display before I press into her. Her grip on me is so tight and wet it takes all my strength to not come right then and there. I growl as she pushes against me until she's down to the hilt, and I realize once again that I could die like this. Gripping her hips and sliding her up and down my dick until my heart gives out.

She feels so good I feel my legs shake, and I wrap my arm around her once more, my fingers finding her clit and drawing tight circles there. I know I'm close to the breaking point, and with each pump into her I know I'm closer and closer to release. Just when I feel like I can't take it anymore, I feel her walls clench against me and a cry rip from her throat as she orgasms.

"That's right baby, come for me," I groan as I pick up pace. Moments later I feel the tightening at the bottom of my spine, and I feel like I could black out from pleasure as my release rips through me.

The only sound is our heavy breathing as I pull out of her warmth, and I see sweat sliding down her spine before I turn her head and kiss her deeply. She turns around to face me and pulls me down to kiss her once more. "Gimme a man after midnight indeed," she laughs. I quirk my eyebrow up in confusion and she laughs harder, "It's an ABBA song."

"Just when you think the ABBA jokes are over…" I chuckle, my words trailing off.

She nuzzles my neck so sweetly I feel like my heart could shatter, "Stay the night?" she asks in a whisper.

"Depends, are you a blanket hog?"

She grins at me wickedly, "Oh I most definitely am, but I sleep naked if that makes up for it..." she trails off.

"Sold!" I yell before picking her up as she laughs hysterically and walking her to her bedroom cradled against my chest.

Chapter Twenty
Ella

I wake up to the new light of the sunrise peeking through my purple curtains, my head groggy from lack of sleep. *Last night...* it comes to me in flashes of heat and pleasure that make my toes curl against my amethyst-colored satin sheets. I rub the sleep from my eyes, needing the warmth of him against me once more, I turn over to lay my head on his chest, only to find the other side of the bed empty.

Fear roils in my gut, panicked thoughts of him regretting the past two days and leaving without a word in the middle of the night flooding my bloodstream. I jump out of bed and tug my navy floral robe around my waist, praying to whoever's up there that I didn't make a mistake, when the smell of coffee faintly wafts into my bedroom from the kitchen.

Relief washes through me at the realization that he's still here, and a smile spreads across my lips. I pad through the small hallway lined with pictures of friends and family that spills out into the kitchen to see Liam grinning widely at me from the stove, wearing nothing but his black boxers and an apron that says 'I like my butt rubbed' with a pig on it. "Good morning beautiful," he says while wielding a spatula in his hand.

I walk toward him and wrap my arms around his neck before planting a kiss on his lips. I look down to the stove top to see a pancake sizzling, and the familiar smell of dough crisping fills my nostrils, making me grin wildly. "What's all this?"

He nuzzles his nose with mine before turning to face the stove once more to flip the pancake. "I made pancakes," he beams. It's so fucking cute that he did this, the fact that I've never had a man make me anything after fucking me notwithstanding.

"Of all the dirty things you said to me last night, that might have turned me on the most." I say while leaning on the counter next to him.

I watch as he leans over, lips brushing the shell of my ear whispering, "I made coffee too," before removing the pancake from the pan and ladling more batter in its place.

"That's it. Ravish me on this counter right here right now," I say, grinning at him wickedly.

He chuckles at my comment, "If I would've known it was that easy, I would've started making you coffee a long time ago," he muses before placing a small kiss on my nose and flipping over the new pancake.

A realization dawns on me, "Wait where did you find pancake mix? I don't think I've ever bought it before." I walk toward the cabinet and stand on my tiptoes to grab down my 'Tears of my students' mug before filling it with coffee, adding my cream and sugar to make it the tawny brown color I love. I take my first sip and the warmth glides down my throat while the smell wafts into my nostrils, I release a contented sigh.

He places the last pancake on the plate piled with them next to the stove and turns off the burner. "I ordered Instacart when I woke up this morning," he remarks before bringing the pancakes to the table and setting it next to the butter and syrup.

I open the pantry to grab my jar of peanut butter and sit down at the table next to Liam, where I'm met with that familiar lift of the eyebrow. "And here I thought you summoned it with Mjolnir."

I watch as he smears butter and syrup onto his pancakes before cutting into them, "I try to keep my hammer use strictly for making you moan," he says smirking around a bite.

"And a fine job you do," I chuckle before spreading peanut butter on my pancakes and covering them with syrup.

"Wow. High praise," he grins.

I take a bite of my pancake and the perfect combination of the salty peanut butter and the sweetness of the syrup makes me moan, "five stars. Ten out of ten would recommend."

"So, are you saying I Ragna-rocked your world?" he smiles while waggling his eyebrows at me before taking another bite of his pancake.

A cackle rips from my throat, "God I'm loving how you're actively participating in this now."

"I'm considering putting it on my LinkedIn profile," he muses before looking back at my plate, "peanut butter?"

"Peanut butter makes everything better. Don't knock til you try it," I quip.

"Fair enough," he replies before taking the jar of peanut butter and spreading some on a pancake. I watch closely as he takes a bite and moans, the sound sending familiar tremors down my spine.

"Told you."

"You were right. I'm never eating a pancake another way ever again." he responds before shoveling another bite into his mouth.

"A man who cooks, makes me laugh, says I'm right, and dicks me down like the lady that I am. Who says you can't have it all?" I muse.

I watch as a grin spreads across his face and then turns into something I can't quite figure out. Like he's trying to determine whether to say something and is deciding if he should. His fork clatters to the plate as he steeples his hands on the table, "Speaking of having it all… it's our spring break…" he trails off.

"Yes?"

I watch him hesitate before forcing himself to talk once more, "And I obviously want to spend as much time as possible with you, but at some point, we're going to have to tell work."

Dread coils in my stomach, and familiar terror threatens to scrape against my skin at what might happen next. I sigh, "Can't I enjoy my peanut butter and syrup-soaked pancakes in post coital bliss without thinking about Bledsoe?" I try and make it sound like I'm joking, but it falls flat. I'd like to think he doesn't notice, but I know he does.

"What a complicated tapestry of images you weave," he deadpans.

I shift in my seat, trying my best not to let my fear show. "I'm just saying… Can't we figure out what's happening with us first before we drag Bledsoe and the entire faculty into the bedroom with us?"

I can almost feel it, the eyes boring into me, the whispers, the dread of never knowing who is saying what about us. I've been down that road, and while I know it has to happen at some point, I'm not ready yet.

He quirks an eyebrow at me then, "I didn't realize I was fucking the entire faculty."

I roll my eyes at his comment, "You know what I mean."

I watch as he runs his hands through his inky black curls, his amber eyes taking on a worried look, "Okay. I get needing time. We can wait until we figure this out, but I want it on the record that I'm pro sooner rather than later."

I shove the last bite of my pancake in my mouth, relief

flooding my insides, "Record duly noted," I remark before shoving back from the table and walking up to Liam's chair, positioning myself in his lap. I turn his head slightly while trailing kisses up his neck. I'm met with a groan rumbling in his chest and a familiar hardness coiling against my center. "What do you have planned today?" I ask between kisses.

"Well, I have some labs to grade..." he trails off on a moan.

I nibble at the crook of his neck, "Uh-huh...?"

I both feel and hear the sharp intake of breath as my teeth meet his sensitive skin, "And I'm supposed to play basketball with Max at four..."

I rock my hips against his hardening length, the friction sending electricity through my body, "And tonight...?"

A hiss escapes him, his hips tilting upward to give me better access to undulate against him. "I'm keeping it open in case a succubus decides to call upon me..." he grins,

I let out a small giggle against his throat, "And I'm the succubus in this scenario."

He pulls away slightly to look me in the eye, his thumb tracing my bottom lip, "Oh yes, and I'm pretty sure I'd do anything you asked me to," he muses before scooping me up and taking me to my bedroom once more.

Chapter Twenty-One
Liam

I drag the back of my wrist against my forehead to wipe off the excess sweat on my brow, stemming from the fact that Max is once again kicking my ass at basketball.

My sneakers squeak against the polished gym floor as I move to pass the ball to Max. "She wants to wait to tell Bledsoe..." I trail off in between deep breaths as I run to block his shot. "I'm trying not to read too much into it."

Max wipes the sweat from his face with the bottom of his shirt as he grabs the ball that bounced off to the side, "What you think she's embarrassed by you or something?"

I catch the ball as he flings it toward me to shoot, "No not that, I'm just worried I'm reading too much into it. Maybe I like her more than she likes me."

Max watches as I attempt to shoot a 3-pointer and miss, smirking at me before his face turns serious. "You're doing that shit again where you don't think it's possible that someone could like you as much as you do them. You've always been scared you'll love someone more than they do you and you won't see it coming when they leave you. It's classic child abandonment issues that stem from your adoption and are exacerbated by the fact that your last girlfriend dumped you."

"Wow, thank you Dr. Freud. Super fucking helpful. I didn't realize I was getting a therapy session with today's workout. Should I be paying you hourly?" I deadpan.

Max narrows his eyes at me before retrieving the ball, "Hey, I have a degree in psychology."

He dribbles the ball as he walks it back to the center, "Yeah, and you're really putting it to a lot of use swinging your dick around in every place you travel to. Tell me, do you get into the childhood trauma before or after you have sex with someone and never contact them again?"

Max snorts as I try to steal the ball from him, and he runs to the basket to shoot, just barely missing. "No comment."

He catches the ball off the rebound and gets ready to shoot, "Okay, last shot, I've got an article to write." He looks at me with a cocky smirk and sends the ball swishing into the net. "I should've played for the Pacers."

I roll my eyes at that, "Yeah, that checks out considering the Pacers haven't had a good season in years."

He chuckles at me as he picks up the ball and stores it under his arm, "Jealousy isn't a good look for you. It makes your eyes all bulgy."

I narrow my eyes at him, "You're very obviously baiting me, so I'm not responding. Same time next week?"

"Yessir. And don't worry I'm sure she feels like you do, just maybe, she doesn't know it yet," he shrugs.

I grab my gym bag and sling it over my shoulder, "Wow... look whose being encouraging. That must've been physically painful for you."

"You have no idea," he says with a smirk as he gives me a small wave before heading to the locker room.

I send a small wave back before grabbing my phone out of my bag and seeing I have a text from Ella.

Ella: Georgetown Movie Plex is doing a showing of 'The Breakfast Club' tonight. Want to go?

Me: If you mess with the bull, do you get the horns?
Ella: ... So that's a, yes?
Me: What time am I picking you up?
Ella: seven?
Me: I'll be there. Bring a big purse to smuggle candy into.
Ella: *Oooh...* I do love a bad boy.
Me: Just wait, until I get comfortable enough with you to smuggle entire dinners in...
Ella: Just when I thought I was with Anthony Michael Hall, here comes Judd Nelson.
Me: Hey I can be both!
Me: Nobody puts baby in a corner.
Ella: Not you throwing a 'Dirty Dancing' reference into the mix.
Me: And yet the sentiment is the same!
Ella: I'll see you at seven, my big bag in hand.
Me: See you then El.

*

After I pick up Ella, we pull into the parking lot of Georgetown Movie Plex to find that the lot is nearly abandoned, but to be fair it is on a side of town that the rest of the city seems to have forgotten about. It's a veritable ghost town of a parking lot, but instead of tumble weeds it's old candy bar wrappers and flyers for a nearby Cash for Gold store blowing around the parking lot.

I grab the empty bag that Ella brought and put the candy inside, waving a bag of peanut butter M&Ms so she could see, earning a squeal of delight from the seat next to me.

"You remembered?" she asks as I shut the bag, hiding the evidence. Pure excitement is radiating from her face over something so small. I know it's wrong to compare, but as I look around this near-abandoned parking lot, stuffing contraband candy into a bag to see a $5 movie, I can't help but realize just how different Ella and Blair are. I can't for the life of me ever imagine Blair suggesting a place like this. It's just further proof that around Ella I can be myself, that I don't have to plan an elaborately expensive date for us to have fun.

As we get out of the car, I walk hand in hand with Ella as she leans into me for warmth. In typical Indiana fashion, it's a spring day, but the billowing wind and dark clouds make it look like winter. I look down at the woman clutching my arms for warmth as the wind whips her blonde hair up and around her face while she tries to keep her skirt from blowing in the same direction.

"I think I picked the wrong outfit..." She winces, looking down at her black Def Leppard shirt, black skirt, and black sandals.

I chuckle as we walk through the doorway, the push bar shoddily attached with duct tape and... napkins? I honestly can't tell. I lean down to the shell of her ear and whisper, "Don't worry. I'll keep you warm."

Her bright gray eyes meet mine and look as if they're simmering at my comment. I watch a shiver creep down her spine, and I can't tell if it's from the chill of the wind or the innuendo of my comment.

The inside of the Movie plex is as empty as the parking lot, and I can't help but wonder if Ella misunderstood and 'The Breakfast Club' screening was actually thirty years ago before the theater was promptly abandoned shortly after.

I'm about to tell Ella that I don't think they're open when a surly teenager with black and purple hair, a septum piercing, and a black polo with a nametag that says Rhonda on the front appears from the wall behind the counter. Rhonda, it seems, is quite inconvenienced by us being here. If Ella notices, she says nothing, and smiles as she tells Rhonda we need two tickets for 'The Breakfast Club.'

I hand her the money for the tickets and she has us follow her to the snack counter. "Popcorn? Candy? Pop?" Rhonda asks in the flattest tone I think I've ever heard a human being use.

Ella smirks at me, a smile that says we've got all the contraband we need, but I get us popcorn anyway. A decision that as I watch Rhonda scoop a red bag full of popcorn that looks like it's been there since they bought the machine, I wonder if I'll regret it. Rhonda sets the popcorn on the counter and pulls out her phone, stating "Theatre two," before her fingers move rapidly over the screen. It seems we've been dismissed.

As we walk down the slightly darkened hallway Ella leans in and whispers, "Do you think she's the only person working?" A fair question since I've seen not one other person since we've gotten here.

As I listen to the ripping sound of my shoes on the sticky floor echo through the hallway, it seems like all the confirmation I need. "I can't imagine leaving a teenager as the only person running my business, but I also don't see anyone else."

As we walk into the theater, it becomes clear that our suspicions are correct, and there's no one else here. At least not to watch 'The Breakfast Club.' "Just us then?" I ask Ella as I look down at the place where her arm is looped through mine while commercials play in the background.

I watch the side of her lip quirk up and we head toward the back of the theater, "I guess we can't be shocked that a movie theater playing a forty-year-old movie on a Monday night isn't packed."

I chuckle as we sit in the middle, the seats shockingly not as bad as I thought they would be. Though they're clearly old, the wine-red suede of the seats are clean.

Ella keeps her arm locked with mine, "I know this isn't the fanciest place, but Josie and I love it. My mom and Hank used to take us here when we were in high school on dollar movie night. I remember being so happy, sharing my love of movies with my favorite people. We didn't have a lot of money back then, but it was one of the first places I really felt like my mom, Hank, and I were an actual family. We had so much fun."

I smile down at her, "I don't care about fancy. Being here, a place that makes you so happy, is all I can ask for."

Ella gazes at me with a watery look in her eye before grabbing the bag of popcorn and tossing a handful into her mouth. She immediately becomes rigid next to me before gagging and spitting the popcorn back into the bag. "Oh my God do not eat that! It tastes like Styrofoam had a three-way with a sewage drain and a stick of butter."

I give her an incredulous look, suppressing a laugh, "You know some people would just say 'It tastes bad'."

"Um, yeah, well some people are boring," she retorts while trying very hard to not laugh at her own joke. "Moral of the story. Do. Not. Eat. It."

I grab the peanut butter M&Ms for her so she can get the taste of Styrofoam sewage butter out of her mouth and hand them to her. "Well, I wouldn't anyway now that you spit your popcorn back into it."

She narrows her eyes at me, "If you wanted it that bad you could eat around it."

I can feel my face contort into a look of disgust, "I would

most certainly not do that!"

She pops a few M&Ms in her mouth and her eyes narrow into slits even more, "Have you, or have you not, put your tongue in my mouth?" she asks between bites.

The lights begin to dim as the opening credits begin to roll, and I feel heat creep up my neck at the thought of her tongue twining with mine. "I have."

I watch as the side of her mouth quirks up, "And have you, or have you not, used your tongue on my pussy?"

The heat in my neck spreads all over my body, and I feel my cock stiffen at the thought of just how good her pussy tastes. I could die happy with the taste of her on my tongue. "I have..."

She smiles then, "And that's different... how?"

I adjust in my seat, trying to relieve the pressure of my dick straining against my zipper. "It just is," I smile back at her.

One look into those stormy gray eyes tells me one thing, she definitely noticed. Her eyes seem to blaze back at me before she turns toward the movie as it begins. I will myself to get my erection under control, and it almost seems to be working, until I feel Ella's hand on my thigh. Her fingers go lightly upward, and I feel my control slip. Her hand moves inward toward my now painful erection and rubs against the bulge there.

All self-control leaves my body as she firmly grips my cock on the outside of my pants. I lean back into the seat more, allowing her better access. I watch pink painted nails rub up and down, before moving to the button of my jeans. My hips flex upward in response, and I look over to see need in her eyes that matches mine. "El...?" I ask. The unspoken question, are we going to do this?

I watch her teeth tug at her pouty pink bottom lip, nodding silently, before wiggling down my pants and pulling my cock from the opening in my boxers. I feel a grunt come from the back of my throat as my dick bobs against the cold air of the theater.

Delicate hands wrap around me, and Ella leans over to guide me into her mouth. I could scream from how good this feels, the slick warmth of her tongue licking up the vein in my cock while she takes me to the back of her throat. My hips rut up to meet her mouth, greedy for more of her as she teases me by licking the pre-cum from the tip and letting me sink to the back of her throat once more.

"Oh, fuck El," I moan. The pleasure of her slick tongue so good I can barely stand it. The heady combination of her hot mouth and swirling tongue in a public setting leaves me so turned on I feel like I can't see straight.

Feel her. I need to feel her. The desperation I feel is clawing at my skin. Using the angle she's at to my advantage, I extend my arm to reach beneath her skirt and gently toy with the already damp fabric there. She pushes her hips against my hand urgently, silently begging me to push past the fabric and slip my fingers into her slick heat.

I do as she wants and move her already drenched panties to the side before lightly guiding my fingers up the seam of her, meeting her already hardening clit with a light circling of my thumb. With my cock still in her mouth I feel her moan around me, and the feel of it against my straining skin is almost enough for me to explode down her throat.

"If you keep moaning like that, you're going to feel my come spill down your throat." I groan.

She responds with an even deeper, more exaggerated groan. "Brat." I gasp as I rut against her mouth relentlessly.

If the movie is even playing, I wouldn't know, because my vision and hearing are blurred at the edges, the places where our bodies are joined the only thing I can see, the moans and heavy breathing coming from our throats the only sound I can hear.

I buck into her throat rapidly now, but she meets me each time, taking me excitedly with every thrust in her mouth. I slide my two fingers into her tight pussy, so warm and wet it threatens to become my undoing. She rapidly fucks my fingers, timing it with the fervent thrusts of my cock in her mouth.

The thought of my dick filling her mouth, my fingers filling her tightening pussy, spurring me on. I lean over, close enough that I can smell the lemon scent of her, and my voice comes out like a rumble. "You like when I fill both holes baby?" A whimper comes from her then with an ardent shake of her head in agreement.

"Just wait, until I fill all three." she cries out at the very idea of it, but I won't. Not yet anyway.

"More. I need more," she whimpers.

This woman is my undoing. The end of any sane or rational decision I'll ever make. From the first night I met her, I should've known. I should've known that the scent, the feel, the taste, of her would give me tunnel vision with the singular focal point being her. Hump each other on a porch with her perfect tits in my face where anyone could see? I would've gone as far as she wanted and not even cared. Fuck each other on a field trip we're the chaperones for? Sure, no problem there. Fuck each other in a public movie theater? An adamant yes. The stark realization that I would do anything for this woman, do anything to make her happy, even when it meant I couldn't be with her.

With all the strength I can muster I pull myself from her mouth and her aching heat before guiding her to my lap, her skirt parting as she straddles me, my cock pulses against the soaked panties there. A mischievous grin spreads across her lips, her molten gray eyes filled with lust meeting mine.

Her knees bracket mine and it reminds me of the first night together, how she straddled and writhed against me, and how I ached to finish what we started. How I would've given anything then to be inside her. Her eyes say she remembers too, and her lips capture mine passionately. We're all lips opening to tongues as hers silkily tangles with mine before she moves her panties to the side and guides my throbbing cock to her entrance.

She isn't delicate or gentle as she sinks down onto me, the walls of her pussy grip me like a wet, hot, vice as she takes me all the way to the hilt. She slams down on me again and again while my hands guide either side of her hips up and down.

"So full," she murmurs as she slides up and down in rapid succession, and I thrust to meet her each time. I'm so close to coming I can feel my vision blurring at the edges, so I move one hand from her hip and move my thumb close to where we're joined, against her clit, already stiff to the touch. I circle her there, my other hand moving from her hip to her ass, using the leverage to guide her more and more rapidly up and down my length.

My thumb circling her clit is her undoing, and she lets out a sharp cry as she bounces on top of me, the walls of her pussy taking me in a pulsing grip that sends me spiraling. We both ride out our orgasm before her chest collapses against mine, with her head in the crook of my shoulder. The sounds of our gasping breath and the vague dialog of the movie are now creeping at the edge of my senses.

I feel her chuckle against my neck, her head lifts so her eyes can meet mine. "Gotta says, that was a first."

I kiss the tip of her nose as I slide out of her and put her panties back in place. "I'm all for new experiences," I chuckle back.

She straightens her skirt and moves back to the seat next to me, lifting up my arm so she can snuggle into my side. "We missed the first half of the movie," she says matter-of-factly.

"El, I could not give any less of a fuck about 'The Breakfast Club' when my dick is in your mouth."

She buries herself into my side more, the smell of lemon and heat filling my nostrils as she laughs at the corny dancing montage in the movie. My chest feels like it could crack open as realization dawns on me. I want this every day, every week, every month, and every year for the rest of my life. I want to laugh, and kiss, and fuck, and watch movies, and eat snacks with Ella, and I'd never tire of it. The realization that I'm in love with this woman dawns on me as I watch her laugh hysterically when Judd Nelson continues to bait the principal.

Chapter Twenty-Two
Ella

The morning after our date I wake up in Liam's bed with my body wrapped around his in a tangle of limbs and sheets. When I saw his apartment for the first time, I was in shock. I've never seen a single man with an apartment that was both clean and decorated.

We walked up the stairs to the second floor, and to my surprise the small one-bedroom apartment had plants, furniture, and pictures on the walls. One of the guys I slept with only had a bean bag chair in his living room and a Jessica Simpson 'Dukes of Hazzard' poster that even then hadn't been relevant in over a decade, so again, I was shocked.

When I mentioned it to him, he just smirked and said, "What's the point of having gay dads if you don't learn how to decorate?" To which, I had no reply.

He took me to bed soon after we got there, laying me out on his black silk sheets and lapping at my pussy gently before he slipped inside me slowly.

When we fucked in the movie theater, which I still can't believe I did, it was hurried, frantic, and unhinged. This time though was different. It was slow and tender, like we had all the time in the world. Like time had no meaning, and we could've stayed wrapped in each other forever. I had no idea how much time had passed, but I knew I didn't want to leave. I asked if I could stay the night, to which he replied he was hoping I would ask.

We showered together, and it was a different kind of intimacy that I've never shared with anyone before. I'm starting to realize what I have with Liam in general is something I've never shared with anyone before. He lathered my hair, and pressed light kisses down my body as he washed me with a damp cloth that smelled of the soap I recognize as his.

He told me about how all the times he fucked his hand while thinking of me while he was in the shower. In return I lathered his body, paying excruciating detail to his already hardening cock as I pumped it up and down lightly, telling him about all the night's I'd spend trying to convince myself not to want him, only to orgasm with my vibrator wishing it was him moments later. The idea elicited a groan from somewhere deep in his throat before taking me against the cold wall of the shower while the warm water sprayed at our backs.

After the shower I put on one of his T-shirts that hung to my knees and fell asleep on his chest with the smell of him filling my nostrils and his warmth like a blanket surrounding me.

It took all the strength I had to leave this morning. I truly didn't want to. I could've stayed in that bed until I became fused with it, but he and I both have a ton of grading to get done. We're both days behind and progress reports are due next week, and considering how when he's around all I seem to be able to think about is tasting every single inch of him, I had to leave so I could get some work done.

So, here I am, sitting cross-legged on my dilapidated blue couch, my hair tied up in a haphazard bun and surrounded by stacks of midterms. I grab my pack of glitter gel pens I use for grading and play Fleetwood Mac on my Spotify before getting to work.

I move through the papers as quickly as I can, trying not to think about the fact that I have to read every single essay question in the back, which takes longer than correcting all the multiple-choice questions combined. I roll my eyes; I only have myself to blame. I'm the one who assigned it after all.

I have no idea how much time has passed, but I go as long as I can before my arms are coated in smudges of glittery ink. I realize I am truly bored out of my mind, and that grading is by all accounts the worst part of teaching. Well, besides the lack of funding, resources, and respect.

I decide to take a much-needed break and pad into the kitchen to grab some coffee from the pot in the kitchen. As the coffee soothingly burns down my throat, I send a text to Liam to check in.

I feel like I should be afraid by the fact that I'm already missing him, when I just saw him this morning. I try and tamp down the self-loathing I feel crawling up my throat and burning at the back of my eyes at the fact that I wasted so much time not being with him. It's only been days, and I'm kicking myself.

I am preternaturally exposed to self-sabotage, but that's the plight of an anxious mind. I think I'm protecting myself, afraid of what may happen if I act on something, only to sabotage another part of my life by "protecting myself." Rationally, I know I should forgive myself. I was trying to protect my heart and my job, but when I think about all the time I could've spent with him... *No. No don't think about that. You're happy now. Enjoy the now. Letting the past burrow beneath your skin like a tick never helps anything.*

I walk back into my living room with my coffee in hand and grab my phone only to see he texted me first. I feel my heart squeeze with excitement before I even read his message.

Liam: How goes the midterm grading?

Me: Probably as well as your labs are going.

Liam: Ah, Hindenburg then.

Me: Now, who's the history teacher, me or you?

Liam: I can know things besides science!

Me: Get your own thing.

Liam: No, I don't think I will.

Me: Ooh feisty.

Me: We go back in a couple days, and I've done maybe, a third. So yeah, Hindenburg.

Liam: Procrastinator

Me: I blame you. If I wasn't spending so much time sucking your dick in movie theatres, I'm sure I would've gotten more done...

Liam: What I read is that you procrastinated and it's my dick's fault.

Me: I said what I said.

Liam: Come over and grade with me.

Me: *Oooh* demanding... kinky.

Me: We're not going to grade and fuck instead, aren't we?

Liam: Who said it had to be one or the other?

I feel my toes curl and heat pool in my belly at the thought of seeing him again. I grab a bag and start putting all the papers in it, making sure to pack my pens.

Me: Say less, I'll be over soon.

Liam: Can't wait.

*

After I pull the Prius into the visitor parking at Liam's apartment, I grab my bag and head up the stairs. I tug on the sleeves of my sweatshirt to try and cover my hands as a gust of wind blows through the open alcove of exposed stairs. Thankfully, Liam opens the door quickly, and the warmth from inside rushes out to greet me.

As usual, Liam looks handsome as ever, with one of his inky black curls threatening to fall into the glasses hovering over gleaming amber eyes. *Yeah. If I get any grading done, it'll be a miracle.*

I try and restrain myself by giving him a quick kiss after he shuts the door, but I fail spectacularly at it the moment his hands cup my face, and his tongue traces the seam of my lips. A small whimper comes out as his hand skates down my spine to grab my ass. I feel his smirk against my lips before he pulls away slightly, tracing my bottom lip with his thumb.

"First, we grade, then I lay you on the bed and lick your pussy until you beg me to stop," he says before he leaves the doorway.

I feel like someone kicked me in the shin and scoff at him, "That's hardly fair! You did that on purpose!"

He chuckles, the sound coasting down my spine in the places he just touched and pulls something from the oven. "Yes. Yes, I did."

"Tease," I groan in protest.

The same chuckle comes from the kitchen in response to my complaints as I marvel at the place where his sweatpants are hanging low on his hips. "Waiting makes it better baby. Like I said, I want you to beg."

"Bastard," I mutter, the only thing keeping me from throwing myself pathetically at this man is that the small apartment smells like a baked good.

"Ooh, are you making something?" I ask barely hiding my

excitement.

"I am," he smiles at me then. "Banana bread, okay?"

I grin widely at him, "Yes, I love banana bread."

My response makes him smile in return, "Perfect, it's my Pop's recipe. He used to make it for my brother and I when we were younger," he replies while leading me to the couch in the living room with a coffee table in front of it covered in papers, I'm assuming they're the labs he was telling me about.

I sit on the gray suede couch and set my bag full of papers next to my feet while Liam crosses the room to turn on the small Bluetooth speaker. The music trills through the air as the sound of ABBA fills the room, making a smile break out across my face. "ABBA?" I question.

"Seeing you in an ABBA shirt and a tiny scrap of cloth really created a newfound appreciation for them in me recently," he says as his eyes crinkle at the edges of a smile. That smile could convince me to do unspeakable things.

He grabs a stack of papers off the coffee table and sits cross-legged next to me on the sofa. I'm trying very hard not to notice how good he smells, or how close his proximity is to me. *Be patient Ella Jesus, you're being feral again.*

"Is that so?" I reply, trying not to let him see how pleased I am that he said that.

"Oh yes," he says as his eyes look like they could burn a hole right through my shirt. *Good to know he's not the only one that's horny right now...*

"How about we play a game?" I say coyly, my eyes burning right back at him.

"*Hmm*... a game? What kind of game?"

"For every ten papers we grade, whoever gets done first gets to make the other take off an article of clothing. The first one naked loses," I say with what I know must look like a wolfish grin.

"*Oooh...* I like this game," he purrs. "Prepare to lose, Ms. Jacobs."

"We'll see about that, Mr. Scott," I reply before grabbing a stack of papers and getting started. We work in companionable silence, both of us reading and scribbling on the papers furiously. Much to my chagrin, Liam got through his first set of ten faster than me.

"Okay El, what'll it be?" he asks with a cocky smirk.

I bend down to take off my left shoe before throwing it off to the side of the couch. I look back to see that his cocky grin has faltered slightly, before he mutters, "Boring."

He wins a second time, forcing me to take off my right shoe, and now I'm starting to realize that the essay question at the end of the midterm is royally going to fuck me over. Again. *This is why I should've just done all multiple choice;* I say rolling my eyes at myself internally.

I'm not sure what's happening in the third round, but one of the labs is clearly taking up a lot of time, and I finally win. I let the cocky grin spread across my face, "Okay fork it over," I said while sticking my hand out.

He grins at me before grabbing his shirt by the back of the collar and pulling it over his head, and there he is, sitting next to me shirtless. He notices my ogling and grins even wider. *Damn him! He did that on purpose to distract me.*

I watch as the muscles of his chest flow into tight stomach muscles and then drift into the V-shape of his hips where his sweatpants are hanging. I have to physically restrain myself from licking my lips. *Yep. His strategy is working, but two can play that game.*

Sure enough, Liam wins the next round, and I grin internally as I grab the hem of my shirt and pull it over my head, leaving nothing but a black bra that encourages an obscene amount of cleavage. I grab each breast and fluff it in its cup so that everything but a millimeter of my nipple is exposed. I hear a sharp intake of breath from Liam on the cushion next to me and I know my evil plan is working.

I can feel my competitive streak coming out, and I purposely lose the next round so I can rid myself of my bra and play with my nipples in pretend absentmindedness.

I feel the heat radiating off him, and I notice that he's adjusting in his seat more and more frequently. I finally have my edge, and I'm damn well going to use it to my advantage.

He loses the next four rounds, leaving him only in his black boxers with the last round upon us. Even his glasses have been used in a last-ditch effort, and he's very obviously going to lose the game no matter what the outcome of the final round is going to be.

I realize I might as well let him win this last round, so I do just that, and as I finish my last test, I look next to me to see Liam's fists are bunched at his sides. I gently set the pen down, his eyes boring into mine.

"Pants. Now." he growls. Not a question, a demand.

If I was a woman that had more self-control, I would take my jeans off at a painfully slow pace. However, luckily for him, I'm not, and when he starts demanding things of me in that growly voice with his eyes full of savage amber energy it makes me feel like I could melt into a puddle on the floor.

I lock eyes with him and quickly pull off my pants and my panties along with them. I stand in front of his appraising gaze and try not to fidget. I feel his eyes rake up and down my body and see his erection straining against his boxers. He spreads his legs slightly, clearly noticing I can't help but stare at the bulge that's making my mouth water.

"I want you," I moan helplessly, but I stand still noticing he hasn't made a move toward me.

A wicked smirk plays on his lips, and the brief time in which I held the upper hand is clearly gone. "What do you want to do to me?"

My tongue licks along my bottom lip, "You know what I want."

"Say it."

"I want to take your cock all the way to the back of my throat and run my tongue up and down the length of you until you spill down my throat," I say matter-of-factly, not breaking eye contact even once.

He moans at my words, and I can see his dick physically twitch at the thought of it. He rubs his hand down his length, palming himself outside of his boxers. "Good girl. Now come do it," he says while crooking his finger at me.

I sink to my knees in front of him where he sits on the couch. The tile floor biting into my flesh, but I want him so badly I couldn't care less. I grab each side of his boxers and push them down his legs, dragging my nails lightly along with it as I watch his cock become completely free.

I moan at the sight of the bead of cum glistening at the top and desperately want to taste it. I lick from the bottom of his balls and along the underside of his dick slowly before reaching the pre-cum at the top. I lightly lick it off as a hiss comes from behind Liam's teeth and he digs his hands into the couch cushions.

In an instant I take him to the back of my throat, running my tongue along the length of him as I bob my head up and down and my hand massages his balls. I watch as his eyes become glazed and unfocused, and he grinds his hips in time with my mouth. The amount of the control I have over this man and the effect I have on him is almost enough to send me spiraling.

I watch as he grips the couch cushions harder and his jaw tenses with what has to be the most self-control I've ever seen in a human as he says, "I believe you're supposed to be the one on your back and begging." With that he removes himself from my mouth and picks me up to take me down the hall to his bedroom, kissing me deeply as he walks with my legs wrapped around his hips.

He lays me out on the bed, the cold of the silk sheets caressing me down my back as I wiggle in anticipation. Liam climbs on the bed, his cock so hard it makes me realize how empty I feel without him filling me. He pushes my knees up to my stomach, my pussy on full display before him.

"Fuck El, you're so fucking wet," he moans moving his tongue at an achingly slow pace up the seam of me before sucking my clit into his mouth, wrenching a guttural moan from the deepest part of me. The sound acts like a gunshot ringing out at the beginning of a race, and his pace quickens.

He flattens his tongue against my clit before swirling it rapidly while he plunges two fingers inside me, curling them against the spot that sends me reeling. All the sensations at once send me crying out as I fist my hands in his curls and buck against him.

His pace quickens even more, and I know I'm not long for this world, that I'm no longer capable of rational thought or anything besides unabashed desire for this man. The familiar feeling of nearing a cliff is fast approaching, and before I know it noises are coming from my mouth that I've never even heard myself make before.

His fingers curl against my G-spot in time with his tongue lapping at my hardened clit. My vision blurs and focuses down to this one singular point as waves of pleasure crash up and down my body, causing me to spasm. "That's right, baby, come on my tongue. Jesus Christ, you taste so fucking good," he says against my clit as I clench around his fingers.

I'm half dazed, half crazed, and both completely sated and yet it will never be enough. I've come to realize that Liam is an addiction, his plump lips, the dark curls that fall over his glasses, the amber eyes that could light the deepest part of me on fire, the possession of my body.

I'm unwell.

I'm unhinged.

I'm going to want to fuck this man until the day that I die.

"I could look at you like this all night," he growls, "laid out bare and glistening for me, and I'm going to, but first I'm going to fuck you until you come again on my dick." His words have me wiggling against the sheets, and I'm already feeling molten and aching for more.

"Yes, baby please I need it," I moan.

He chuckles while he kisses up my body, only stopping to suck lightly on my nipples before continuing upward. His strong hands grab my chin and tilt my head to the side so he has access to my ear. "On your stomach El. I need to be able to smack that perfect ass while I take you from behind," his voice is gravel against the shell of my ear.

My cheeks heat as I whimper and become liquid at the thought. "That's new... I've never... um... been spanked before..." I remark nervously as I put a pillow underneath my hips so I'm on full display for him.

I feel his cock at my seam as he lightly grinds against my behind and trails a finger down my spine. "You mean to tell me you have an ass this perfect, and no one has ever spanked it before?" he asks as his hand lightly trails around the curve of my backside before he gently smacks.

A sharp inhale of breath comes from me at the light pain that initially comes from his hand, but then he soothes it. Shock turns into want. I want more.

"Harder," I whimper.

He fists my hair in his hands and groans into my ear from behind, "I knew you'd like it when I smacked that beautiful ass. You'll love it even more when I smack it while I take that wet cunt from behind." This man's mouth. Filthy. This can't be the same man who carried me through the hallways when I hurt my ankle, who took care of me afterwards, who volunteered to help me peel an ungodly amount of apples just because I needed help. I fucking love it. I love that he can be both.

Shit. Do I love him? Later Ella. Later. Maybe think about this when your head is clearer, and you aren't at the point where you would bark if he told you to. As I'm having an existential crisis, Liam lines his dick up to my entrance and shoves into me all the way to the hilt in one thrust.

"Fuck," I cry as I adjust to the size of him.

"So, fucking wet El. I can't get over it. You're dripping." He grunts as he slowly moves inside me, dragging his cock out almost to the tip before plunging back into me. The measured friction against my inner walls is like a slow torture.

"More baby please. I need more." I beg.

"Good girl El, tell me what you want," he praises while picking up the pace of his thrusts.

I feel his hand gently round the curve of my ass, and then

smack. The sting sends a line of pleasure up my spine.

"Harder," I beg.

Smack.

Soothe.

Smack.

Soothe.

The perfect pattern as he thrusts back and forth inside me, this is both torture and pleasure in a rhythm I've never known. "So good," I cry out.

I feel Liam's long arm wraps around to the front of my body, his thumb rubbing circles around my clit. I can't take it. Too much. Too good. My vision blackens at the edges again, and I'm on that cliff, and I'm falling off. Free falling as adrenaline and pleasure dump into my bloodstream in droves and I scream.

I literally scream.

I thought that was something porn stars did to be over the top. Apparently not.

My walls clench around Liam's thick shaft and he grabs my hips to better pump in and out of me. His thrusts are punishing as I rapidly move up and down his cock until he cries out, coming inside me.

My breath is coming out in ragged stints as he peppers kisses down my spine before he pulls out of me. I slump into a heap of melted nonsense onto the bed and feel empty with him no longer inside me. I don't know who or where I am. I could be told I had been transported to another dimension and I would believe it. That orgasm wrecked me.

"Holy shit," I grumble as Liam brings me a washcloth from his bathroom to clean me up.

He lays back on his bed and pulls me onto his chest from the place where I became a heap of existentialism. "Agreed," he chuckles while placing a kiss on the top of my head.

I nuzzle into his chest, wrapping my arms and legs around him because I can't seem to bear the thought of a part of my body not touching his. We lay in quiet, his hands playing with my hair, while I breathe in the scent of his skin.

Laying here in this bed, I realize it then. I love him. I love this man. I think I've loved him for a very long time, and once again I'm cursing the fact that there was ever a time that I thought being with him wasn't an option.

My heart strains at the thought of him, we can have this. We can be this together, in love, having amazing sex, grading papers together, watching movies, and snuggling.

I want that. I want this life that I can picture so clearly now. The only thing left to do is tell him. Which I will definitely do, when I'm not being a total anxious coward. So probably never.

Chapter Twenty-Three
Liam

Today has been just so fucking long, but any teacher can tell you that the day before break and the day students get back are always the longest. Why? Because in teenager-time a week away from each other is forever, and they all want to talk about what happened while they were gone. All day my students seemed like they were truly out to get me. It was like they leeched all the energy out of me to fuel themselves, which is why now by the end of the day I'm a shell of a human being and they all act like they could run a 10k.

The day isn't over yet, I still have a whole Activities Committee meeting to get through, but at least I'll get to see my girl. My girl, I never thought I'd get to say that, never thought I'd get to call her mine.

Spending the last week with her was actual paradise, and how I was able to go so long without being near her I'll never know, because now going a day without seeing her, touching her, kissing her, makes me feel empty. I could spend every day for the rest of eternity alternating between being buried inside of her and feeling her body wrap around me while she lays on my chest.

I want the whole world to know she's mine, and the urge to claim her, to touch her, any time I'm near her is so strong that I have to physically plaster my arms to my side when we're at work. Pinning her to the wall is definitely not appropriate. Hell, thinking about all the things I want to do to her at work probably isn't appropriate either. Especially, since no one knows we're even dating yet, although, I'm pretty sure Sergio suspects something because he kept looking at me funny in the lounge this morning.

I let all my classes use the period to prep for the science fair that's in two weeks, which leaves me with far too much time on my hands to think. I try and work on lesson plans, but then my brain drifts to Ella laying naked on my bed, the taste of her on my tongue, her perfect ass taking every slap so perfectly, smelling the lemon scent of her hair while she snuggles into me. Everything about that woman is pure perfection. I've never met anyone that's made me laugh one minute and then make me want to immediately fuck them the next until I met her.

I check my watch and see it's almost time for the meeting, so I collect my things and lock up my classroom before walking across the hall to Ella's.

I lean against the doorway, watching her stuff papers and random items into her bag before I gently wrap my knuckles against her door. "Are you ready for the meeting Ms. Jacobs?" I ask wryly.

She tucks a piece of her blonde hair behind her ear and grins at me, "My goodness Mr. Scott so professional," she remarks before slinging her bag over her shoulder and grabbing her keys.

"That's me, the epitome of professionalism." I say while bowing at the waist dramatically.

She chuckles as we head into the hallway, and then locks the door behind us. I fight the urge to grab her hand as we walk together and grip the legs of my pants so I don't accidentally do something that will get us caught.

God, I hate the feeling of sneaking around, but I also don't want Ella to feel pressured into saying something before she's ready. We've only really been together over a week, but I'm already paranoid about us getting caught. It's not like we're lying really, but it feels like it. Bledsoe isn't necessarily against staff relationships, they've happened before, but what he is against is lying, and HR violations. Hence my paranoia.

"How was your day? Anything of note?" she asks while looking up at me with curiosity dancing in those beautiful gray eyes.

"Oh, you know, I tried getting some lesson planning done while they worked on their science fair projects, but I was exceedingly distracted today." I reply with a wry smile.

I see a grin spread wide across her face, and I can tell she's trying to play it off. Too late, I already saw it, and it's adorable. "Oh really? What was so distracting?"

I'm pressing my luck, I know it, but I can't help myself. I lean down close to her ear so that only she can hear me and whisper, "Any time I tried to do anything productive, all I could think about was how perfectly red your ass was while I spanked it."

Her eyes go wide, and I see a blush spread like wildfire across her cheeks. Was it risky saying that? Probably. Worth it? Absolutely.

She smirks at me then, "If I had pearls, I'd clutch them."

I chuckle as we enter the auditorium, and I see Josie sitting toward the front and waving for us to come sit next to her. We make our way down the aisle and sit in the red cushioned seats while we wait for Bledsoe to arrive.

Ella loops her arm through Josie's and rests her head on her shoulder as Josie jokingly sticks her tongue out at me. She just has to rub salt in the wound, doesn't she? She's the only person as of right now in the entire school that knows we're together, she's Ella's best friend so I assumed she would be the only one who knew until Ella was ready to tell people.

Josie and I were cool before Ella ever even came into the picture. She and I started at Valley the same year and joined the activities committee at the same time too. If anyone was going to be the only person to know about us, I'm glad it's her. I stick my tongue out at her right back, and she laughs.

"Welcome everyone," I hear Bledsoe's deep baritone say as he walks down the aisle to the front. "Please take a seat if you haven't already, we'll be starting shortly."

Everyone takes their seats and Bledsoe clears his throat. "Welcome to the last activities committee meeting of the year. As we plan the last event of the school year, let's really try and end it with a bang. The 8th grade dance has always been a great way for us to fundraise for the following year's 8th grade trip. We rely very heavily on these events, and the generosity of the businesses within our community, to help fund the 8th grade trip for anyone who wants to go. Since it began, we have yet to miss a year due to lack of funds, and that's because you all volunteer your time and resources in order to create a memorable time for your students, a lot of whom have never even left the state of Indiana before. These are experiences and memories that will last a lifetime, and I am so thankful for each and every one of you, and all the work that you put into these events. Give yourselves a hand," he says as he claps his hands.

We all return the sentiment and clap as well. Once the noise settles Bledsoe continues, "With that being said, let's open the floor for discussion about a theme for this year's dance. Josie, I believe you mentioned to me earlier this week that you had some ideas?"

Josie claps her hands excitedly, her curls bouncing with

excitement. "Yes! So, if everyone recalls earlier this year the sixth graders had a winter concert, and Mr. Lennox had a friend that donated a ton of very pretty white lights to decorate for it. Well, I spoke with Jack, and he still has them stored away in the choir room and is willing to let us use them for the dance."

"*Oooh* I love that!" Ella coos.

"Right? So, I was thinking we could make the theme 'A night under the stars,' and hang tons of lights all over the gym."

A murmur of approval rings through the crowd and Bledsoe responds as well, "Excellent idea Ms. Jones! I love an idea that saves us money. If no one else has any other ideas, we should go with that. Are we all in agreement?"

Everyone nods or says yes, and I hear Ella lean over and whisper, "Great job Jos," and nudge her shoulder. It makes me smile.

"Well then that settles it. I spoke with Mrs. Hammond, the P.T.A. president, and they've already decided on the date May 10. They're working on the fliers now but were just waiting for us to give them a budget and theme so that they can post them."

"Do we know how much we're charging per ticket?" Someone sitting behind me asks.

"We're thinking $15 a person. It would give us a great head start on the funds for next year, and more than cover the cost of supplies." Bledsoe responds.

"Crap," I hear Ella whisper.

"What?" I ask in a whisper back.

"May 10 is Stella's retirement party."

"Shit."

Ella's hand shoots up next to me to ask a question. When Bledsoe points at her she asks, "Do we know what time the dance is supposed to be?"

"Mrs. Hammond said they were planning on six p.m. to nine p.m.," he replies.

Ella gives him a thumbs up and whispers to me when Bledsoe is no longer paying attention, "It ends at nine... we should be good by then right?"

"You two sure are whispering a lot," Josie leans in toward Ella and me. "In a totally inconspicuous way by the way," she says sarcastically.

Ella whispers to Josie, "May tenth is Stella's retirement party."

"Shit," Josie mouths.

"If the dance is done by nine, then we can just go after, right? I'm sure her party will still be going by then," I reply.

"I don't know, it is a retirement party after all. Won't dinner be at like four p.m., and the party end around 8?" Josie says with a smirk.

"Don't be a dick Jos," Ella chuckles and playfully shoves her friend on the shoulder. "When we see Stella next, we'll just ask her..."

*

"What the hell do you mean? Of course, the party will still be going! Just how old do you think I am?" Stella wraps her satin purple scarf around her neck dramatically.

It's the next morning, and Stella, Sergio, Jack, Ella, Josie, and I are all talking over coffee in the lounge before the first period bell rings. Ella is standing next to me, and I have to force myself to wrap both hands around the new Garfield mug that she got me in order to keep from touching her. I can't help myself when I'm around her. I spent months and months not allowing myself to touch her, not going against her wishes, but now that I have her it's an impulse that I have to physically stop from doing.

I roll my eyes at how dramatic she is, "We didn't mean anything by it Stell, we just want to make sure we don't miss it."

"It's eighty's themed right Stella?" Ella asks after taking a sip of her coffee. She looks so damn beautiful I know I must be staring. Her red-blonde hair is clipped up exposing the slope of her neck and her collar bone, the mascara on her eyelashes makes her gray eyes look piercing, and her pink sweater contours her breasts so perfectly it should be illegal. How could one light pink sweater that covers her completely still make me this fucking needy. I think I'm broken.

"Damn right it is!" She grins widely, "The best decade by far. I was in my prime, fresh into teaching, and looking fine as hell!"

Her response makes all of us chuckle, because that was the most Stella answer that she could have responded with. Josie is sitting on the arm of the couch and takes a big gulp of coffee before responding. "Don't worry Stella, we have to chaperone the 8th grade dance, but if the party will still be going on then we shouldn't miss it."

"Oh, it will be!" Stella replies while shaking a maroon painted fingernail for emphasis. "I didn't spend the last forty years forcing surly teenagers to learn how to sketch a self-portrait to not celebrate my retirement with tequila shots and dancing to Pat Benatar."

Ella giggles and gently elbows my ribs, "We wouldn't miss it." She must've realized her error because I see her eyes go wide. I can feel the anxiety in my stomach begin to roil and I know I have what must be a panicky look in my eyes as I look over to Josie, who responds by widening her eyes and gritting her teeth.

A nonverbal que for me to calm the fuck down.

Jack narrows his eyes at us, pointing a dark green nail between us, "You two are being weird."

I feel my back go stick straight. I'm not good with the lying or playing it cool shit. I glance over at Ella whose wringing her hands together in front of her stomach, something I know she does when she's feeling anxious.

"No one's weird," Ella says in a voice that comes out with a slight squeak that definitely alludes to us being weird. We're caught. I can feel it.

"We're being normal…" I say without looking Jack in the eyes. See? This is why I wanted to tell people right away. I'm not good at this.

"What totally normal responses that you both are having…" Jack says with an eye roll. "Not even a little bit suspicious." I'm really not appreciating his particular brand of sarcasm right now.

"You're being weird!" Josie shouts in a completely irrational tone for the moment while pointing her finger at Jack. Yep, we're fucked.

*

When we're done for the day, I meet Ella in the hallway after we lock up our classrooms and we walk to the teacher parking lot together. There's finally some reprieve from the cold of the winter air, and the sunny chill that comes from early spring in Indiana is in full force today.

We're careful not to hold hands, even though I'm sure everyone was on to us in the lounge today, so as not to raise any more suspicion. Doesn't mean I can't appreciate how her brown bomber jacket is tight in all the right places and her jeans hug the curve of her ass perfectly. When we get back to her place tonight, that ass is mine.

When the Prius comes into view, I follow her as she unlocks the car with the key fab and I open the door for her. Standing on the other side of the door her gray eyes meet mine with a smile, "You didn't have to do that."

"You know I want to baby," I reply, a low tone to my voice.

The thought makes her smile more, "Yeah I do..."

We're both quiet for a moment, and I know I've got to say something to her about what happened this morning. It's eating at me, and I want us to be able to enjoy our night together without my awkwardness hanging over us.

"You know that we're going to have to mention that we're together at some point, right?" I force myself to look her in the eyes, and I can see worry lacing hers as they meet my gaze.

"I know..." she says quietly.

"If Bledsoe finds out before we report it... it won't go over well," I respond in an almost pleading tone. I'm feeling desperate at this point to convince her to report us to Bledsoe, not just because I'm terrified of getting caught, which I am, but because I'm just so proud that she's mine. I want everyone to know.

She lets out an exasperated sigh, "I know, and we will. I just want to enjoy our bubble with only the two of us a little while longer. Well, the three of us, I guess if you count Josie, who we know won't say anything. I just want to have enough time to figure out how to approach everything. I want to be in control of the narrative. Even though we're together, I'm still terrified history's going to repeat itself."

I feel my brow tug together with worry, "Okay El, if that's what you want, but you know this isn't the same as what that literal definition of a prick did to you."

She takes her hand and settles it on my face, rubbing her thumb lightly against my cheek. "I know that rationally, but I just need time for the rational and irrational parts of my brain to get together and agree."

Hell, I'd be lying if I said I didn't understand that. At the end of the day, I'm letting her take the lead on this, and if she's not ready, then she's not ready.

"Okay babe, meet you at your place?" I ask while checking my surroundings before giving her a kiss on the forehead.

She grins up at me widely, and that smile of hers has me grinning like an idiot right back. "See you in a bit," she responds before shutting the door behind her and driving away.

Twenty-Four
Ella

The month of April came and went in the blink of an eye, but I guess that's what happens when you feel so happy you feel like everything has a rose-colored hue to it.

No matter how much Liam and I are together, it feels like it's never enough, and we start most nights with him inside me before he wraps me in his big strong arms or with me nuzzled into his chest. The mornings that I wake up next to him are always my favorite, and the longer that we're together the more I crave it. Hell, at this point it feels more like I need it. I sleep better with him next to me.

I've never known this feeling before, the one where a man has my whole heart. I know I've mentioned this before, but I've never really been a relationship person. I'm sure if I had a therapist, they would tell me it's because I spent a large portion of my childhood without a stable or consistent home, so I never really had a good relationship modeled to me until Hank came along. It's been a lot of not so serious flings, or dating guys, but an actual boyfriend? It never happened to me, not until Liam anyway.

I didn't have any idea what I was missing, how lonely I was, until he showed up. Sure, I had my mom, Josie, and Hank, but having someone to hold me, watch movies with, laugh with every night, has filled a hole in my heart I didn't know was empty. There's no doubt in my mind that I love this man, and it scares the absolute shit out of me. He deserves every good thing in this world, and I want to tell him, I really do, but I just haven't had the vagina flaps to do it yet. I'm a chicken.

I can tell he's getting antsy about the fact that I'm still not ready to tell Bledsoe about us, and I really keep meaning to, but it never seems like the right moment. I've actually gone to his office twice in the last month, walked all the way to the other side of the school, only to have my stomach twist and turn into anxious knots so badly that I panic and don't do it.

Rationally, I know that this situation is different than the one I was in at my last school, I wish my rational brain was the one that always held the reins in my head, but it's not. In fact, it's frequently irrational, hence the reason I'm a medicated queen.

I can't shake the feeling that if I tell Bledsoe he'll get pissed and then tell the entire school, and then once the entire school finds out everyone will talk shit about us, and I'll have to leave school again. How does changing schools twice in two years look on a resume? Terrible. I can answer that, it looks terrible. No one will hire me, so I'll be forced to stop teaching, which I love so much. Without a job, I won't be able to afford my mortgage anymore, so I'll have to move back in with my mom and Hank. Do you think Liam would want to be with a loser with no job or future? No, of course, not, I would just drag him down, and I'll lose him too.

See, how easily I spiral? This is why the default setting in my brain is panic, because I can very easily turn a situation that seems fairly straightforward into a complete nightmare in approximately three minutes. If it wasn't so damn inconvenient, I would actually be impressed with myself.

Which is why it's May, and the school year is almost over, and I still haven't told Bledsoe about Liam and me. I feel pretty confident that at least a few of the core teachers that we hang out with have an inkling that something is going on, mostly because Liam and I are both terrible at not being completely obvious. We're trying so hard to make it look like we aren't together that it's like we're making it even more awkward.

The 8th grade dance is a week from today, and now that the school day has ended the activities committee is meeting in the gym so that we can work on decorations.

Josie and I are clipping magnets to the "stars," aka the lights, so that when we go to hang them next week they just attach to the bleachers and metal beams surrounding the gym.

Josie huddles next to me so we can talk without anyone hearing us. "El, you need to say something! It's been well over a month. What if Bledsoe finds out?" She whispers while clicking a magnet into place.

I groan audibly, "Ugh, okay, I know. I just keep procrastinating it. I'm just so stupid happy and I'm afraid once we tell Bledsoe the whole school will find out and everything will go to shit. I can't handle losing him Jos. I can't."

"El, no matter what happens people will talk, but who gives a shit? If you're the one that tells people, then you control how it gets out." She says while tying her curls out of her face with an orange silk scrunchie.

I pinch the bridge of my nose, feeling a stress headache behind my eyes beginning to develop. "Fuck, okay you're right. First thing Monday morning I'm doing it."

Josie lets out a grateful sigh, "Oh thank God because you guys really aren't being as covert as you think you are. People that are 'friends' don't look at each other like they're cartoon mice with hearts for eyes. The amount of damage control I've had to do has been overwhelming."

I look up to see Liam attaching magnets along the bleachers, his broad shoulders straining against his collared shirt with beakers printed on it as he leans over. I watch as he stands up and pushes that curl of dark hair that falls into his glasses out of his eyes, and I feel myself audibly sigh with what I know has to be the biggest grin on the planet. God damn it that man is so hot. He must feel me staring at him or something, because at that moment his amber eyes connect with mine and he smiles right back at me, giving me a small wave.

"See! This is exactly the shit I'm talking about!" Josie says in an exasperated tone while rolling her eyes at me.

I turn back to my task and snap another magnet to the back of the bulb, "Okay fine. I'm a pile of mush."

Josie snorts and starts looping the long strings of lights around her arm so she can put them back into the storage container. "Oh, I think we've surpassed mush and have gone straight to liquid."

"Well, he certainly makes me wet…" I mumble.

"Ella Jane!" Josie mockingly chastises me and shoves my arm before we bust out in a fit of giggles.

"You ladies almost done?" I hear the deep tone of Liam's voice asks from behind us. I feel his presence becoming increasingly closer before he leans close to my ear from behind and whispers, "I have plans for you when we leave here."

My teeth graze at my bottom lip in response to his alluding tone, and I feel my blood begin to heat beneath my skin. His eyes dip down to my lips, and I know what he's thinking, and he's not the only one.

"See!" Josie says in an annoyed whisper while flailing her arms between us. "You two are so obvious! How could I even begin to try and perform damage control on this? You both might as well get matching shirts with arrows pointing toward each other that say I'm fucking him/I'm fucking her labeled on them."

Liam's eyes get wider, and I can tell he's trying his best to contain his laugh while I snap the last magnet into place. "And on that note, I'm leaving," I say while glowering at Josie.

"Bye I love you too," Josie says with a grin. She just thinks she's so fucking funny.

As we walk to the parking lot we head toward the Prius, and I itch to hold his hand, but I know I need to wait until we're out of eyesight before I can touch him. A situation where the irony is not lost on me, considering I'm the one that's been keeping us from saying anything to Bledsoe in the first place.

The sun was out in full force today, and in the glow of the sunlight as it dips into the horizon, I look up to the man next to me. He's breathtaking, and he's mine. How? Literally how? I don't think I'll ever be able to understand.

He looks down at me and gives me a grin that extends all the way to his wire framed glasses, and I fight the urge to melt into the black top as we reach the car.

I decide then that I am one hundred percent going to tell Bledsoe on Monday, because this man is perfect, and I realize almost painfully that I would do pretty much anything to make him happy. Does he want me to sing every song from the soundtrack of Moulin Rouge at the Grand Ol' Opry while playing the kazoo in nothing but a feather boa and a driving cap? If it would make him happy, I'm pretty sure I would do it. I try and not let the thought send me into a tailspin as I lean against the car door and look back at Liam.

I worry at my lip, and I see his eyes follow the movement. I can't tell if it's worry that etches his face because he knows I'm feeling anxious or if it's because he wants to be the one biting my lip, but I decide to go for it.

I lock eyes with him before saying, "I'm ready. I think we should tell Bledsoe on Monday."

A huge smile spreads across his face then, and his eyes dance with excitement. "Wait really?" His eyes crinkle at the corners, and a pain aches in my chest at the thought of how patient he's been with me. He's been wanting to do this for so long now, and I know it's been eating at him. The sneakiness of it, the lying, he hates it, and yet he still did it just to make sure I was comfortable.

"Really babe," I smile back at him.

He rolls his lips slowly between his teeth and boxes me in between his arms before leaning down to the crook of my neck. I inhale a sharp breath at the nearness of him, the smell of his cologne sending sparks to all my nerve endings. He nuzzles his nose against my neck before his lips meet the shell of my ear, where he whispers because he knows it drives me absolutely crazy with need. "Well, it looks like those plans for tonight just got even more special. Maybe I should give you a preview?"

My breathing picks up speed at the thought of what he's alluding to. Excitement sending shivers down my spine and my nipples hardening in anticipation. "*Mmm...* A preview would be nice..." I trail off.

In the next second, he encloses what little space remains between us and grips the back of my neck while his thumb extends beneath my chin, holding me in place. His strong hand against my throat makes me liquid, and I swallow beneath his grip. I know, he feels the small movement in my throat because he grunts as his eyes become dark and he crushes his lips to mine.

His lips press urgently against mine, sliding his tongue against my lips, begging to enter my mouth so that it can tangle with mine. I let him in greedily and open my mouth even wider so I can have more of him. Fuck. This man tastes so fucking good.

His hips press against mine, and I can feel just how much he wants me pushing against his zipper. I gasp as the hand not holding my head grazes down my body, cupping the curve of my ass.

This is absolutely insane. We are in the parking lot for crying out loud. My vagina has a mind of her own when it comes to this man. All semblance of social preservation or self-awareness goes right out the window, eclipsed by how much I need Liam touching, caressing, tasting, every inch of my body.

As if he too realizes that we're in the parking lot at our place of work, he pulls his lips from mine and he looks me in the eye. "You're such a good girl, you're going to get it tonight. I'm going to make that beautiful pussy come on my tongue until you force me to stop."

I shiver at his promise, mentally giving myself a high five. If I would've known just how far this would have gotten me, I would've told Bledsoe a month ago.

I squirm at the chill that grazes my skin once he pulls away, and the heat of him is no longer encompassing me. "I'll hold you to that," I say with a smirk.

He straightens then, a smirk playing at the corner of his lips. "So, I'll see you soon, Ms. Jacobs?"

I lightly rub my hand down his tall, broad, chest. "See you soon Mr. Scott," I say with a smile.

"I'll pick up Dragon House on my way, I believe I still owe you a plate full of crab Rangoon," he says before shutting my door.

I squeal with excitement and turn my car on, blasting my Fleetwood Mac playlist as I drive home, grinning like an idiot the entire time, because everything is finally falling into place. I have a job that I love at a school that is perfect for me, amazing colleagues, a great support system, I'm finally on a medication that's working for me, and I have a man that is better than any rom-com star or Disney prince.

A small bubble churns in my gut, the thought that maybe, things are too good. That at any moment the other shoe is going to drop, and all hell will break loose, and there's no way anyone deserves to be this happy, but I quickly shove those worries down deep.

I'm taking ownership and control of my life, and while I'm at it on Monday and finally coming clean to Bledsoe, I'm going to tell Liam how important he is to me later that night. I'll do something cute, like cook him dinner or something, and express what I've known since before we ever started dating. Shit, if I'm being honest, I've known for months that I love him more than I ever thought I could love another human being. He deserves to know, and even if he isn't ready to say it back just yet, I can't keep it inside anymore. I love him, I love him, I love him, and I don't care who knows any more.

Chapter Twenty-Four
Liam

Today's the day. It's Monday morning and we're finally, finally, going to tell Bledsoe after school today. I'm a little nervous sure, but I'm also excited, excited to not have to hide my relationship with Ella anymore.

It's been eating me alive. I know a lot of people get off on the whole sneaking around thing, but that's just not me. I spend the entire time waiting for shit to hit the fan, and it feels like once we get this over with, we can move forward in our relationship, because I'm all in. I'm all in, and I've been this way from the moment I saw her on that stage and realized who she was all those months ago. Hell, even in Jamaica if it had been up to me, I would've gotten her number. When I got home from my trip my dreams were plagued by strawberry blonde hair, an insanely curvy body, and steel grey eyes that could melt me down to my core.

I get out of bed, my heart thrumming with anticipation, and get ready for the day. I look in the mirror and try to arrange my dark curls in a way that doesn't fall into my glasses, even though it always somehow manages to. It's crazy to me that I haven't really worn my contacts since Ella told me she thought I looked cute in glasses, back when I thought I was going to have to suffer in silence over my longing for her. I would've done just about anything to get her to notice me differently, so I kept wearing them, and now I'm just used to it. I pick up the wire-rimmed glasses and clean the lenses before adjusting them on my face. Perfect, now I can actually see.

I go to grab my favorite flamingo patterned collared shirt out of my closet, but trip over the duffel bag that's somehow sticking out. I wipe my hand down my face, *Jesus I really need to clean out my closet.* I see a random assortment of flashing lights out of the corner of my eye, *what the fuck?*

The flashing is coming from the duffel bag, weird. I crouch down and find the source of the flashing lights, and a giant grin spreads across my face. I find a hot pink chain with a flashing shot glass on the end, and the script, *swallow like a lady,* scrawled on the front.

I chuckle as I hold the necklace in my hand, and it wasn't until this moment that I even knew this thing lit up. I don't think Ella even knows, because knowing how she is now, she would've been wearing it with the flashing lights going off.

I've never met anyone who is such a confusing mixture of both caring and not caring what people think. It's like if Ella thinks that something will bring another person joy, she doesn't get embarrassed or anxious about it, but when it becomes her that's front and center, the potential for her flaws to be on display, that's when she begins wringing her hands, and gnawing on her bottom lip.

I love her for all of it. I love the joy she gets from bringing joy to others, her kind heart, that no matter how anxious she is she'll push through it if it means bringing a smile to someone else's face. I love how absolutely fucking hilarious she is, how her laugh is the most beautiful sound I've ever heard, and the noises she makes in the back of her throat when I'm seated inside of her.

This is perfect timing honestly, after we meet with Bledsoe

today, I'll tell her how proud I am of her, how much I love her, and how I can't wait for us to start this new chapter together. Because I know that as long as I have her, I feel like I can do anything.

I finish getting dressed and brush my teeth before heading out the door before the sun has even risen yet, and I'm ready to take this day by the balls.

*

This entire school day has been fucking weird. When I walked into my second period class after hallway duty, they all immediately quieted when I walked in. It was eerie. Maybe, I'm just weirdly paranoid or something, but it felt like I had some sort of weird target on my head all day that everyone kept looking at, and when I would get near them, they would get quiet. I decide to just chalk it up to paranoia because of the impending meeting with Bledsoe this afternoon and try not to be creeped out by it.

That is, until halfway through sixth period Bledsoe appears in my doorway, looking very serious and not a trace of a smile on his face. "Mr. Scott, can I see you in my office after dismissal?"

I can feel all the students' eyes on me, whatever random conversations that were occurring during their group work seeming to stop in an instant and replaced with a resounding "*oooh...*" from the entire class. Thanks kids, just what I needed, bring more attention to the situation.

I put on the most professional demeanor I can muster before responding, "Of course, sir, I'll see you then."

He responds with a curt nod, and just as quickly as he appeared, he's gone again. I blow out a low breath to find that every single student is looking at me with wide eyes.

"Don't you all have periodic table assignments due by the end of the week you should be working on?" I try and keep the frustration out of my voice, it's not their fault I'm panicking, but easier said than done.

They quickly get back to work, allowing me to get back to mine, or at least attempt to. There's no way I'm going to be able to focus for the last thirty minutes of the day. *Maybe, Ella mentioned that she wanted to set up a meeting between the three of us, and he was just confirming that it's happening...? Yeah that's it, it must be.*

I'm glad for how forward-thinking Ella is and I've convinced myself of this enough that I at least attempt to finish up the grading I was working on.

When the last bell rings, I'm utterly relieved to get this over with. I watch as the last student grabs his bookbag and heads out for the day, me following close behind before locking my door.

When I reach the hallway, I smile because there's Ella with the bravest face on that she can muster, and I know she must be feeling extremely anxious. I'm overwhelmed by just how much she's sacrificing so we can be together, I know this isn't easy for her, telling Bledsoe. I know she's terrified that what happened at her last job will happen again, which is why I wanted to let her go at her own pace. Saying I was surprised when she decided to finally tell him a few days ago would be an understatement.

She gives me a tight smile before we walk down the brightly lit hallway to the front office, our shoes squeaking against the polished floor the entire way there.

She's so beautiful, it's overwhelming. Today she has her hair twisted into a clip, showing off the collarbone I've kissed and licked more times than I can count by now, with a lavender cardigan draped over a black t-shirt and jeans. Her full lips are coated in a light pink color that plays off her sharp gray eyes perfectly, and not for the first time I remember how entranced I am by her.

The walk down to the office is plagued with silence, and I know it's just because of the nerves. This isn't exactly an easy task, but I'm really proud of Ella for not only agreeing to do this but scheduling it with Bledsoe beforehand.

As we approach the office, I feel Ella's body go ramrod straight and she stops walking, her eyes getting wider by the second. "El? Is everything ok?" I ask as I see her staring toward the front entrance of the building.

"He's... here?" She whispers.

I follow her gaze toward a middle-aged man wearing a tweed suite and a receding hair line that looks like he tried to comb the few hairs left there from one side of his head to the other. Standing next to him is a younger woman that looks roughly our age with long brown hair and a smile plastered to her face, nodding at whatever it is he's saying.

The man looks up at us, stunned for a moment before a creepy grin spread across his face and he starts walking toward us, the short brunette following closely behind. "Why Ms. Jacobs, what a pleasant surprise. How long has it been? A year?"

I feel her nails bite into my skin as she clutches my arm, "Phaser..." she grits out.

The name makes my blood boil, and I feel an obscene amount of rage bubble to the surface. "What?" I snap, lunging toward him before Ella pulls me back toward her.

The arm clutching me starts to shake slightly, "What are you doing here?" she asks, her voice wavering.

A snake-like smile plays along his lips, "Oh, well my

daughter just got a position as the new art teacher. I believe she's replacing the teacher that's retiring at the end of the year. She was just showing me around."

The short brunette smiles sweetly, "Hi! I'm Nikki! I'm so excited to meet everyone. Principal Bledsoe said that the faculty here is all really close."

Ella doesn't even seem to realize someone is talking to her, all she does is stand there staring with her mouth open. I clear my throat in attempt to tamp down my rage, "It's nice to meet you Nikki, unfortunately your father isn't welcome here."

Nikki's face contorts with confusion as she looks at her dad questioningly. "Dad?" She asks in a tone much firmer than she used only a minute earlier.

Phaser's face turns red and is full of rage, "Ah, I see Ms. Jacobs found someone else to whore herself to since I rejected her advances."

I feel my vision turning red, "How dare you talk to her like that?" I ask before lunging toward him once more.

"Liam, please. It's fine let's just go," Ella says quietly.

"Fine," I grit out before whipping my head toward Phaser once more. "The only reason I'm not kicking you out the front door right now is to save your daughter the embarrassment, but if I ever see you here again, I promise you won't get lucky twice. Do you understand?"

Phaser's smarmy eyes narrow at Ella, "What a surprise, Ms. Jacobs remains completely and utterly silent. Relying on someone else to do her work for her, so what if I expected a little compensation in return?" The silent rage behind his eyes burns, any and all awareness that his daughter is next to him is gone. Either that, or he thinks Nikki won't care what just slipped out of his mouth.

Nikki's face becomes horrified as she stares at her father, "Oh my God that is it! I should've known better than to believe you. All those allegations and I stood by your side, refusing to realize the truth right in front of me. Get out!" she shrieks, her voice echoing in the alcove.

I watch Phaser's façade finally begin to crack, a war between who he truly is and who he presents himself to be, "But sugar plum."

Nikki's teeth clench together, "No! Don't call me that and try to manipulate me. That's the reason I came to this school in the first place, I couldn't stand being under your thumb for one more second! I tried bringing you here as a peace offering, but as usual I was just being delusional in thinking you'd ever change. Now. Get. Out."

At this point, I swear Phaser's face turns purple, and I feel Ella's grip tightens even more around my arm. "Fine! Enjoy teaching at this ramshackle school with no funding." He shouts before turning and storming out the front door.

Nikki grabs Ella's hand and peers at her, "Are you okay?"

Ella is still silent, but I watch as a single tear falls down her cheek before she nods in reply.

"Thank you for doing that. She and your father... aren't on good terms to say the least." I respond.

"Of course," Nikki says with a small smile. "You probably don't remember me Ella, but I was a sub your last year there. I heard about you, and I knew something about that entire situation didn't sound right. If anyone knows how much of an ass hole my father can be, it's me. Don't worry though, he won't come back here ever again. I'll make sure of it."

"Thank you," Ella whispers.

"We should get going, we have a meeting. Nice to meet you

Nikki," I say with a nod.

"You guys too," Nikki smiles before picking up a giant canvas bag on the floor and lugging it over her shoulder down the hallway.

When we finally make it to the administration office after that giant fiasco, we're greeted by Gina, the school secretary. She has her glasses perched on the top of her nose attached by a small silver chain draped around her neck.

As we walk in Gina gives us a friendly smile, "Mr. Scott, Ms. Jacobs, I'll let Mr. Bledsoe know you've arrived." Both Ella and I respond with a nod, and I give Gina a smile before she disappears into a door located on the wall behind her desk.

I feel Ella's gaze and glance over at her, meeting her eyes, and the fear in them reflects back at me. I quickly take her hand in mine and give it a squeeze before releasing it. "We're going to get through this El, don't worry. We'll feel so much better when it's over." I can't even imagine how rattled she must feel right now.

Ella responds with a smile, but it doesn't meet her eyes. I'm not sure she's convinced, but I try and keep a brave face. Even though internally I feel like I swallowed rocks.

Gina walks back through the doorway, her smile crinkling at the edges. "Mr. Bledsoe will see you now."

I hear Ella suck in a sharp breath next to me, and I feel my heart rate start to elevate. *This is good. Just get this over with and you'll feel the weight immediately lift off your shoulders.*

When we walk through the doorway to his office, Bledsoe is stern-faced and sitting behind a large wooden desk. His broad shoulders are firmly set, straining against his suit jacket, and he looks tense. That doesn't really make me feel any less uneasy, but I try to keep my composure as we sit in the chairs on the other side of his desk.

The chairs are straight backed to the point where I almost feel like I'm leaning forward, but I try not to fidget. It's hard not to under Bledsoe's appraising gaze, his eyes are so dark brown that they're almost black, and they look like he can read my every thought.

I peek through my peripheral to see that Ella looks like a shaking chihuahua when the wind is blowing. I can only imagine how much these past few minutes have triggered her.

I decide that since we're about to tell him anyway, what's one little touch if it puts her at ease? I take her small hand in mine and give it a little squeeze before bringing it back to the armrest, and I can feel Bledsoe's eyes track every movement.

He leans over to rest his forearms on the desk, and his hands clasp together in front of him. "I assume you know why you're both here?" He says in a tone that conveys no emotion once so ever.

I clear my throat before slightly adjusting in my seat, "Well I'm not sure how much Ella told you when she asked to meet but…"

Before I can even finish my sentence, I feel Ella clasp my arm tightly, her nails digging into my skin once more. I can feel her terror as I meet her eyes once more and they're as wide as I've ever seen them. "I didn't talk to him… I thought you did…" she says, her voice trembling.

I can feel it, her panic. Like its seized her throat in an iron grip, and I can feel it too. *Fuck, this is not good. Maybe this is something completely unrelated to us then? A coincidence? Because the only other person that knows about Ella and I is Josie and I know she would never say anything.*

"What exactly are you wanting to speak about?" I say with

an effort to keep my voice neutral. I'm not sure if I'm succeeding, but I'll play dumb until I can actually get my footing on what's going on right now.

I see a crease form between Bledsoe's dark eyebrows, and he clears his throat. "I know you two are together," he says matter-of-factly.

I didn't honestly think that Ella's eyes could get any bigger, but I was wrong. She goes utterly still next to me, like her fear has completely frozen her in place. In this moment I know that I'm going to need to be the one to talk, because I don't know if she could form words at this point.

"How is that... how?" I ask while pinching the bridge of my nose. It doesn't seem like I can form words right now either.

I see his dark eyes harden at me then, "A student saw you two in the parking lot together last Friday. Considering this is a middle school I'm sure you can guess how quickly word spread." He looks more frustrated than I've ever seen him, at least more than has ever been directed at me.

I obviously can't blame him, because well, we fucked up. "I didn't want to believe the rumor, I figured there was no way that you didn't take the proper precautions and report your relationship, but we have cameras in the parking lot."

I feel my face heat immediately, because I know what he saw. I'm fucking kicking myself because that was so dumb. Why the hell did I have to push her against the car and kiss her like that? I literally couldn't have waited? Jesus, do I have so little self-control? But I know the answer to that already, don't I? Whenever Ella is involved, my self-control is always in short supply.

My stomach is in literal knots, and I look over to see that Ella's entire face is flushed, and she has a look of pure terror etched into her eyes. I can guess what's going on in her head, and what awful memories this is drudging up for her. I feel a sharp pain in my chest at the thought of her feeling any type of hurt, especially, one that I had a hand in creating.

"As you can imagine this is extremely inappropriate. Not only are you required to report any romantic involvement to the administration to keep on file, but a student saw you two together." I can feel his anger, and I understand it, but I don't think he has the capacity to be madder than I am at myself right now.

I look over at Ella, and her eyes are watery. The threat of tears running down her face present, and I know she's trying her best to hold them in. "Principal Bledsoe, I can explain…" Her voice is gravel, and I would give anything at this moment to hold her until her tears dry, but I know this isn't exactly the right moment for that. I notice she starts to hyperventilate, and her breathing becomes shallow and rapid, preventing her from finishing her sentence.

"Frankly, I don't want an explanation. You know the rules, and you very clearly didn't abide by them." If he feels any sympathy for the impending anxiety attack I'm watching before me, he doesn't let on.

"El?" I ask, my voice laced in worry.

She doesn't respond, the only sound coming from her is that of her shallow breaths.

I think at this stage the best course of action is just to get her out of here as soon as possible. "What happens now?" I ask, my eyes meeting his stern gaze, and I try not to let on that I could probably throw up on this desk at any moment.

He adjusts in his chair before responding, "You both will be suspended for the next week without pay. Please make sure your sub plans are emailed to me by the end of the day. Hopefully by the time you both come back on Monday the rumor mill has slowed down. The students are bound to have found something else to gossip about by that point."

His eyes soften as he looks at Ella then, and I think he can feel her terror as he looks at her directly. She doesn't meet his gaze, opting to look at her twisted hands jumbled together. I recognize the gesture well by now, knowing that she does this when she feels out of control. It grounds her, when she feels the impending feeling of drowning in panic. It makes my chest ache.

"Our biggest concern right now is just damage control," he finishes while looking back and forth between us.

I feel hope bloom in my chest, "Wait so we aren't fired?" I look at Ella to see her reaction, assuming she would be ecstatic, but all she does is manage to look back up with a blank gaze.

There's a crack in his armor then, and I see a slight smile tug at the corner of his lip before he forces it back down, straightening his face. "No. I'm obviously not thrilled with you both right now, but there's a teacher shortage. I can't afford to lose two of my best ones."

I feel the fizzing in my blood begin to quiet, *a week suspension, I can work with that.* "Thank you so much," I reply with a small smile.

"Please don't thank me. You're free to go. I'll see you next week," he replies curtly.

Ella seems to unfreeze then, like she's finally aware of what's going on. "Wait, what about the dance? It's Friday."

"As of right now I don't think I'll be able to find any teacher chaperones to replace you both, but I also don't really want to have you in the school after hours while you're still technically on suspension. I'll just have to ask the PTA for two more people," he answers.

"Okay, thank you," she responds quietly, so quietly that it's almost impossible to hear her.

We both leave the office, and despite the fact that I am forced to take a week off unpaid, I feel lighter than I have in months. Bledsoe finally knows, and the feeling of sneaking around won't plague me anymore. Is this the way that I wanted it to go down? Absolutely not, but thankfully it's over now.

At least, that's what I'm thinking as I walk down the hallway toward the parking lot until I look over at Ella. She hasn't said anything since we've left the office, and a blank expression has been on her face since she last spoke. I want to think it's just because of the emotional roller coaster we were just on, but I have an uneasy foreboding feeling rooting deep in my stomach.

I've helped Ella through anxiety attacks before, but this one is different. I don't recognize this expression, and it concerns me. The total shut down of it, if I didn't notice the slight rise and fall of her chest, I wouldn't even think she was breathing.

As we walk toward the double doors leading out to the parking lot, I reach down to take her delicate hand in mine, but she brushes it away. I need to comfort her, seeing her like this, it's physically painful, but I also don't want to push her. Maybe, she's just overwhelmed right now, and the physical touch is too much. She's mentioned to me before that when she gets overstimulated, touch becomes painful. I'm so frustrated with myself, of course, she needs space right now.

"El, what's wrong? I know this isn't how we wanted it to happen, but now we can be together, and we don't have to hide it…" I trail off as I watch a single tear cascade down her cheek. I want to reach out and wipe it off with my thumb. I want to kiss her pink lips until that smile that makes me grin like an idiot is on her face again. This isn't about me though, and if she needs space, I'm not going to push it.

"Baby...? Talk to me. What can I do?" I ask, no plead really. I'd give anything to help her, if only she could tell me what she needs.

The single tear turns into a waterfall then, like something inside her has broken, and the sobs that are coming out are wracking her chest. Like with every exhale more tears flow out, and the reality of us being in the alcove of doors before the parking lot is unnerving. Although, I guess if an entire school is talking about how we were making out in the parking lot, this probably isn't such a big deal is it? I'm so conflicted. Do I hold her anyway? Do I wait for her to speak? Do I push her to talk and hope that it makes her feel better, or do I not push and let her talk about it when she's ready?

Before I can figure out what the right move is, she speaks, albeit through pauses in gut wrenching sobs. "They all know. The students know, the teachers, everyone. They're all talking about us. And he was here, that fucking monster that made my life a living hell was in this building."

My hand twitches at my side, itching to touch her. I force myself to put my hands in my pockets, so they don't get any ideas, when I remember the necklace is in there. I smile internally, knowing that once she's calmed down, I'll give it to her. *It's going to be okay, just help her through it...* "El..."

But I can't even finish my sentence before she speaks again. "We almost got fired!" She yells before burying her face in her hands. She's trembling now, her voice shaking with panic.

"But we didn't baby," I say while bending down, so her face is closer to mine.

She tears her hands from her face, and she glares back at me.

Her eyes are already bloodshot and red-rimmed, and I wish I knew what the right words were, because I can see it. She's angry now. "Because there's a shortage! I can't... I can't lose this job Liam! These kids are everything to me. This! This right here is why I said I didn't want to date coworkers."

I feel my face begin to heat, anger threatening to bubble over, but I don't let it. She's panicking. That's it. She doesn't mean it, so I try and give her an out. Maybe I'm misunderstanding what she's saying... "What are you saying El?"

I watch her face contort from angry back to sad, her hands turning to fists at her side. "I'm saying that I obviously can't control myself around you, and I need this job. I can't be the person that the whole school looks down on again. I just can't. Seeing him again just confirmed it even more for me." She exhales a shaky breath before continuing. "Liam, I care about you so much, but I don't know if that's enough."

I feel like someone just punched me in the gut. This pain... I don't know if I've ever felt it before. She can't end this. Not now. Not when we've finally come this far. "El, I would risk anything for you. Even my job if I had to. You're the most important person in my life."

I feel it, the anger bubbling. I can't do this. I should've known this was going to happen, that I've always cared about her more than she has me. Shit, I've been a fucking puppy dog following her around since August. How embarrassing. I was literally about to tell her I love her, and she's about to end it. I'm close to groveling, and I don't even care.

"Damn it El, I love you!" I yell.

She jumps, her eyes wide, but she says nothing. She just stands there, staring at me. Wordless. That gives me all the answers I need, and now I know she doesn't feel the same. "I guess my fears were right all along. I clearly care about you more than you do me."

I feel my eyes begin to water, tears collecting in my ducts, threatening to fall at any moment. This ache in my chest is turning into a deeper and deeper pain by the minute. I have to get out of here, now.

I reach into my pocket and pull out the hot pink shot glass necklace from that first night I met her. The night she immediately had me hooked, and before I ever knew I'd see her again, I knew I'd never forget her.

"Looks like I finally found you, but you weren't ready to be found." I say before placing it in her hand. I watch as recognition crosses her face, and more tears fall down her face.

She holds the necklace in her hand and looks up at me as I back away out the doors to leave. "Liam, wait!" She calls after me.

"El, I can't. It hurts too much. I need space, not you stringing me along again. I'm too weak." I reply, and I know how pathetic I sound, how defeated, but I don't even care. All I can think about is getting out of this doorway and to my car before I embarrass myself any further.

I let the door swing shut behind me, and I walk out to the parking lot. Ella's sobs echo in my head, and I fight the urge not to have a complete breakdown right here. All of this, all the things we went through. Finding out we were teaching at the same school, deciding to just be friends, making out and then not speaking for months, back to friends, then a relationship. All of it just to not end up together. This isn't how stories are supposed to end.

You don't just work this hard for love, only for it to not work out, but even as I think it, I know that's not how real-life works. Sometimes, there aren't any happy endings. Sometimes, you just break up, no matter how in love you are, and it doesn't work.

    I try and shut these thoughts out of my brain, because they aren't going to do me any good right now. When I get home, I'll stew and drown in my own thoughts as much as I want, but not now. I've done enough embarrassing things in this parking lot to last a career. I climb into my car and try to make it home before I start crying.

Chapter Twenty-Five
Ella

This pain is unbearable. I don't know what I expected honestly, of course, I feel this way, and I deserve it.

It's been a long time since I've spiraled this badly. Last time when Liam and I stopped talking, I thought it was bad, but that was nothing. That was before I knew how good being with him could be. Before I knew what it would be like for him to wrap his arms around me and hold me while I sleep. I didn't know then how his dark curls fell into his eyes while he slept, or how he could love me as hard as he did. I don't even bother texting my mom the typical tornado emoji. It's just embarrassing. My God how often can someone mess up so badly that they spiral and need their mom? I couldn't stomach it this time, not when I ruined any chance I've ever had at love.

Oh God, love. He said that to me. That he loves me. No guy has ever said that to me; hell, it's never even been close. Those words were like a balm on my heart that was beating entirely too fast, trying to keep up with the panicked thoughts racing through my brain. I couldn't even properly process it until it was too late.

Now here I am, almost a week without him, and the pain still feels as fresh as it did when Liam and I had to leave the school for the week's suspension six days ago.

The only company I've had is the constant palpable humiliation that seems to hang around me at every turn. Sometimes the shame is so potent it feels like it's an actual person with a vice grip on my windpipe that's preventing me from taking in any air. That's when the hyperventilating begins.

I've been taking my meds, but even 100 milligrams of grade A panic prevention can't fix it all. I spend a lot of the day being thankful that I'm on them now, because thinking about how bad I would feel without the pills is too scary to even consider.

Most of my days this past week have been me watching Netflix reality shows where everyone finds love in the most unlikely of scenarios, because I need to torture myself even more than I already am. I'm a masochist clearly. I binge watched an entire season of Friends or Benefits in a day for crying out loud.

It's nothing more than I deserve. These are the consequences of my own actions, after all. I'm the one that kept insisting that we put off telling Bledsoe about our relationship. I'm the one who didn't support Liam at all during the entire interaction with Phaser and the meeting with Bledsoe because I was so frozen in fear. It was me who heard Liam say, 'I love you' and couldn't even form the words to respond back to him. I chose to end things because I panicked so badly that I made a horribly rash decision instead of just taking one fucking second to think, so like I said, this pain is nothing more than I deserve.

I deserve to feel like someone command stripped a 30lb barbell onto my chest. To feel like my whole body has been submerged under water, the pressure enveloping me, burning my lungs and gasping for air without any chance of taking a breath. The shame, grief, and pain are all encompassing. I haven't left the house in days, because I know that no matter where I go, they'll all follow me. They haunt me.

The hard truth that I've learned, one I unfortunately learned when it was too late, was that Liam is more important to me than any job could ever be. I love him, and I didn't even get the chance to tell him. I didn't even get to experience what it might be like to be in a relationship where we both knew exactly how we felt about one another. I fucked it all up before I even got the chance, and now I'll never know.

Considering that I've been living in my shame hovel for almost a week now, I'm not expecting anyone to show up unless they're delivering a pizza or ice cream. By the end of the week the Door dash drivers are going to have my address memorized, so when I hear a knock on the door, I walk quietly toward it and look out the peephole. I know I didn't order anything.

I see a bundle of dark springy curls tied up in a bun with an orange scrunchie, and instantly I know who it is. "El, I know you're there. I could hear those flat ass feet slapping against the floors."

I groan loudly as I open the door, Josie beaming at me with a smile that would be infectious if the muscles around my mouth could even remember how to make one. I look at her with narrowed eyes, "The comment about my feet seems like an unnecessary evil."

She snorts and pushes through the doorway, plopping down on the over-stuffed blue couch in the middle of my living room. She unloads a reusable bag from Aldis and starts piling various items on the coffee table in front of her. "I think it's time for an impromptu M^3 intervention."

I pinch the bridge of my nose and try not to sigh, I know, she's trying to help, but I just don't know if I'm ready to deal with my shit quite yet. "Jos, I appreciate this, I really do, but Millennial Movie Marathon just seems like a lot of work that I'm not up for right now."

She stops unpacking her bag to glare up at me, "A lot of work? El, you're only expected to sit on a couch and eat M&M's

while watching a corny film from the early 2000s. The most work you'll be doing is lifting a handful of M&Ms into your mouth."

"You know what I mean Jos. I just... I can't right now."

That comment earns me a classic Josie Ann Jones eye roll, "That's cute that you think you have a choice. Now shut up and come watch 'Easy A' with me."

I groan loudly, knowing I should just give up now. I'm not strong-willed enough to go toe-to-toe with Josie, that would take a special kind of stubbornness I've never had. "Damn it Jos, you know I can't say no to Emma Stone or Amanda Bynes. It's like my kryptonite."

She chuckles lightly, grabbing a white fuzzy blanket from the back of my couch and wrapping it around her body. "Yeah obviously, that's why I picked it. However, intervention first, movie second. Now, what the shit is wrong with you?"

I feel my eyes narrow at her, she's not exactly one to beat around the bush, like ever. "Blunt as always, Jos."

She leans her head on her hand that's propped against the back of the couch, her dark brown eyes boring into mine. "I'm serious El. I love you, you're my chosen family, but you're being a dumb idiot."

I feel the prickle of annoyance at her words against my skin, knowing that she surely has a point to make that's not just going to be her insulting me. "How exactly am I being a dumb idiot?"

She scoffs at me, "You're being a dumb idiot because you're about to throw away a chance at actually being happy because you can't forgive yourself!"

"What am I supposed to say Jos? I fucked up. My immediate reaction was to panic, and now I've lost him for good." If I could take it back, that entire interaction, I would, but I can't. I don't blame Liam for not wanting to be with me anymore.

Josie lets out an exasperated noise, "Just go to him and apologize! He loves you El, it's so obvious. I'm sure he hates being away from you as much as you do."

I shake my head, feeling a familiar burn behind my eyes. "There's no way he'll forgive me…"

"Don't do that! You messed up one time, that doesn't mean it's over. I know you think that when you mess up its unforgivable and you have to punish yourself forever, but you don't! You do this all the time. You feel like it's impossible to earn forgiveness and so you don't even try." She's sitting up right, her face as serious as I've ever seen her, her dark eyebrows pinched in the middle.

"I don't…" I trail off. I'm not even sure what I'm going to say.

But no fear, Josie's not done with me yet. "You do! Not to psychoanalyze you or anything but your mom moving you around constantly, bouncing from guy to guy fucked you up."

"My mom…"

"Don't start that 'My mom did the best she could' bull shit. She did, and I love her dearly, but she also messed you up. It's why you don't ever feel like things are fixable, why you've never had an actual relationship up to this point, because shit gets hard, and you cut and run. Just like she did." She looks at me with the corner of her eyebrow lifting, this is clearly her version of a mic drop.

"Oh, shit…" I grumble, the full weight of what Josie just said hitting me all at once.

"There she is, now you're getting it. A real epiphany huh?" she smirks at me cockily.

"Oh, shit…" I repeat again. Apparently, it's the only phrase I know how to utter right now as my mind is currently being blown. That's it. Right there. My mom never stayed to fix any of the messes she was in. She hopped from relationship to relationship until she found Hank because moving constantly with a child in tow was somehow easier than staying and fixing the relationship she was in. I've never known how to deal with conflict, or feelings of failure, because my mom never sat back and dealt with her shit.

"El, do the hard things. Stay at the school and fix things with Liam. No one at Valley is going to pull the shit that they did at your last school. Everyone's already moved on."

"Jesus you're really putting that degree in counseling to work, aren't you?" I deadpan.

She chuckles at that, "Yeah well the shit ton of student debt says I damn well better be!"

I smile at that, "Oh my God. I was going to cut off the man I love like a dead tree limb instead of trying to talk to him? What the fuck is wrong with me?" I scrub my face with my hands, feeling like I just woke up from a week in a coma.

Josie crinkles her nose at me, "Honestly, so much, but we can do a deep dive on that later. Also, you just said love."

I roll my eyes dramatically, feeling lighter than I have in days. "I love him. I really, really, do. I just can't believe it took me almost losing everything good in my life before I figured out what that means."

"Well regardless of what happens, you know you'll always have me." She smirks while grabbing the bag of popcorn and shoving a handful in her mouth.

"And popcorn. The most important things obviously," I grin back at her.

"Okay now that the time for playing bad cop is over, and we've both realized that I'm a psychological genius that even

Freud would have to acknowledge as one of the greats, it's time to watch 'Easy A' and figure out what our cheesy grand gesture is going to be." She says matter-of-factly.

"Our cheesy grand gesture?" I ask, slightly confused.

"All good rom coms have them," she says with a wink before turning on the movie and shoveling another handful of popcorn in her mouth.

Chapter Twenty-Six
Ella

I feel like my stomach is in my throat. Is that a thing? It feels like a thing, but Josie stayed last night until I felt less like a lizard in a human suit, and I feel more like a person than I have in the last week. Watching movies from our teenage years, eating junk food, and plotting was exactly what I needed. Leave it to Josie to know what I need better than I do. Typical.

Seeing our plan through requires me to actually leave my house, so for the first time in a week I make it past my doorstep. The only fresh air I've had is when I've walked onto said doorstep to get whatever food I ordered. I'm surprised my lungs didn't adapt to breathing in whatever dust motes collected in my stupor and seize up the moment I step out the door.

When I get to Goodwill, I search the racks endlessly until I find exactly what I'm looking for. Say what you will about thrifting, but nothing ever quite 'asks and ye shall receive' like Goodwill will. Considering the very specific type of dress I'm looking for; I was shocked I found it after only one walk through.

After my second stop to the discount aisle at the craft store, I go home to work on my outfit for tonight. I have plenty of time before Stella's party starts, so once I'm done putting together my outfit, I decide to get my shit together in more than just the romantic and career aspects of my life.

I'm manic cleaning before I fully come to and realize what's happening. I've done this before, when my anxiety shuts me down so hard that I'm barely capable of feeding and cleaning myself, let alone cleaning the house.

It's like in the movies where there's a giant spaceship and someone presses the self-destruct button when shit is already hitting the fan, and the whole time you're like 'who the hell would install something like that?' Well, both are me. My brain is somehow both the spaceship in turmoil where I press the self-destruct button, while a small part of me is still stifled in the background asking, 'who the hell installed that button?' The result? A human blob that disassociates to the point where time is both non-existent and also all consuming. I'm a fun time.

The aftermath that ensues after one of these anxiety spirals can be any multitude of self-destruction that I'll end up having to clean later. Hence the reason I'm currently on my hands and knees scrubbing congealed sweet and sour sauce out of my carpet.

Before I know it, my house looks like Michelle Obama is coming over for tea, and I have sweat dripping down my back. Although I'm sweaty and red faced, my muscles sore from all the different positions I contorted myself into while cleaning, I feel better than I have in what feels like a long time.

I make my way up to the shower and scrub the sweat from my hair and body. I take my time, doing the full-on shower routine, or what Josie and I call 'the works.' Aka, we shave, deep condition, and use a body scrub. The stuff that isn't ever really the priority, but when you do it, it feels like you're treating yourself to the fancy wax coat at the car wash.

Despite how ridiculous I might look in this outfit, I still want to look like a four-course meal, so when I emerge from the shower, I blow out my hair and take my time with my makeup.

After what feels like an eternity of waiting, Josie finally texts me and tells me that Liam's at the party. We agreed that she'd get there to scout for when he showed up, because our plan involves him needing to be there before me.

I take a deep breath and wiggle the poofy pink chiffon over my body and fasten my flower crown over my big '80s style barrel curls. I truly think there's now a hole in the ozone layer after all the hairspray and teasing that was required of me in order to achieve this level of height.

I go to my full-length mirror to get a better look at myself, and if it wasn't for the fact that I have long blonde hair and quite a few more curves, I'd say I've achieved the desired look.

After talking with Josie last night, I told her about how Liam and I went to go see 'The Breakfast Club' for our first date, and how he and I both love Molly Ringwald. Since there aren't really any iconic outfits from 'The Breakfast Club,' she thought it'd be cute if I dressed up like the main character Sam from 'Sixteen Candles' at Stella's party. Something sweet and simple.

I might embarrass the shit out of myself, but I need to show him what I couldn't that day. That I'd risk anything to be with him, including embarrassment in front of all my colleagues, and I don't care who knows that we're together. I'm proud of our relationship, that is, if there's still a relationship to be proud of.

The sinking feeling that I fucked everything up beyond repair claws at the back of my mind, but I try not to think about it too much. Even if I feel like my stomach is in knots and trying to take up residence in my throat.

I leave the house, lock the door behind me, and get into my car. I turn on ABBA through my Bluetooth to get my mind right and pull out of the driveway toward everyone's favorite dive bar.

The familiar crunch of gravel beneath my tires greets me as I pull into the parking lot of Crenshaws, and I steady myself. I gulp air as much as I can despite the feeling of having a boulder on my chest. *You can do this. You can do this. Go get your man, nothing else matters. No more fear.*

Yeah, easier said than done brain.

I go around the back entrance where Josie told me that Lola would be waiting for me. She's leaning against the back door, her dark eyes only visible by the glow of the ember at the end of her cigarette and her salt and pepper curls bundled on top of her head. The familiar leather jacket with her name etched on the lapel draped over her shoulders.

"Josie told me the plan. You ready for this?" she asks, a dark eyebrow upturning with the question.

I attempt to swallow down the lump in my throat, "Yeah, I think so."

"He was really messed up you know. I've never seen him so sad before, and I've seen him go through a breakup he had with a woman he once thought he would marry," she says flatly while flicking the ash off her cigarette.

"I hate that I hurt him, Lola. I never meant for it to happen, and it's not like this past week has been all sunshine and rainbows for me either." I reply quietly. I know she can hear me though, because understanding reflects in her eyes, and they soften.

"Everyone fucks up Ella, but it's what you do after you fuck up that determines the kind of person you are. I'm sure if you go in there, I have no doubt in my mind that he'll want to get back together with you." She takes one long drag of her cigarette before she stamps it out on the brick wall behind her.

I feel the rapid thrum of my heartbeat slow down slightly as her words help calm me down. "Thanks Lola. That makes me feel a lot better actually."

"Anytime hon, now let's get in there and go get your man

back," her smirk makes me chuckle, and I follow her through the back door that leads into the kitchen.

I stand on the other side of the wall where the kitchen meets the back of the bar and try to will my heart not to beat out of my chest. Hiding until Josie gets everyone's attention is probably my best bet, considering I look like a puffed-up bottle of Pepto I'm not exactly able to blend in.

Josie grabs the karaoke machine and turns on the microphone, the feedback crackling through the speakers. I see Liam on the other side of the room, and even though his eyes look heavy and exhausted, he still looks so handsome. His dark curls are gelled together so that one singular curl falls onto his forehead, and he has on what looks like layered polo shirts with collars popped and khaki pants. He's adorable.

"Attention people! We have a special little performance one of our very own would like to put on for us tonight! Let's give a round of applause for the one and only Ella Jacobs!" cheering from the crowd ensues, and I try not to picture how many people are actually going to be out there and watching me.

Oh fuck. It's happening. I walk out behind the bar and my eyes immediately find Liam's; the shock is evident on his face. He had to know I was going to be here, but I doubt he expected it in this capacity.

I go up to the little makeshift stage area where the karaoke machine is and grab the microphone. I take a deep breath trying to settle my nerves one last time and see at least half of the faculty in the crowd, not to mention Stella's friends and family are here too.

I smile brightly and get ready to embarrass the shit out of myself. "This one is dedicated to the man I love, and Stella approved. Liam, I don't ever want you to think that you love me more than I love you. This week without you has been unbearable. I fucked up, but when you love someone, I know now that when you mess up, at the end of the day, they'll still love you, so please accept my classic '80s rom-com style grand gesture. Josie, if you please!"

Josie starts up the music, and the song 'Don't You (Forget About Me)' by Simple Minds blares through the speaker. I try and contain my laughter as Josie lifts up the karaoke machine over her head in a very 'Say Anything' manner and sways with the music.

I know as I start to sing, I sound like shit. I mean truly, I have never in my life been able to carry a tune, but as I look out at the people in front of me, they're drunkenly swaying to the music and holding up the lights from their phones. I even see Lola flick the light on her lighter, and it makes me go even harder. I put every ounce of my terrible singing voice into the song, and when I lock eyes with Liam, he's grinning so wide that his amber eyes are crinkling at the edges.

Once the song is finished, everyone in the room starts whooping and clapping, Josie sets down the karaoke machine and yells at the top of her lungs, Liam cups his hands around his mouth and cheers for me. I pick up both sides of my Pepto pink dress and curtsy dramatically before hopping off the little ledge that doubles as a "stage" and run toward Liam.

When I get to him, he's still grinning widely, and I feel like my heart could explode from how happy the sight of him makes me. I want to kiss his face until my lips go numb, but apology first, kiss after.

"Baby, I'm so sorry I reacted like that. I love you. You were right, and I know now that I really would risk anything to be with you. I'd even wear a giant fluffy pink dress and a flower crown while singing at an octave that I'm assuming only the ears of local wildlife could hear. I filled out all the paperwork and gave it to H.R. and all you have to do is sign on Monday. That is, if you still want to be with me?"

He chuckles, his eyes bright and glassy. I feel every eye in the bar on us, waiting to see what his response will be. "That performance was completely unhinged, and I loved every second of it, but more importantly, I love you, El. This past week without you was a living nightmare, and I never want to do it again."

I feel tears begin to well up in my eyes out of sheer joy, and before I can even lean in to kiss him, he grabs my face in both hands and pulls himself down so that his lips meet mine. I missed the feeling of his lips on mine, and I wrap my arms around his neck, needing to be closer to him.

His kiss is gentle, and he nuzzles his nose with mine before planting a kiss on my forehead. The entire bar erupts in a fit of cheers, while Liam gives me a smoldering glance that I know means that I will be reaping the benefits with him later tonight.

I hear the tapping of silverware against glass and look over to see Stella grabbing everyone's attention, Lola's arm draped over her shoulders. I must be the world's biggest idiot, because I just now put two and two together that they're married.

It makes perfect sense, and just when I think I can't get any happier, seeing them together and so in love sends my happiness over the edge. The way Lola looks at her, like she's a work of art, fitting, considering that's what she just retired from. "Okay everyone enough of this mushy shit. I'm retiring bitches! Let's get fucked up!" An echo of cheers reverberates around the bar, and I can't help but think that in this moment, I might be the happiest I've ever been.

Epilogue
Liam

I grunt as I try to balance on the ladder and hang up the last picture. I moved into Ella's place a few days ago, and now we're finally settled in. Mostly due to the fact that we wanted everything to be done so that when we have everyone over tonight, the house looks like the perfect mesh between the both of us.

My lease is up in a few weeks, and although it may feel fast, and the school year just ended last week, Ella asked me to move in with her. I obviously jumped at the opportunity, living with my best friend, the love of my life, was a no-brainer.

With everything we went through this year, it feels like we've been together for so much longer. Technically we didn't really start dating until a few months ago, but she and I both know that we caught feelings way sooner than that. While we might have been friends, we both secretly wanted more, and after all this time, we finally got it.

I climb down the ladder and fold it up to put it back in the shed, passing Ella in the kitchen on my way out. Her perfect pink lips peel back in a smile as she sees me walk through the doorway. She's cutting up veggies for our housewarming party tonight, so I lean down and give her a quick kiss on the cheek before going out to the yard.

Max and Josie are out back stringing bulb lights and sniping at each other. I'm sure they're currently regretting volunteering to help set up the party, but oh well.

"Oh, for the love of all that is holy, just fucking wrap it around the pole! If you can't figure it out, I'll do it myself!" Josie yells at Max in an exasperated tone.

Max chuckles, ever the cocky bastard that enjoys needling Josie far too much, replies with a smirk. "Baby you can wrap whatever you want around my pole," and winks at her.

This, very clearly, makes her even more irate. "How about a pair of pliers you insufferable ass!"

That makes me cackle as I walk back inside and go the counter to where Ella is finishing up the veggie tray, smirking. "I think Max enjoys getting a rise out of Josie far too much. If he turns up dead at the bottom of a well, she's my first suspect."

I chuckle and pop a baby carrot in my mouth, "I don't know, they say there's a fine line between love and hate." I wiggle my eyebrows at her, and she nudges my chest with a laugh.

"Are you nervous for tonight?" I ask while gently running my thumb along her shoulder.

She crinkles her nose at me, a gesture that I find utterly adorable. "A little... I really want your dads to like me."

"El, I promise that they're going to love you. I'm nervous to meet your mom and stepdad too, but the most important thing is that we love each other. I'm sure that's all our parents want for us."

She smiles at me, a stray piece of blonde hair falling out of her low bun. "You're right," she replies before standing on her tiptoes and planting a kiss on my cheek.

"Of course, I am," I say while giving her perfect round ass a light slap. She squeals and lets out a giggle, the sound is nothing but pure joy. I can't believe that this smart, beautiful, funny, perfect woman is all mine. Not for the first time, I thank the universe for highly improbable meet cutes.